Praise for *Blue Thread*

Ruth Tenzer Feldman has created a rare gem—a story that looks into the heart and the soul of the suffrage movement in Portland, Oregon, a hundred years ago.

—Rosanne Parry, author of *Heart of a Shepherd*, awarded a Kirkus Reviews 2009 "Best Book of the Year"

Hooray for Miriam! Just the kind of young woman I like—curious, compassionate, intelligent, independent, and determined. Her story is told in *Blue Thread*, a wonderfully written novel about her struggle to be herself, to be honest, and to be just. In an intriguing blend of fantasy and historical fiction, Miriam finds the battles of the past informing her present and inspiring her future. I cheered her efforts, her courage, and her rewards—and so will you.

—Karen Cushman, author of *The Midwife's Apprentice*, awarded a 1996 Newbery Medal

A "blue thread" crossing generations, from ancient Israel to early twentieth-century America. What a creative way to introduce young adults to women's struggles in their pursuit to achieve equal rights.

—Sylvia Frankel, Adjunct Professor of Religious Studies at Lewis and Clark College

Like Miriam herself, *Blue Thread* interweaves elements of faith, history, and politics; but what I loved most about this young adult novel was the even more powerful element of family. From the dominant conflict and connection between Miriam and her father, to the more fantastical tie between the women of the Josefsohn family, Ruth Tenzer Feldman does a beautiful job peering into the bonds that bring us together, tear us apart, and allow us to travel beyond ourselves.

—Anne Osterlund, author of *Academy 7*, Oregon Book Award finalist

Ruth Tenzer Feldman compellingly portrays life in Portland, Oregon, at the turn of the century. The details she includes about the sights and smells of city life, social conventions, and travel by streetcar bring the story to life. This is a believable picture of a young heroine learning to take a stand for her own rights and the rights of others. She is a compelling protagonist whose adventures in two different historical periods both inform and entertain.

—Anne LeVant Prahl, Curator, Oregon Jewish Museum

D0957167

BLUE THREAD

Blue Thread

Ruth Tenzer Feldman

ISBN13: 978-1-932010-41-1

Ooligan Press
Department of English
Portland State University
P.O. Box 751
Portland, OR 97207-0751
www.ooliganpress.pdx.edu

Interior design: Brandon Freels
Cover design: Kelsey Klockenteger
Title design: Matthew Wilson
Author photo: Colleen Cahill

Set in Adobe Caslon Pro.

Photo on page 294 courtesy of the State Historical Society of Iowa. Images on page 297 courtesy of the University of Oregon Libraries.

Printed in the United States of America.

For additional educational materials, see our website.

For Anna Bertha Koritansky Tenzer, my "Nana,"
who introduced me to boiled chicken feet and a wider world.

People like us, who believe in physics,
know that the distinction between past, present, and future
is only a stubbornly persistent illusion.
—Albert Einstein

Well-behaved women seldom make history.
—Laurel Thatcher Ulrich

Prologue

THE UNFORGIVING SUN SPARKS AND FLASHES against the deadly edge of a raised spear. The desert air hums with the hisses and curses of my kinsmen. Miriam calls to me in a language that only I can understand.

"Serakh, I need your power to speak to him."

I struggle in vain against the men who keep me from Miriam's side. "I do not have such power to give you," I shout over the noise. "Come away. Now!"

She does not answer. I raise my voice once more, this time to the one man who can save her. I use the ancient language that is his mother tongue and mine.

"Miriam pleads on behalf of Tirtzah and her sisters," I explain. "She pleads for all daughters who seek a better life. I have brought her here. She is a messenger who deserves respect, not punishment."

He says nothing. He does not look in my direction. Could it be that he has not heard? He turns his eyes to Miriam and strokes his beard, frowning.

I beseech her again, "Come away, Miriam."

But she does not.

I turn my face toward the heavens, close my eyes, and pray—for all of us.

May Miriam's spirit remain unbroken.

May she find strength in the blue thread that unites us.

And may it be Your will that our people allow her to live.

One

Portland, Oregon
Friday, September 20, 1912

"YOU SHOULD NOT HAVE ENCOURAGED THEM, Miriam,"
Mama said, once again dividing my life into her *shoulds* and
should nots.

I touched the bright yellow VOTES FOR WOMEN bow
Charity had pinned to my navy jacket, and I looked back
at the small shop with its hand-lettered sign: Osborne
Milliners. Then I flung one of Mama's favorite mottos at her:
"It pays to be polite."

With no school and Florrie away, Portland was lonely. I
didn't bother to explain that Charity Osborne had friendship
potential. Charity and her sister Prudence were practically
my age. All I did was smile and offer to help them get settled.
It was Mama who admired their fancy hats.

"I have no notion where the Osbornes come from," Mama
countered. "But in Portland, women expect milliners to sell
millinery and not lecture their customers about suffrage."

"They come from Chicago. They're businesswomen." I liked the way *businesswomen* rolled around in my mouth. Mama reached for my elbow to cross the street. Linking arms between one curb and another goes in her *should* category for proper young ladies. I stepped away and skirted a batch of horse droppings baking on the cobblestones. Once we made it to the other side, Mama shot me a disapproving frown. She tucked one of her blonde curls into a hat as fussy as a Rose Festival float.

"Businesswomen? I'd call them spinsters. You would think there were enough bachelors in Chicago to go around. They needn't have bothered with Portland."

Her remark wasn't worth answering. I retied the ribbon that tamed my unruly brown frizz, then smoothed my gloves.

Mama fixed her eyes on Charity's bow. "I'll thank you not to aggravate your father when we get home for dinner. You know how much he enjoys a relaxed meal."

And I don't? I thought. Still, I buried the bow in my jacket pocket, lest Papa see it. Why spoil my last meal before our Yom Kippur fast? I commenced to hum, which Mama regards as most unladylike—definitely in her *should not* category. She pursed her lips all the way to our front door.

§

AT DINNER, MAMA ENTERTAINED PAPA WITH the tale of our maiden voyage to Osborne Milliners—and nary a whisper about Charity and Prudence's efforts to win voting rights for Oregon women come November. Naturally.

"Hilda Steinbacher says she plans to wear an Osborne *chapeau* to temple tonight," Mama said. *Chapeau*—as if "hat" wasn't fancy enough for the dinner table, as if French instantly turned chatter into conversation. Papa dabbed his mustache with a corner of his napkin. He gave her The Adoring Look, as usual. They eyed each other as if I weren't even there. I took an extra dollop of whipped cream and savored my last bite of peach cobbler.

Two hours later, we crowded into a pew at Temple Beth Israel for the Yom Kippur evening service. I smoothed the narrow brim of my simple navy hat and searched the congregation. Mrs. Steinbacher was easy to spot, owing to an eruption of ostrich plumes and felted roses spewing from her head. Florrie would have been appalled by her mother's hat. Surely Charity hadn't created that monstrosity. It must have been Prudence. I settled into my seat and prepared for boredom. Then I noticed the temple's new prayer books. I picked one up and opened it eagerly.

What a wonder! I thought. White space and text covered each page in perfect proportion. English words printed from left to right balanced Hebrew words printed from right to left. Tiny dots and dashes straddled the Hebrew with exquisite precision. And the typefaces—inspirational. I might only be a printer's daughter now, but one day soon I'd be a printer as well.

Rabbi Wise prayed for peace, justice, and mercy. He urged us to vow that we would be better people in the coming year. I vowed to improve my typesetting skills.

After services, I told Mrs. Steinbacher her holiday suit looked lovely. I didn't mention the hat.

"We so miss our Florrie, don't we, dear?" she asked, as she waved to another of Mama's friends in the congregation.

"I can't wait for her to come home for Thanksgiving," I said, looking around for anyone I might really want to talk to. I noticed an odd-looking girl who stood by the front door. Not odd as in scary. Odd as in intriguing. The girl's bronze-colored skin reminded me of the brown and gold pigments

Papa added to the printer's inks that he never let me touch. She looked about my age, yet the thick braid that fell to her waist was old-woman white. No hat, no hair ribbons. Her plain gray dress was a size too small, several years out of fashion, and missing a button. She certainly hadn't come to flaunt her finery. It's possible she had come to pray.

I smiled at the girl as Mama, Papa, and I walked toward her. She glanced at me, and for a moment it looked as though she wanted us to meet. Something about her made the hairs on the back of my neck stand on end. Then she shifted her gaze to Papa, who had stopped to talk to Mr. Steinbacher. Her face seemed to harden. She turned away and folded into the crowd.

I kept thinking about the strange girl during the ride home. From the back seat of our Oldsmobile, I saw a sign on the Orpheum Theatre advertising a vaudeville show featuring ragtime piano. Perhaps she was a performer—there were plenty of Jews in vaudeville. I dubbed her Fantastical Fannie from Frisco and began designing a handbill in my head. Once we were back home, I went up to my room and put the design on paper. I copied ideas from the typographer's Bible: *The Art & Practice of Typography: A Manual of American Printing* by Edmund G. Gress. My design was mediocre. To be honest, it bordered on wretched.

Frowning, I rubbed my aching shoulders. Dispirited, I turned to the front of the book, and read aloud:

> To the typographer who,
> seeking knowledge and inspired by ambition,
> goes about his work with a stout heart and
> sensitive conscience,
> succeeding in spite of every discouragement,
> this book is dedicated.

Papa was my main discouragement. I erased half of Fantastical Fannie's handbill and started again. By midnight, my design bordered on professional.

I went to bed feeling proud of my efforts, but awoke knowing I was doomed to a full day of Yom Kippur services on an empty stomach. We rarely went to services—we hadn't even gone to Rosh Hashanah services earlier in the month to celebrate the Jewish New Year. But Papa always insisted that we observe every minute—sundown to sundown—of the Day of Atonement.

§

BY EARLY AFTERNOON I HAD LOST interest in the new prayer book. The congregation droned. The rabbi exhorted. The cantor sounded like a one-man opera. I counted twenty-four ringlets on the little girl sitting to my left and breathed in the spicy pomade of the man in the next pew. I listened to the organist pound out majestic melodies, and I watched daylight inch across the stained glass windows. Sundown was taking forever.

But when I turned to page 291, the prayer book once again caught my attention. I stared in adoration at the capital M in "Memorial Service." Its apex had a concave dip, so the top of the letter seemed to be smiling. The left foot serif was angular and the right one curved, like oddly matched shoes. Fanciful yet solid, that M was an answer to a typographer's prayer.

"Miriam, we are reading responsively on page 294," Papa said, as if I were six and not sixteen. Color rose in Mama's cheeks. She coughed quietly, and I turned to the correct page in my prayer book.

After the final "amen," Papa slid his prayer shawl from his shoulders and tucked it inside its black velvet bag. When

Mama started a conversation with the woman behind us, I escaped to the social hall downstairs and broke my fast with a deviled egg.

I heard a shuffling noise behind me, turned, and almost choked on my food.

There she was again, that odd girl, wearing the same gray dress and stuffing cucumber sandwiches into a large handbag. Who was she? I hadn't seen someone so exotic since my friend Florrie and I snuck into the fortune-teller's tent at the Lewis and Clark Exposition when we were nine years old.

The girl looked up and caught me staring. She nodded and made her way closer. Barely managing to swallow the egg, I couldn't take my eyes off her. Maybe she was from Persia or Afghanistan. She looked like she belonged in *National Geographic Magazine*. When she reached me, she touched my arm.

In an instant, I forgot how hungry and tired I was.

Her eyes were hazel, like mine, but flecked with gold. Her eyebrows and eyelashes were as white as her braid and looked as mismatched with her young skin as italics in a block of roman capitals. She was thin, like me, but a head shorter, and she exuded a faint odor of farm animals. *Goats?*

"These eggs are delicious," I said, hoping to engage her in conversation.

"I have a passion for cucumbers," she said. Her voice was deep and strong, and her accent was slightly guttural like Papa's, but different from his familiar German accent.

"I have come a long way for you, Miryam," she said, staring straight into my eyes.

How did she know my name? Maybe Fantastical Fannie was a new student at my old school, and they told her to meet me at services. How many tall Jewish girls with brown frizz and hazel eyes could there be in Portland? Three?

I extended my hand. "It's Mi-ri-am, not Mir-yam. Miriam Josefsohn. Pleased to meet you."

"Mi-ri-am." She said my name slowly, as if struggling to get it right. I stood there, not wanting her to leave, not knowing what else to say. She devoured her sandwich and resumed speaking as if there were no awkwardness between us.

"Where are your *tzitzit?*"

"Excuse me?"

She frowned. "*Tzi-tzit,*" she repeated. "Fringes. The garment of fringes."

"Do you mean my father's prayer shawl?"

She shook her head. "The fringes that belong to you."

I pictured everything in my armoire. "I do have a silk shawl that belonged to my grandmother. It has tassels at the corners."

"Tassels? Yes, perhaps you call them tassels. Is there a single thread of blue?"

"Not as I recall."

"This blue thread you would remember. You must have this garment." She squeezed my arm and stepped even closer. "Do your elders deny you your fringes?"

I frowned at the bronze hand crushing my sleeve.

She released me and stepped away. "A thousand pardons," she said. "Come with me. We must talk." When I paused to collect my thoughts, she held out her hand. Her fingernails were short and her skin calloused. "Please come, Mi-ri-am. I have something to show you. Let us meet outside."

I cradled another deviled egg in a paper doily and watched the girl wobble up the steps in old-fashioned, ill-fitting shoes. I hardly knew her. Unease grew in the back of my mind.

She slipped once and grabbed the banister, looking like a child in her mother's shoes.

I decided to follow. If need be, I could outrun her.

Two

THE CORNER OF TWELFTH AND MAIN was quiet, despite the nearby streetcar lines. The sun touched the West Hills, and the warm evening air smelled of late-blooming roses. I nibbled my egg. The odd-looking girl picked cucumbers from another sandwich and showed me the spread slathered across a slice of crustless rye.

"Curds?" she asked, looking at me with wide, gold-flecked eyes.

"Cream cheese, Miss...um..." She didn't take the hint. "Excuse me, but I didn't catch your name."

She laughed. "I did not throw it to you. Call me Serakh, S-E-R-A-K-H." It sounded like "Sarah" with a gagging noise at the end.

"Serakh," I repeated, trying to get it right. I searched for a topic with which to make polite conversation as she chewed her sandwich. "After services last night you seemed to recognize my father. Do you know him?"

She chewed on a cucumber, ignoring my question. "You must tell no one that we have met, not even your mother and father. They would only pester you with questions." Then she reached into her handbag and handed me something flat and thin wrapped in waxed paper.

"See for yourself. Tirtzah and her sisters have been remembered."

Inside was an old newspaper article. The headline read:

SUFFRAGISTS PARADE STREETS
HUNDREDS IN LINE THIS NOON LED BY MISS SHAW

I glanced at the first paragraphs, which contained nothing about a Tirtzah. "I'm sorry, I don't understand. Are Tirtzah and her sisters members of the congregation?"

Her eyes sparkled. "The same tribe, yes. Tirtzah needs you, Miriam. You must find your fringes. Now go in peace." She walked away, leaving the article in my hands.

"Wait!" I lifted my skirt and petticoat and followed her.

She looked back, her white braid snaking over her shoulder. "I will return when you have your *tzitzit*. You must find them or I have traveled in vain. Do not follow me, Miriam. When we meet again, I pray you will come with me, for the sake of our people."

Our people? I didn't race after her, even though I wanted to. Serakh seemed to expect obedience—like Papa, only nicer. I watched her disappear around the corner, and then I slipped the article into my handbag and returned reluctantly to the social hall. Keeping my encounter with Serakh to myself, I asked my parents if they had heard of a girl named Tirtzah.

Papa rubbed his chin. "No, I do not know this person. Lillian?"

Mama shook her head. "Why do you ask?"

I pretended to brush a crumb from my suit jacket. With

Mama I thought it better to volunteer a half-truth than to be forced into the entire truth or an utter falsehood.

"Oh, I heard the name today and wondered where it comes from."

"Curiosity killed the cat," she said—another of her favorite mottos. "You should avoid what isn't your business, Miriam." My parents wouldn't comprehend curiosity if they saw it printed in seventy-two-point Franklin Gothic.

I held my tongue and said nothing more.

§

UNCLE HERMANN AND MY LITTLE COUSIN Albert were eating appetizers in the parlor when we arrived home.

"Lillian, my dear, I am delighted to see you." Uncle Hermann smoothed his mustache and kissed Mama's hand. He ignored Papa, but smiled at me and gave me a quick embrace.

I happily returned the smile and the hug. Uncle Hermann was so much easier to get along with than Papa. "How are Aunt Sophie and the baby?" I asked.

"Resting nicely," Uncle Hermann replied. "She's sorry she couldn't come to dinner."

Papa eyed Albert, who was busy extricating an unsightly yellow glob from his ear.

"Soon you must share your toys like I had to when your papa Hermann was born. Now we share a printing business," he said, reaching into his breast pocket.

"I won't share my tin soldiers," Albert said, ignoring Papa's proffered handkerchief. "Or my rock collection. The baby can find his own rocks."

I looked at Mama. She had that familiar sadness in her eyes—The Danny Look. I hugged myself, feeling the ache of loss in my own chest. How many of those tin soldiers had been Danny's before Albert claimed them?

"Tell us about school, Albert," I said, steering the subject away from big brothers.

Albert wiped his fingers on his knee pants and commenced to recount his adventures in first grade. A moment later, Mrs. Jenkins called us to dinner. Excellent timing.

"This new cook is Lutheran," Papa told Uncle Hermann, "but she makes chicken soup better than any of our Jewish cooks did. And her apple strudel is the best since you and I came to America. You will taste it tonight. Delicious."

During dinner I asked Uncle Hermann about Tirtzah. He was helping to settle the new Russian and Polish Jews who had come to Portland, and Papa always said how Uncle Hermann took his Judaism so seriously—maybe he knew something useful. Uncle Hermann tapped his fork in contemplation. "I am fairly certain she was one of the daughters of Zelophehad. Julius, where is your Bible?"

Papa sipped his wine. "My brother the scholar, fresh from Yom Kippur services at Ahavai Sholom, because Temple Beth Israel is too modern for him. Satisfy your thirst for knowledge another time, Hermann. I have had enough religion for one day. For one year even. Lillian, kindly refresh our glasses."

Uncle Hermann raised his wine glass. "Here's to my brother, the part-time Jew and full-time American businessman."

Mama winced, but Papa didn't seem to mind. "Every penny I earned, *ja?* From scratch I started and now look. Beautiful house, beautiful wife, beautiful daughter." He counted out each accomplishment on his fingers. "When your Albert and little Nathan own Precision Printers one day, you will thank your penny-punching brother."

Penny-pinching, I thought, annoyed at his English and

his attitude. But I didn't correct him. Papa hates to have his English corrected, even in private.

"Nah-uh! I'm going to be a fireman," Albert announced. "Tell them I'm going to be fireman, Aunt Lillian." He sounded not the least bit interested in the printing business, part of which should come to me. I tried to remind myself it wasn't Albert's fault I was born a girl—he was only a child, the little twit.

"Albert will be a fireman," Mama placated. "By the by, Hermann, Miriam is free these days, and I'm sure she'd enjoy helping Sophie with the new baby."

I crushed my napkin against my lap and answered Uncle Hermann's puzzled look. "I was supposed to go away to boarding school with Florrie Steinbacher, but at the last minute Papa said no. Now I don't even get to go back to St. Mary's here in Portland."

"Well, this is a surprise." Uncle Hermann eyed Papa, who continued to eat as if we were chatting about the weather. "St. Mary's Academy is such a fine school, Julius. Even a religious Jew like me would send his daughter there."

Papa stabbed at his creamed cauliflower. "Ah, but you do not have yet a daughter, nor the expense of providing for her in the proper manner."

My temper flared. "Didn't they tell you? Mama is grooming me for New York society this winter. Papa can afford a month for Mama and me in a posh Manhattan hotel, but not another term at St. Mary's."

Papa scowled. Mama fiddled with her wedding ring and said, "Miriam, let's not start this again. The decision has been made."

That decision and millions more. Stop controlling every jot and tittle of my life! I cleared my throat and reached for the pickled beets. I thought of Serakh and those fringes, and a chance to have an adventure my parents knew nothing about. Uncle Hermann smoothed his mustache and smiled at me. "Please stop by to see us anytime. You're always welcome."

I dabbed my lips with my napkin. "Thank you, Uncle Hermann." *Who knows what kind of mischief I might get into this fall…*

§

"Have you read about someone in the Bible named Tirtzah?" I asked Mrs. Jenkins as I sat in the kitchen later that night, nibbling strudel crumbs. "She has sisters," I said. "My uncle thinks she might be a daughter of someone called Zelo…um…"

"Zelophehad. Gracious me, I didn't know you were interested in Scripture. Yes, Zelophehad's five daughters. They are in your Old Testament. The Book of Numbers, I believe. But I must run, or I'll miss the last streetcar."

I thanked Mrs. Jenkins for dinner and called a "good night" in the direction of my parents. In my room, I lounged against the feather pillows on my bed and read Serakh's article. It came from an Iowa newspaper dated October 31, 1908, and reported on a Dr. Anna Shaw and suffrage marchers. A faded photograph showed women waving signs and holding banners. I leaned closer to the lamp and focused on one banner in particular:

LIKE THE DAUGHTERS OF ZELOPHEHAD
WE ASK FOR OUR INHERITANCE

This banner had to be what Serakh wanted me to see. Of course, if the Tirtzah I was supposed to meet was Zelophehad's daughter, she would be in the Bible, and that made no sense at all. Serakh surely meant someone with the same name, maybe someone from my temple. We didn't usually go to services, so it was quite possible there was a Tirtzah in the congregation. *What would be the harm in finding those fringes and meeting her?*

Three

MRS. JENKINS HAD MOST OF THE day off on Sundays, abandoning me to leftovers until dinner, and to my parents from morning until night. I took my time coming downstairs to face them in the library.

Mama studied me head to foot and stopped cranking the Grafonola. "Good morning at last." She had an edge to her voice. "*Rigoletto* or *Carmen?*"

I headed for the tea biscuits and lemon curd. "*Carmen,*" I muttered, although to me one opera record was about the same as another. "It's only half past ten. Are there plans for today?"

Papa turned a page of *The Morning Oregonian* without looking at me. "Your mama wishes for an outing to the Washington Park Zoo in the Oldsmobile. I will indulge her until a quarter before two, when I go to the Club."

Even though Papa grumbled about muddy roads and every-man-for-himself intersections, he kept his word, and we left shortly after breakfast. I had no say in the matter and felt as caged in as those poor grizzly bears at the zoo. We also stopped at the statue of Sacajawea striding westward with her baby on her back. I read the inscription aloud: "Erected by the women of the United States in memory of Sacajawea, the only woman in the Lewis and Clark Expedition. And in honor of the pioneer mother of old Oregon."

I pointed out that Sister Margaret said Abigail Scott Duniway and a whole passel of suffragists attended the statue's unveiling at the 1905 Lewis and Clark Exposition. "Even Susan B. Anthony was there," I told my parents. Not that it did any good. Oregon women still couldn't vote.

Papa looked at his pocket watch. "Sister Margaret filled your mind with useless politics," he said.

I clamped my mouth shut and climbed into the Oldsmobile. Papa cranked the motor and we bumped our way back home.

As soon as we arrived, I headed upstairs in search of those fringes Serakh said my parents should have given to me. Pink tassels, not blue ones, dangled from Grandma Goldstein's silk shawl. Forget that. I tiptoed into the guest bedroom, breathed in the sweet cedar aroma of Mama's hope chest, and commenced to rummage through it. Buried under a bolt of brocade were two silver candlesticks, an embroidered linen tablecloth, and several lace doilies. No fringes, nothing in blue.

Mama stayed home the rest of the day, making it impossible to snoop around. Frustrated, I suspended my search and composed a letter to Florrie. Even though she was far away in California, Florrie felt closer as soon as I set out my ink blotter and picked up my pen. Using my favorite blue-black ink and ecru linen stationary, I began:

Dearest Florrie,

I met the oddest girl at services this week. She's got something to do with votes for women, and—it's the strangest thing—she insists I have a shawl with a blue thread. I've started to search for it, but so far no luck. Honestly, I'm not

quite sure why I'm searching—I just feel as though I must,
somehow. At least it's something to do while you're away.

There's not one whit of progress with Papa about school.
Mama takes his side—doesn't she always? He refuses to let
me go to St. Mary's this term because he wants Mama to take
me to New York City for the winter season. You know how
I hate to be pushed in front of "good prospects," and this is
going to be ten times worse than when she foisted that banker
on me at your mother's garden party. "Bad prospects" are
so much more fun! I still miss Richard, our favorite book-
store clerk, don't you? No doubt clerks like Richard fall into
Mama's "bad prospects" category.

Two suffragists own the new hat shop—Charity Osborne
and her sister, Prudence. You'd like Charity. She's about
twenty, I should think. Prudence looks older and rather tired.
They're both Plain Janes like me, except with brown eyes
instead of hazel. I don't dare get involved in the suffrage
campaign, because I don't want Papa to be angry with me.
He might refuse to let me work at the shop, when I finally
get the courage to ask him. But if he thinks women are too
dimwitted to vote, how am I ever going to convince him I
can run Precision Printers someday?

I must end my letter here. Take care, Florrie, and please
write me back soon!
In friendship forever,
Mim

§

MAMA INSISTED ON TAKING ME SHOPPING Monday for
more clothes for the New York trip. She bought me a hatpin with a pearl stud, yet another pair of white gloves, and
a lacy handkerchief. *Accoutrements* she called them—French

for doodads. We dined out for lunch, though, and for dessert I ate an entire *éclair*—which is French for the most delicious pastry on Earth.

The smell of fresh bread lured me to the kitchen the next morning. Mrs. Jenkins was adding something to sourdough starter. "I feed you up good, Miss Miriam, but you never gain an ounce."

"Keep trying," I joked. I took two sweet rolls from the sideboard and reached for the crock of butter. I figured my luck with staying slim made up for my prominent nose and blotchy complexion.

Mrs. Jenkins asked, "Did you read about the daughters of Zelophehad?"

"Not in the Bible, not yet. But I read an article about a suffrage march and it mentioned those daughters. I don't know why. Voting rights for women is on the ballot in November. Do you think it will pass this time?"

"Can't rightly say."

I offered Mrs. Jenkins one of her own sweet rolls. "Well, do you want it to pass?"

"Don't mind if I do," she said, meaning the roll. She set the starter aside and served us coffee. "*Ladies' Home Journal* is against women voting. Big magazine like that, who am I to say otherwise?"

I added evaporated milk to my coffee and imagined Sister Margaret lecturing Mrs. Jenkins on the need for women to think for themselves. "What did Zelophehad's daughters do? The ones in the Bible I mean."

"As I recall, they wanted a place of their own in Canaan—the Promised Land." Mrs. Jenkins took two lumps of sugar. "When Mr. Jenkins and I came to Oregon in 1898, we called our farm New Canaan. We were so blessed!" She dabbed her eyes with her apron. "He passed away two years come December. Our boys have the farm now."

I offered her my handkerchief. "Do you have any daughters?"

"Married off, thank the Lord. Ethel's in Oregon City and Harriet moved to one of them new homes in Laurelhurst."

Marrying off daughters. Not my favorite subject. I finished my roll, excused myself, and headed to the parlor, where Mama was playing the piano. She raised her cheek, and I kissed it while she continued to play.

"This sonata is impossible to master by Thanksgiving," she said. "I should never have agreed to that benefit recital."

Mama was playing fine, as far as I was concerned. I followed along on the sheet music and turned the page when she nodded. When she finished the sonata, she started on scales again. I wondered about Tirtzah, and those daughters, and the fringes Serakh insisted I had.

"May I borrow your wedding Bible? I don't think Papa has a Bible in English."

"It's packed away with my bridal gown. Why do you want it?"

"Just to look up something." I picked at a fingernail. My search for that shawl had turned up nothing. Perhaps Mama had it. "Is…um…anything else packed away for me? Another shawl, perhaps?"

Mama didn't skip a beat. "There's not another shawl, but I have started on your wedding *trousseau*."

"Mama!" Was MARRIAGABLE MAIDEN stamped on my forehead today?

She glanced my way without stopping her scales. "Don't roll your eyes at me, young lady. You'll meet some very charming gentlemen this winter—Guggenheims and Schiffs. You should keep an open mind. You're nearly seventeen, as old as I was when I met your father. He was already a successful businessman, cultured, *debonair*…he was my German Prince Charming."

I'd heard it all before. She neglected to add that Papa had been thirty-two—nearly twice her age—and losing his hair. Time to escape. "I'm going to the Stark Street Library today," I announced, determined to sound as sure of myself as that odd girl at the temple. I couldn't stop thinking about her.

Mama started back in on the sonata with renewed fervor. "We'll take the streetcar together. I have a luncheon with friends at the Portland Hotel."

"It was perfectly fine for me to take the streetcar to St. Mary's and back every day for three years," I said. "Now you never let me go anywhere alone."

"Young women do not go gallivanting around the city. You should know by now how important it is to avoid a compromising situation."

I couldn't help my temper. I knew it was useless to talk back to Mama, but the thought of being chaperoned everywhere until I could be suitably settled with some "charming gentleman" set me on edge. "Oh, jolly. I'll be a prisoner in my own house until you and Papa marry me off."

Mama pounded out one last chord. I crossed my arms over my chest. One long moment of silence wedged itself between us.

"We'll go to the library together and you'll come straight home on your own."

"Fine," I said, although I didn't mean it.

Four

You would think a library, of all places, would have a Bible. You would be wrong. The librarian explained that the Front Street Mission had Bibles, but she doubted I'd want to go there. I asked whether she had any new books on type-faces and design.

She shook her head. "Have you tried Hopewell's Bookstore?"

My face answered for me. "I imagine you have. A pity Mr. Hopewell no longer has that fine clerk. Such a nice and in-triguing young man—what was his name?"

"Richard Broxburn," I mumbled, and I could feel my cheeks turning pink in spite of myself.

"Ah, yes. Mr. Broxburn. What a breath of fresh air..." She touched a cameo brooch at the base of her throat. "Now then, are you a Jane Austen fan?"

"I prefer fantastical fiction and mysteries."

"We have a new one from Arthur Conan Doyle. *The Lost World*. Mr. Broxburn would have liked it, and I imagine you will, too."

If Richard had told me to read *Encyclopedia Britannica* I would have done so gladly. Still, when I started *The Lost*

World on the streetcar, I knew I would enjoy the book. The first chapter was about a young woman who wasn't ready to get married. *Good for her!*

When I got home, Mrs. Jenkins told me Papa was in the back garden. I took a deep breath and let it out slowly. *Maybe today is the day to ask about the print shop,* I thought as I straightened my posture, retied my hair ribbon, and headed outside. Without Mama around, Papa might pay more attention to me. Maybe he'd realize I could be both a proper lady and a competent businesswoman.

After the expected pleasantries, I said, "How is our new printing press, Papa?" I ignored his frown and kept going. "Uncle Hermann says we took delivery of a 1911 Chandler & Price. It's supposed to be safer than our old presses. What do you think?"

"I think our plum tree does well this year. I hope this new cook makes plum pudding."

"I should like to see the new machine in operation," I persisted, my heart pounding. I addressed Papa with as much authority as I could muster. "Since I'm no longer in school and it's the start of the fall social season, I should like to assist you at Precision Printers. I can make myself useful typing, filing, and taking messages. I already have some knowledge of typefaces and print design, having studied Mr. Gress's typography book."

Papa decapitated a wilting aster. "Not this week, Miriam. Mr. Jacobowitz and I are reorganizing our records, so I do not have one extra minute."

"But Papa, I have a lot to offer you, and I'm eager to learn every aspect of the printing business. Surely I can be of assistance. I could help Miss Svenson."

Papa shook his head. "She will be as busy as the men. One woman in the shop is more than enough, except that her small fingers are useful."

"You let Danny and me spend hours at the shop, dozens of times."

I remembered when Papa gave us tiny bits of old metal type with pictures of flowers or crowns, even a skull and crossbones. I made scrapbooks from old printer's proofs, and Papa called me the apple of his eye.

"You were a child, Miriam, with an older brother to care for you. The shop is not a playground, and Mr. Jacobowitz does not have time to keep an eye on you."

I don't need a babysitter. And Mr. Jacobowitz is as exciting as an algebra lecture in an overheated room after lunch. "I have no intention of playing, Papa. If I'm old enough to leave school and old enough for you and Mama to look for a suitable match for me, then surely I am old enough to—"

His annoyance darkened into anger. "Not this week, I tell you."

I answered him with silence and left him to his precious garden.

At dinner, I managed to be polite. I asked Mama about her luncheon and offered to help Aunt Sophie the next day. Mama pronounced my idea "excellent." Papa complimented me on my initiative and generosity. I silently congratulated myself on finding a way to get out of the house and to borrow a Bible from Uncle Hermann's collection. If I couldn't go to the print shop, I could at least find my shawl and read about those daughters of Zelophehad.

§

"Borrow as many as you like," Aunt Sophie said Wednesday morning. "Hermann must have a dozen different translations, plus the Book of Mormon and that Moslem holy book."

I thumped baby Nathan's back. He gave a satisfying burp.

Aunt Sophie fiddled with her bedclothes. "I must look a fright."

"You look fine." She needed a kind lie. "I'll change Nathan's diaper and put him down for his nap."

"That would be lovely." Aunt Sophie was asleep before the baby was. I tiptoed into Uncle Hermann's library, surveyed his Bible collection, and picked the book with the most attractive lettering on its spine. When I turned to go, I nearly collided with Uncle Hermann in the front hall.

"Miriam!" He glanced up the stairs. "There's nothing wrong, is there?"

"No, not at all. Aunt Sophie and Nathan are napping. I came by to borrow a Bible. How's everything at the print shop?"

"Your father has business well in hand as usual, so I took the afternoon off."

"I thought you were very busy there this week."

"Your father makes every week busy." He reached for the Bible I'd selected. "King James, I see, not the Isaac Leeser translation we use at services."

"Oh, I didn't notice. Why do you have so many different kinds?"

Uncle Hermann thumbed through the pages. "If we want our non-Jewish neighbors to respect our religion, shouldn't we learn about theirs? The first five books of the King James Bible are essentially the same as our Torah. Did you know the Jewish Publication Society is working on a new translation?"

"I'm looking for the daughters of Zelophehad," I said, hoping to avoid a discourse on Bible translations. "We talked about them at dinner."

"Ah, yes, the daughters. That would be in Numbers. Give me a moment."

I studied his hands as he opened the Bible, hands that used to play cat's cradle with me when I was little. Uncle Hermann knew even more string games than Florrie. "What exactly are *tzitzit?*" I asked before I stopped to think about it.

"They're the fringes on a *tallis*, Miriam. A *tallis* is a prayer shawl, you know."

I nodded, though he probably didn't see. He turned page after page. Serakh had warned me against telling my parents about her. *But Uncle Hermann is such a dear*, I thought. *What harm can it do to tell him?*

"It's the strangest thing," I said. "I met someone after Yom Kippur services, and she was surprised I didn't have these *tzitzit* with me. I thought Jewish women don't wear them."

"That's true. Only men wear them—and some don't bother to anymore." Uncle Hermann closed the Bible and frowned. "A woman spoke to you about your prayer shawl?"

"Not a woman exactly. She's about my age, I should think."

"Did you discuss this with your father?"

"Papa would be the last person I'd tell."

Uncle Hermann stared at me, color draining from his face. "Miriam, did she mention a blue thread?"

He read the answer on my face before I could utter another word.

Five

UNCLE HERMANN TURNED THE DIAL ON a wall safe in his study. He extracted a white woolen bag, beautifully embroidered, that looked like a pillowcase folded in half.

"This belongs to you." His voice shook. "They told me that one day someone would ask about the blue thread, but they didn't tell me why."

His attack of nerves was contagious. "They?"

"My mother and Savta." Uncle Hermann stared at the woolen bag. "They told me to watch over this shawl. They didn't trust your father because he was afraid. It's not his fault, really. He said our sister Raizl died in this shawl."

"She died?" I stepped back.

Uncle Hermann closed the safe. "I don't remember much about Raizl. Your father was fourteen then. I was only five. I should have told you sooner, but Julius was adamant. Still, you are old enough now. You have a right to know."

He presented the woolen bag to me, treating the moment like a ceremony. "This prayer shawl came from your great-grandmother, my dear Savta. She wanted you to have this— her most precious gift." He placed the bag in my arms.

"I thought my great-grandmother was called Miriam. Mama said I was named for her."

"Yes. Her name was Miriam Seligmann. *Savta* means grandmother in Hebrew—at least the Hebrew that the rabbis wrote centuries ago. Who knows what they speak in the Holy Land now. In our town everyone called their grandmothers *Oma* or *Bubbe*—either German or Yiddish. She told me that *Savta* reminded her of her travels, so Savta became her name."

"I didn't know you had a sister named Raizl."

"Your father keeps things to himself—things that are painful to remember." He kissed my cheek. "Mim, please, we'll talk another time. Handle this carefully and never show it to your father. Never. Open the bag when you get home. Now go before I change my mind." He looked so torn that I almost gave the package back to him. But I didn't.

Instead, I clutched the bag and Bible to my chest against a sudden drizzle and raced home. Easing open our front door, I heard Mrs. Jenkins humming in the kitchen. Perfect. She only hummed when my parents were gone. I put the Bible on my nightstand, closed my bedroom door, reached inside the embroidered bag, and spread the shawl across my bed.

Large as a child's blanket, the shawl was made from a rectangle of the finest wool, cream-colored and woven into a delicate white-on-white pattern. Someone had embroidered the edge of the shawl that was meant to touch the back of my neck. Six tiny flowers in shades of ochre and orange and two clusters of purple grapes with green vines bracketed a set of curved marks stitched in crimson. The marks reminded me of Hebrew lettering from the prayer book, and they were grouped in a pattern that could have made words. Some curves and angles looked different from Hebrew—and what's a letter but curves and angles? I brushed my fingers across the embroidery, as if it were Braille. What was the language? What was the message?

Swirling the shawl over my head, I draped it across my shoulders. A strange sort of peace cocooned me. Everything seemed right. The prayer shawl fell to just below my knees. Like Papa's *tallis*, it had short white fringes on the narrow ends, each tied in a special knot, and a longer knot of fringes dangling from each corner. One long fringe had a single thread dyed a vivid sky blue. I let that blue thread glide through my fingers. My hand tingled. I closed my eyes.

I jumped when I heard a knock on my door.

"You have a visitor," Mrs. Jenkins said. A moment later she knocked again. "Miss Miriam? Are you all right?"

"I'll be downstairs in a second," I managed to choke out.

"It's a young lady for you. She's in the parlor. There's lemonade in the icebox and fresh gingersnaps."

The visitor had to be Serakh! How could she have known? I had so many questions for her. Who was Aunt Raizl? Why did she die in my prayer shawl? I hurriedly returned the shawl to its bag and raced to the parlor.

Serakh was nowhere to be seen.

"Happy Blotter Day!" Charity Osborne smiled and thrust a yellow ink blotter at me. "We distributed these downtown, to remind businessmen to support voting rights for women," she said. "I thought you'd like one." Wisps of her straight brown hair peeked out from a plain felt hat with a thin ribbon and a single quail feather. Poor bird.

"Why…um…yes. Thank you." I sat on the settee and tried to hide my disappointment. After all, I would have been delighted to see Charity if I hadn't expected Serakh. "It's lovely," I added, examining a rectangle of porous paper about the size of a large business envelope. The pressed fibers were coarser than the blotting pads I used to set ink when I wrote, and the dye had taken poorly. But the VOTES FOR WOMEN slogan looked professionally designed and printed.

"I have a typography book that says blotters are the newest form of advertising," I added. "Would you care for a glass of lemonade?"

"No thank you, I can't stay long." Charity cleared her throat. "But I do have a request. Prudence and I have joined the Portland Equal Suffrage League, and we wondered if you might help us print materials for the campaign. Mrs. Solomon Hirsch suggested I ask. She's very active in the campaign and she's a member of your church."

Church, not temple—a mistake I often heard, but I didn't bother to correct her. And I took a chance on honesty. "I'm really sorry, Charity. Either Mrs. Hirsch doesn't know about my father's views or she has a wicked sense of humor. He's probably the most anti-suffrage person on Earth. He thinks women should handle housekeeping and social calendars and play sonatas at benefit concerts."

Charity managed a weak smile as she stood to leave. "And what about you, Miriam?"

"Women should definitely have the right to vote. Definitely. But...um...I'm not sure I can help with the campaign right now. Much as I'd like to." I couldn't risk involvement with the campaign—then Papa would never let me work at Precision Printers.

I waved my hand toward the kitchen in the hope that food would cement our friendship even if politics didn't. "Won't you change your mind and stay longer? Mrs. Jenkins baked gingersnaps today. I'm sure she'd brew some fresh coffee for us."

Charity shook her head. "Prudence hates to be alone at the shop." As we walked down the front hall she added, "There's a rally for Dr. Shaw in Portland this Saturday. Anna Howard Shaw. She's president of the National American Woman Suffrage Association. It's a mouthful, I know. Would you like to go to the rally with Prudence and me? Dr. Shaw is due in on the train from Pendleton about five."

I opened the front door. "My parents usually make me do something with them on Saturdays, but maybe I'll get lucky. Thanks for the blotter."

"This part of Johnson is quite lovely," Charity said as we crossed the front porch. "Your rhododendrons and rose bushes are gorgeous. And your house is so…spacious."

Spacious is the word, I thought. Not charming. Unlike the other homes in the neighborhood, ours was a box of a house, all efficiency and right angles, like Papa. No curves. No ligatures or serifs. Everything in a straight line.

We exchanged waves before she crossed the street. I did like Charity, and going to that rally could be exciting, maybe as exciting as meeting this Tirtzah person now that I had my shawl. I hurried inside, thanked Mrs. Jenkins (none of our other cooks had answered the door for me), tossed the blotter on my desk, and hid my prayer shawl in a hatbox on the top shelf of my armoire. It was a temporary solution. Mama had a habit of poking around in my things—no telling what she'd say to Papa. She came home two minutes later and called up to me.

I reached for the Bible and pretended not to hear. The daughters of Zelophehad. Why stick their name on a suffrage banner? It was too late now to ask Charity.

Mama called again. If she needed me that badly, she could climb the stairs and knock on my door. I opened the Bible to Numbers, chapter one. The text was set in two tight columns, in a tiny serif typeface, and read:

> 1 And the Lord spake unto Moses in the wilderness of
> Sinai, in the tabernacle of the congregation, on the first day
> of the second month, in the second year after they were
> come out of the land of Egypt saying: 2 Take ye the sum of

all the congregation of the children of Israel, by their families, by the house of their fathers, with the number of their names, every male by their polls

I scrutinized the names on line after line. Zurishaddai, Zuar, Zebulun, but no Zelophehad. Mama finally stopped calling. I skimmed fourteen more pages. Finding Zelophehad's daughters was going to be harder than I thought.

The front door slammed toward the end of Numbers, chapter ten. Curious, I rushed to the top of the stairs. Papa was in a fury.

"Blotter Day!" he shouted up at me from the foyer. "If I am pestered by one more silly woman with yellow ink blotters, I will treat her like a man and punch her in the nose!"

I stared down at him open mouthed, not knowing what to say. I must have looked like a dead fish.

"*Ach!*" He stormed into the library, slamming the door so hard the dining room chandelier sounded like a wind chime. Mama swooped in from the parlor. I retreated to my room and tucked my own yellow blotter under my pillow.

By the time I went downstairs, it was decided. Papa, Mama, and I were to dine out—Papa's answer to all things stressful. Mrs. Jenkins had the night off. I did not.

I kept a civil tongue all through dinner, which was easier to do in a restaurant with people watching. Papa was in a better mood by the time we came home, so I decided to take a chance and mention the print shop again.

"Papa, I know you are busy this week, but may I work at the print shop next Monday?"

Mama sighed as she pulled off her gloves and handed her coat to Papa.

"Mondays there is always disarray," Papa said, taking my coat as well.

"Please. I won't be any trouble." Papa gave me a long, almost searching look. I held my breath.

"Perhaps Tuesday. Do not pester me, Miriam. And do not expect me to wait while you dawndle in the morning."

Dawdle, I thought, correcting him automatically in my head. I nodded and tried to look professional. *He might just let me go!*

"I leave the house by a quarter past eight," he continued. "My employees must be at their desks by nine, and I set for them a good example."

"Certainly, Papa."

Back in my room I danced a congratulatory waltz with Mr. Gress—well, with Mr. Gress's typography book. Finding that prayer shawl today was a sign of good things to come. *An invitation to a suffrage rally with Charity, a chance to see Serakh again and meet Tirtzah, and now...* I flopped on the bed and imagined how lovely it would be at Precision Printers. I tried not to think about Uncle Hermann's solemn face when he gave me the shawl, or about the girl who died wearing it.

Six

TUESDAY, TUESDAY, TUESDAY... MY FIRST DAY at Precision Printers was eons away. I filled part of Thursday practicing layouts and designs in my copybook and trying on several outfits for the print shop. I settled on my light gray gabardine suit. It made me look older and more sensible, especially with my small silver brooch. I managed to read a few more chapters of the Bible, with nothing to show for it. No Tirtzah. No Zelophehad.

Friday's highlight—if you could call it that—was a visit from Mama's seamstress. She measured me for two holiday gowns, lowered the neckline on my taffeta dress, and pinned the hem on six outfits, including the light gray one. The new fashion let my ankles show, so I wasn't always dirtying the bottom of my skirts and dresses.

"I need the gray skirt by Monday evening, please," I told the seamstress, who knelt before me with straight pins clamped between her lips.

Mama came to her defense. "Mrs. Sablovsky requires at least a week, Miriam. And stop moving. Look straight ahead."

"But this is the perfect outfit for Tuesday."

"What's happening on Tuesday?"

"Mama! I'm going to the shop on Tuesday. How could you forget?" Sister Margaret would have called that a rhetorical question. Mama rarely remembered anything related to Precision Printers.

She sighed. "All right then. Would you kindly hem this one skirt by Monday, Mrs. Sablovsky?" The seamstress smiled, even with pins in her mouth. I think she understood—one businesswoman to another.

At dinner that night, Papa announced that he had to go to the print shop for most of Saturday. I looked up from my soup, but he shook his head before I could frame the question. "Tuesday," he said, as set in his ways as indelible ink.

Mama put down her soupspoon. "Julius, dear, since you'll be downtown tomorrow, I'll go to the art museum with Hilda, and then let's dine out with the Steinbachers. When shall we meet you at your office?"

Papa gave her The Adoring Look. "A quarter after five."

Mama turned to me as if she'd forgotten I was still in the room. "Oh, Miriam, would you care to join Mrs. Steinbacher and me at the museum?"

And miss the perfect chance to go to a rally with Charity? "No thank you, Mama," I said, trying to keep my expression casual.

"Then I'll tell Mrs. Jenkins there will be only one for dinner."

I pretended to rearrange the napkin on my lap, lest they see the annoyance on my face. "I suggest we give Mrs. Jenkins the evening off, Mama. Surely I can fend for myself. I don't need looking after."

After a moment's hesitation, Mama said, "No doubt Mrs. Jenkins will be delighted."

§

AND SHE WAS. "I'LL MAKE A double portion of salmon cakes for lunch," Mrs. Jenkins told me the next morning. "You have a good time this evening."

"I will, and you do the same, Mrs. Jenkins. I won't disturb Mama's piano practice now. When she's done, please tell her I went for a stroll and will see her and Papa after their dinner."

I tucked my frizz into my favorite hat—the navy one with a narrow brim and nothing fancy—and headed for Temple Beth Israel. I'd had my shawl since Wednesday, but there had been no sign of Serakh. Since it was Saturday morning, I peeked in at the temple long enough to satisfy myself that she wasn't among the congregation. I asked Mr. Olsen, the caretaker, if he had seen a bronze-skinned girl with long white hair while he was getting everything ready for Sabbath services. He hadn't, but he suggested I check at the First African Methodist Episcopal Zion Church down the street.

Refusing to fret on a parent-free Saturday, I hopped back on the streetcar and headed to Osborne Milliners. Prudence and Charity were helping customers when I arrived. Apparently Portland women aside from my mother didn't mind suffrage material mixed in with their millinery. Charity waved, and I settled into the corner by the ribbons.

"I'm free for the rest of the day," I said, after the customers left, "so I thought I'd go to the suffrage rally with you after all. It is today, isn't it?"

"Absolutely!" Charity beamed. "We're so glad you can come."

"Before we go anywhere, I could use an extra pair of hands," Prudence said. She brought me several hats and hatboxes, tissue paper, and a ball of twine. "We're shipping these hats to Roseburg."

Charity answered my puzzled look. "Most of our business is by mail order. Prudence says it will take another year before we can compete with Meier & Frank and the other big stores."

"So, why did you move to Portland?" I asked, genuinely curious.

Charity told me about how she and Prudence wanted to help with the suffrage campaign. She talked and talked, like Florrie does when she's describing her latest boyfriend. I didn't mind. That's what friends are for.

When we finished with the hatboxes, Prudence closed up the shop and proposed that we walk to Union Depot rather than take the streetcar. Mama would have been appalled.

"The iron works puts out an awful smell," I said, trying not to sound surprised at the prospect of crossing the railroad yards and factories on the way to the depot.

"We go the bakery way."

I had no notion what that meant.

Charity handed me a VOTES FOR WOMEN sash and studied my hat. "It needs something a little extra," she said.

"Charity, it's fine. I prefer handbills fancy and hats plain." But she was already fussing with it behind the counter.

The end result was a narrow burgundy-and-navy ribbon gathered around the crown with a simple hatpin and a burgundy rosette.

"The burgundy matches the highlights in your hair and complements your hazel eyes," she said. "Like it?"

I glanced in the mirror. The same scrawny me with the same small chest and frizzy hair glanced back, but the hat did make me look professional. "Definitely," I said. "When I saw Mrs. Steinbacher's hat…um…" I didn't want to be rude, but Charity just laughed.

"Well, you should have seen the things we didn't put on," she said. "Mrs. Steinbacher wanted every doodad, geegaw, and whatsit in the shop. That one hat must have paid a week's rent."

Prudence touched my shoulder. "I'm sure you won't say anything to Mrs. Steinbacher, Miriam. Charity and I need all the customers we can get. It will be a miracle if we manage to make ends meet this year."

The bakery way turned out to be down Seventeenth to Glisan, then east toward the river. My nose soon reminded me how close we were to the Pacific Coast Biscuit Company at Twelfth and Davis.

Charity chatted about her uncle's farm in Indiana. She told me how her father had died in a threshing machine accident and how her mother later succumbed to pneumonia. She explained that Prudence yearned for big-city life in Chicago and refused to leave her behind to work in the fields.

"Prudence promised she would make a better life for us," she said. "We worked in a millinery factory and squeezed six cents out of every nickel until we saved enough to start our own shop here. You don't know how lucky you are to have parents who can provide for you."

"How long were you in Chicago?" I asked, feeling a little guilty about how easy my own life seemed in comparison.

"More years than I'd like to remember. I'm nearly twenty-one now, and Prudence is twenty-nine. We started at the factory when I was fourteen. Thirteen actually, but we lied to the foreman. Prudence never let me handle the blocking solutions or the dyes. They still sicken her."

What could I say? I had never met anyone who worked in a factory. I concentrated on stepping across a patch of uneven cobblestones. "Charity, you must let me pay for the ribbon and rose you added to my hat."

"It's my gift. Please. I'm happy you like it." Charity offered an encouraging smile, sealing our friendship.

It was nearly five when we crossed Seventh Street and joined the crowd at the depot. Parked nearby was an empty automobile festooned with yellow roses and VOTES FOR WOM-EN streamers. I supposed it was waiting to take Dr. Shaw to her rally at the Multnomah Hotel. Everyone seemed in a festive mood, as if the Ringling Brothers' circus had come to town. There were banners everywhere, including one that read COLORED WOMEN'S EQUAL SUFFRAGE ASSOCIATION.

"That's Hattie Redmond holding the banner," Charity pointed out. "She's the president of their association." Charity was in a jolly mood, as if these people were all her best friends, although she and Prudence had moved to Portland only two months ago. She told me about Suffrage Day at Oaks Amusement Park the previous Sunday. And she explained in detail how Esther Pohl Lovejoy had persuaded Dr. Shaw to come to Oregon. "Well, they are both physicians, Miriam, so it stands to reason. Isn't this exciting?"

Charity's enthusiasm enveloped me. I linked my arm in hers and took it all in. The people around us commenced to recite a poem and Charity joined in, her voice high-pitched and clear. Prudence touched my sleeve. "This poem has been popular since the textile strike this past winter." She searched my face. "In Lawrence, Massachusetts? The strikers there kept walking in a picket line. They didn't stand still, so they couldn't be arrested for loitering. Clever women."

I nodded, unwilling to admit to Prudence that I didn't know about that strike.

"I remember hearing about that terrible fire in the Triangle Shirtwaist Factory in New York last year," I said. "Dozens of women died."

"One hundred forty-six to be exact," Prudence replied. "Mostly girls, Miriam. Many of them were Jewish girls even younger than you."

I nodded again and shuddered, remembering the newspaper account of them jumping to their deaths. We all stood

together as Prudence, Charity, and the rest of the crowd recited the last lines of the poem:

As we come marching, marching, we bring the greater days.
The rising of the women means the rising of the race.
No more the drudge and idler, ten that toil where one reposes,
But a sharing of life's glories: Bread and roses! Bread and roses!

Charity wiped her cheek. Then I heard a familiar voice say,
"Miriam Josefsohn, what an unexpected pleasure!" I nearly
jumped out of my skin.

Seven

KIRSTEN SVENSON, THE ONLY FEMALE EMPLOYEE of Precision Printers, was waving and walking toward us, accompanied by a burly man with a pockmarked face. With their matching straight blond hair and blue eyes, they could have been brother and sister.

"Kirsten, I didn't see you," I said, catching my breath and forgetting my manners.

Charity leaned forward. "I'm Charity Osborne, and this my sister, Prudence." I could almost hear Mama telling me I should have made the introductions.

Prudence extended her hand to Kirsten. "We own the new millinery shop at Seventeenth and Marshall. We'd welcome your business."

Kirsten shook hands. "How nice to meet you. Kirsten Svenson. I work in Mr. Josefsohn's print shop. This is Nils Kuula, my...intended." Her face reddened.

Nils touched Kirsten's cheek. "Soon Kirsten here will be Mrs. Nils Kuula, staying at home with our beautiful babies."

I looked at Kirsten, who pursed her lips. Prudence coughed. Charity frowned. Nils seemed quick to realize his mistake. "Kirsten can stay on if she wants to. I am a modern man."

"Does my father know you're leaving Precision Printers?" I asked.

"Not yet. I'll stay until at least late June, after the Rose Festival invitations."

"How long have you worked in the printing business?" Prudence asked.

"I started with Mr. Josefsohn six years ago, right out of school. He has been very kind to me."

Papa? I found that hard to believe.

Nils chuckled. "Remember those VOTE NO cards in '06? You were so mad, Kirsten."

"What cards? Vote no for what?"

"It's nothing," Kirsten said. "Nils, you are embarrassing me. So, Miss Osborne, you have a hat shop?"

Prudence gave Kirsten a sympathetic look and commenced to describe life in the millinery business. By the time she was through, Nils had excused himself to check on the train, Kirsten seemed relaxed, and Charity looked bored. I was still wondering about those VOTE NO cards.

Nils came huffing back and reported, "The train from Pendleton is late. At least another hour, maybe two. There's nasty weather in the Gorge."

Charity wrinkled her forehead. "The Columbia River Gorge," I explained. "It gets very windy there; here, too, sometimes. Just wait until winter."

Charity practically snorted. "It can't be a bad as Chicago."

"One day I'll find out for myself," I said. "I've never been out of Oregon except for a few trips to Seattle." I didn't mention my upcoming trip to New York City. Marriage markets don't count.

Nils suggested we while away the next couple of hours over a soda or beer. I looked at my watch. "You'd best go on without me. I'll have to miss Dr. Shaw. My parents..." I bit my lip, feeling foolish and quite young. They were grown and I still lived at home. Kirsten smiled. "The way your father acted at the shop on Blotter Day, I am surprised you had the gumption to come in the first place."

"Suffrage lost here in 1906," I said, gratified to show Prudence I knew something about politics. "Did those VOTE NO cards refer to that?"

"I'm afraid so," Kirsten said.

I winced.

"Oregon will come through this time," Charity asserted. "Women have the vote in Idaho, Washington, and California. We won't take no for an answer."

Prudence cocked her head. "It's going to be a tough fight."

"Nils and I will do what we can," Kirsten said.

"Me too," I added. And I meant it, especially since Papa had printed that VOTE NO card. "May I keep the sash?"

"Certainly." Charity seemed pleased.

Nils laughed. "Don't show it to your father." Kirsten cuffed him, but she laughed too.

§

I WOULD HAVE LIKED TO STAY and see Dr. Shaw. Annoyed at my own worries about antagonizing Papa, I decided to cheer myself up on the way home. I sipped water from Mr. Benson's new outdoor bubbling drinking fountain by the depot and discovered a new confectionery, Rose City Candies. I bought a cone of licorice nibs—an indulgence Mama says I shouldn't buy unwrapped from a seller I don't know. She says you can't trust what might be in licorice, which is never served at the best of bridge games or dinner parties.

The house was still quiet when I returned. I put my sash in my hatbox in the hall closet, lest Papa see it. Then I put the rest of my nibs on the kitchen table—and there she was, sitting on the floor in front of the open icebox.

"Ah, Miriam," Serakh said, rising to her feet. She wore a loose-fitting caftan and sandals. She stretched her hand toward me. In her palm was a half-eaten salmon cake. "I have never eaten such a food."

"Serakh!" I leaned against the table, my heart pounding. "How did you get in? The door was locked!"

"I had no trouble getting inside." Serakh licked her lips. "A food that is pink—in all my times and places this is new."

"It's just salmon," I took another step toward the hall. "Is a window open?"

"Perhaps. Salmon is a lentil?" Her voice was friendly and soothing, as if the nicest people barged into empty houses, opened the icebox, and made themselves at home talking about pink foods.

"Salmon is a fish," I said. *Who didn't know that?* Serakh took another bite and offered the rest to me. "No thank you," I replied, as if this were dinner-table conversation, as if everything were perfectly ordinary—which it wasn't. I paused to collect my thoughts, then ventured, "I have the shawl, Serakh. My uncle had it locked away in his safe."

She stroked the end of her braid. "He understands the value of your *tzitzit*."

"My uncle has heard about you. And he says my father was afraid to give the shawl to me."

She nodded. "Poor man."

I was getting nowhere. "My aunt Raizl died in the shawl. She *died*, Serakh. What's the mystery? I have to know."

"Much in this world we cannot explain," she said with a sigh, as if Aunt Raizl was none of my concern. "I will finish this tasty fish while you get your *tzitzit*," she said. She eyed my hat. "You have added small ornaments to your head covering. Is that a custom here, like the woman with the many feathers where you pray?"

"Mrs. Steinbacher? No, not really. Mrs. Steinbacher's hat is…um…exceptional." I took a deep breath. Probably Mrs. Jenkins had forgotten to lock the back door. Serakh's clothes were odd, and so were her manners. Maybe she really did come from Persia or Afghanistan. Perhaps I was feeling anxious for no reason.

"Serakh, please sit at the table. That's the custom in Portland."

"I will do as you say, Miriam. I am eager for another portion of pink fish."

I put a salmon cake on a plate, closed the icebox, and handed her a fork.

Serakh ignored the fork. Even Cousin Albert had better manners, but I really didn't care about her table etiquette at the moment.

"Where are your fringes?" she asked again.

"Stay here, I'll be right down."

My shoulders tensed as I climbed the stairs, and I wondered whether to ask Serakh to come back another time. Still, if I was old enough to leave school and old enough to go to a suffrage rally, I was old enough to have another girl come calling, even a strange one like Serakh. Besides, questions were piling up in my mind faster than I could count, and I wanted to satisfy my curiosity.

When I returned with the shawl, Serakh was sniffing my licorice nibs. "What is this?"

"Licorice. Try some. You pop it in your mouth or bite off a piece and chew. Like this."

She followed my instructions. "Excellent!"

"As tasty as cucumbers?" I teased, easing my discomfort.

She smiled. "Cucumbers are pure delight."

"I'm that way about sweet rolls." I opened the embroidered bag and spread the shawl on the kitchen table. Serakh's hazel eyes glistened. She kissed the embroidered edge and draped the shawl around her shoulders and mine. My whole body relaxed as if I were soaking in a warm bath. Then she wrapped the corner fringe with the blue thread around her fingers.

"Many Miriams of your line have worn this shawl. Many have traveled."

"Pardon?" The thread commenced to gleam as brightly as a filament in Mr. Edison's light bulbs. My heart lurched.

"How did you do that?"

"No matter, Miriam. Are you ready to visit Tirtzah? You have only to touch this thread."

I willed my hands to stay at my side. Surely this parlor trick had a rational explanation. "I have to be back before my parents return."

"We shall take no time at all."

"Oh, does Tirtzah live around here? The only Tirtzah I've heard about is supposed to be in the Book of Numbers."

"I do not know of such a book." Serakh hummed to herself. She looked longingly at the licorice nibs, but didn't ask for another piece.

The grandfather clock ticked in the hall. Serakh stroked the blue thread with her free hand. "Miriam," she said softly, "I cannot make you touch this thread, so I ask again for the sake of Tirtzah and our people. Tirtzah struggles to share in her father's dream. Will you come?"

I thought of Papa and that vote no card. "I have problems with my father, too."

Serakh frowned. "Of that I am sure."

I was curious—who wouldn't be? And it wasn't as if Serakh was forcing me. Besides, what was the worst that could happen? I could still outrun her if things got any stranger, and we hadn't even left the house yet. She gestured to the shawl again.

I reached for the blue thread.

An eerie blue glow spread over my fingers. I stared at her as I fought an urge to let go of the thread. "Who in heaven's name are you?"

Serakh didn't answer. Instead she kissed my forehead and covered my hand in hers. My stomach felt queasy and a great crushing feeling squeezed my chest.

Blue lightning crackled before my eyes.

My world turned black.

Eight

EVERYTHING ACHED.

"Do not rise yet," Serakh murmured somewhere in the darkness. "The *olam* is not easily traveled. Let your body rest."

Blackness dissolved into grays and browns. I shut my eyes, then opened them slowly. Stone walls—a cave. I lay on a rough woolen blanket, my shawl folded neatly by my head.

"Do not fear, Miriam." Serakh squatted by my side and smoothed my hair. "I will take you back across the *olam* when we are done. Perhaps I will stay for more pink fish."

"Across what?" I struggled for breath. My throat burned.

"The *olam*—the path through every place and all time."

"The path through what? Where am I?"

She kissed my forehead, smothering me with that goat smell I remembered from our first meeting. "Let your mind rest for now."

I clutched my shawl and shivered. The blue thread had lost its glow. "What's happening to me? Who *are* you?"

"I am the same Serakh who traveled to Port Land. I am Serakh, daughter of Asher. Serakh *bat* Asher. You might hear Tirtzah say *bat*. *Bat* means daughter. My gift of language does not always translate names. Have no fear, Miriam. You chose bravely, and now you are safe so long as you remain with me."

My hands felt like ice. My legs started to shake. "Not your name, Serakh. I mean what kind of a person are you? Where am I?"

"I am a good person, believe me. And we are not far from the River Jordan." She handed me a pair of well-worn leather sandals, an ochre-colored shift with blue and ochre fringes, and an ochre robe with a crimson stripe. "Here. We must hide the clothes of your place and time. These garments I have saved and honored for this occasion. You must put them on quickly."

I pushed the clothes away. "No. I will do no such thing until you tell me what's happening. None of this makes sense!"

Serakh pressed the palms of her hands together and touched her fingers to her lips. She seemed to will her eyes into unaccustomed softness. "I shall try to explain in the short time we have. My father was a son of the man you call Jacob and a brother of the man you call Joseph. You and I are kin through the line of Joseph, my uncle. The daughters come from the line of Joseph directly, through Joseph's son, Manasseh."

"Slow down. This is completely impossible. I don't understand any of this."

"I speak of the daughters of Zelophehad. Tirtzah and her sisters. Here, you must not appear before Tirtzah like this. You must change your garments."

I squeezed my eyes shut, counted to three, and opened them again. Same cave, same craziness. "This is straight out of *The Lost World*."

"Do not feel troubled, Miriam. We are not lost."

My breath came short and fast. "What have you done to me? Where are we exactly?"

"By the river, as I have said. But where you are or when you are is not of great importance. They form only a tiny dot in the *olam*, a spark in the universe. What matters most is who you are."

Think! I rubbed my forehead. Maybe I fell asleep at the kitchen table. The business with the salmon cakes and the shawl never happened. None of this happened. This must be a dream. The girl who stood before me looked very much like the one I'd met at the temple. That made sense. Dreams can be very realistic.

Another voice echoed in the cave. "Serakh?"

"I am coming, Tirtzah," she shouted. "Stay by the entrance."

Serakh dumped the clothes in my lap and grabbed my shoulders. "Miriam, you must go to the back of the cave and change from your Port Land garments. Tirtzah cannot travel as I can. She does not know of your world. Do you wish to frighten her to death?" She left me and strode toward the light at the front of the cave.

Frighten Tirtzah? I was the one losing my mind.

I tried to analyze my situation. Florrie was wild and dramatic about things, but not me. *What did I eat that was out of the ordinary today?* The licorice. Yes, it was entirely possible that the licorice had been tainted with some powerful drug. The neighborhood by the depot was close to the saloons and immoral establishments along the waterfront.

Still, as dreams went, this one seemed harmless. I'd had much worse. This was bound to be over soon. No need to panic. And if changing clothes was part of my dream, then so be it. I rolled my shoulders and felt my jaw relax.

Gathering the robes, I retreated to the back of the cave. It was cooler there, with just enough light to see by. I took off my dress, socks, and petticoat and piled them on a flat rock. I kept on the rest for the sake of modesty. The woolen shift and robe made my back itch. They were quite ample, but short, revealing a bit more of my legs than my regular clothes. I could have sworn the shift had blue and ochre fringes when Serakh gave it to me, but now all the fringes were ochre and white. I couldn't even keep my own dream straight.

It was a relief to unbuckle my shoes and ease my feet into soft leather sandals. I twisted the long, thin straps around my ankles and tied them in a bow. Then I crept closer to the cave's entrance.

The bright sunlight contrasted so much with the cave's dim interior that it was hard to see clearly. I squinted at a girl about my size stepping into and out of the light. I glimpsed her profile and a glint of gold. How could there be gold on her face? Definitely a dream.

I wrapped the shawl around me and inched forward. The girl stepped into the sunlight again. There was no doubt now. A gold ring clasped one side of her nose.

"Oh!" My surprise slipped out of my mouth before I could stop myself. The cave echoed. The girl turned in my direction.

I swallowed hard, draped my shawl over my shoulders, and walked toward her. "Pleased to meet you," I managed to say. "My name—"

Serakh rushed in front of me. "We are blessed with the perfect messenger from another place and time. She is also of the line of Joseph. She brings news that you are on the right path."

I do? The girl bowed deeply and kissed the hem of my robe. She was about my age and an inch taller than Serakh, with the same bronze skin. Her lips quivered. She looked at my feet, which were much smoother and whiter—and larger—than hers. This other dream-girl seemed even more frightened than I was. She retreated a few steps, squatted on the cave floor, and looked up at me with soft brown eyes.

"Blessed messenger, I am called Tirtzah, daughter of Zelophehad," she said.

I nodded slowly, mesmerized by that gold band embracing her left nostril.

"Call me Miriam," I said, before Serakh could stop me.

"Mir-yam?" Tirtzah frowned. Serakh crossed her arms over her chest and said nothing.

"Mi-ri-am," I said. "Um…Miriam *bat* Julius." My father's daughter. What would Papa and Mama do if they found me sick from the licorice and slouched over the kitchen table dreaming?

Serakh murmured her approval. She touched Tirtzah's head. "Arise, my brave one. Let us show our messenger the River Jordan."

Instead of going toward the entrance, Serakh led us along a side passage of the cave. I crouched low to keep my head from touching the ceiling. The rock walls felt cool and slightly damp.

Serakh seemed to disappear for an instant, and then I realized she'd turned a sharp corner. Tirtzah and I followed. Sunlight greeted us. We stepped out onto the ledge together.

Far below, a vast desert stretched toward craggy mountains on the horizon. A wide river meandered through a thin swath of green. I shaded my eyes from the cloudless sky. It could have been eastern Oregon, on the other side of the Cascade Range. I remembered a trip we took to Crater Lake once, and I wondered if the lava beds I saw near there would appear in this make-believe landscape.

Serakh pointed to some low bushes about five yards down a small slope. "Tirtzah," she said. "Please gather fuel for tonight. Take our messenger with you. Hold her hand, and do not be afraid."

I wondered why I'd make up such a fantastical dream about fetching twigs. *How dull is that?* At least the characters in *The Lost World* discovered dinosaurs.

Tirtzah placed her palm against mine. Tiny cuts and scratches marked her skin. She shivered a moment and then covered my thumb with hers. We started toward the bushes. I slipped on loose stones once, and Tirtzah caught my arm to steady me. "You must watch where you place your feet. There are scorpions among the rocks."

Scorpions? I clutched Tirtzah and walked with care. I hated when scorpions showed up in my dreams. Danny always followed the scorpions. Dream would decay into nightmare and I would wake cold and shaking.

When we got to the bushes, Tirtzah told me to hold out the front of my robe like a sack. "Your hands are soft," she said. "I shall do the gathering. There are many thorns."

As I watched her stoop and pluck, I wondered why I'd invented such a creature. She didn't smell of goats the way Serakh did, but more like campfires, and, frankly, the way I smelled after a strenuous hike. Her long black braid peeked out from the wide scarf she'd draped over her head. I felt the sun searing my scalp and covered my frizz with my shawl.

After a few minutes, I said, "Serakh told you I was the perfect messenger. What sort of message am I supposed to tell you?"

Tirtzah paused and looked at me. She cocked her head. Silence.

Our hands brushed against each other as she commenced to fill my makeshift sack with bits of bark and bramble. I asked again. This time her eyes were wide with fear. She clasped my hand. "You do not know the message? Serakh made an oath. She vowed that you would help. She vowed that my sisters and I would be safe."

"I'm sorry," I said, feeling foolish. "I don't know anything about a vow. We'll have to ask Serakh."

Tirtzah gathered more kindling and then took my elbow to guide me up the path. As soon as we got to the ledge, she scooped the fuel from my robes to Serakh's. She started to say something, but Serakh interrupted with, "First we must return to my sleeping quarters."

I followed them back to the cave, and we three sat together on the rough woolen blanket. Again Tirtzah tried to talk, but Serakh stopped her.

"Miriam," she said. "What did you and Tirtzah speak of while you gathered fuel?"

I licked my parched lips. "First we talked about scorpions and thorns. Then Tirtzah asked about a message I was supposed to be bringing her, only I don't know what the message is."

Serakh beamed. She touched Tirtzah's shoulder. "And you, my brave one, did you understand the words spoken to you by our messenger when you two were outside the cave?"

Tirtzah wrinkled her thick, black eyebrows. "Once, while I was gathering, our messenger uttered sounds in a strange tongue. But when we touched again, I understood."

Serakh grabbed my hand and clasped Tirtzah's as well. "Then let us give thanks to The One who has kept us in life and guided us to Miriam daughter of Julius."

I looked at Tirtzah. It was hard to tell which of us was more confused.

Nine

SERAKH RELEASED US AND REACHED FOR my prayer shawl. She gave us a look that reminded me of Sister Margaret before a particularly important lecture.

"In another time and place, I gathered and preserved many blue threads for the fabric of generations that would arise from my uncle Joseph and his kin, including his kin through the line of Ishmael. Each thread has the power to carry a messenger across the *olam*. Tirtzah, this Miriam carries such a thread. I had to make sure she was the right messenger for you."

My dream was getting crazier by the minute. "So you sent us out as a test of the blue thread? Didn't you know I was the right messenger as soon as I met Tirtzah in your cave?"

"No, Miriam. I have a gift of languages, as is needed in my travels through the *olam*. You and I will always understand each other, as in your Port Land. I share this gift with guests in my cave while they are within its walls, though few come to visit. But you and Tirtzah left my cave to fetch kindling and still understood each other when your bodies touched."

Tirtzah frowned. "Miriam is my messenger?"

"Indeed."

"But she bears no message."

Serakh patted Tirtzah's leg. "How can Miriam inspire you if she does not know your plight?"

Tirtzah turned to me. "What do you want to know?"

What don't I want to know? How about what was in that licorice and when am I going to wake up? I looked at the ceiling of the cave for a moment. "Well, I am curious about your nose ring."

She smiled. "Then I shall start there. It is a betrothal gift. I am going to marry Gabi, son of Hezron, of the tribe of Reuben. Their portion is on this side of the river."

"Their portion?"

Tirtzah glanced at Serakh.

"Miriam comes from another spot on the *olam*," Serakh said. "You must explain."

Tirtzah began again. "The portion is the land that The One has given to each tribe of those who were slaves to Pharaoh in Egypt. When it is time to cross the River Jordan, Gabi will help the other tribes to settle the land The One has promised to them on the other side. Then he will take me to be his wife, and I will settle here with the Reubenites." She caressed the gold nose ring. "He has been generous."

I thought of Mama's plans to parade me in front of prospects in New York City. "Do you love him, Tirtzah?"

"Gabi is my life. I long to be by his side." Tirtzah grasped the sleeve of my robe. "But, Miriam, when I am with him, who will care for my sisters? Who will pay the bride price for them? Our father is dead. We have no brothers. My mother is powerless. We have no one and nothing. I will not let my sisters be taken into servitude."

"The bride price? Servitude?"

"Many women who do not have men to care for them have no property," Serakh explained. "They can become the property of someone else. That is why you are here." Before I could reply, she added, "You have done well, Tirtzah, as I knew you would. Miryam the prophetess would have been proud of you."

"Miriam, my great-grandmother?" I asked.

Serakh smiled. "She is a fine woman, a messenger, too, as you are. But I speak of Miryam, the sister of Moshe, from this time and place." She turned to Tirtzah. "Now you must return to your sisters."

Tirtzah looked at me. "I fear Hoglah will whisper against me if I am away too long," she said. I bobbed my head, feigning understanding, although nothing made sense. "Everything will turn out fine," I said. Why not? It was my dream, and so far I liked most of what I'd conjured up. Who doesn't like being told they are special?

Tirtzah kissed the hem of my robe once more. I wanted to tell her to stop doing that, but it seemed like second nature to her. She gave Serakh a questioning look.

"Miriam is right," Serakh assured her. "Will you come again, Miriam, when it is time?"

"Certainly," I said.

"Go in peace, Tirtzah," Serakh said. "When I summon you, bring your sisters. You are on the right path."

Tirtzah covered her head and part of her face with a long scarf. She bowed again and left.

"What's next?" I asked Serakh. Maybe I was beginning to get my footing in this adventure in my mind.

She studied my face. "You do not believe any of this?"

"No, not really. Would you?"

"Come, let me show you something."

I half expected Serakh to reach behind a rock and produce another suffrage article like the one she gave me at Temple Beth Israel. Instead, she linked arms with me and led me toward the entrance of the cave.

Squinting in the bright light, I barely managed to stay on my feet. Just outside the cave was a narrow ledge. Like the view along the side of the cave, the space beyond and below the ledge seemed enormous. But this time we were far from alone.

Tents. I saw hundreds of tents made from what looked like animal skins. And I saw thousands of people, dressed in flowing robes or in loincloths barely hiding their nakedness. And thousands and thousands of sheep and goats.

I braced myself against the entrance to the cave. Strong smells and strange noises drifted up from below. This dream was getting away from me. How could I have imagined this place?

My foot slipped, dislodging a stone. A scorpion skittered across my sandal. Tirtzah had warned me of scorpions. I should have listened to her. I should have woken up then—now it was too late! My mouth turned sour, and I was afraid I might retch.

Squeezing my eyes shut, I heard Serakh's voice, quiet and calming. "Our people. See, Miriam? Finally we rest from our wanderings. During the famine of another time and place, I am among those my uncle Joseph brings into the land of the Mitzrayim, the place you call Egypt. Your blue thread comes from his many-colored tunic—I save it from destruction. Generations later, Moshe comes among us. I remember what my father has told me about a deliverer, and I convince the elders that Moshe is sent by The One. And when Moshe leads us out of Egypt, I alone know where my uncle Joseph is buried. Because I promised—"

"Stop. I want to wake up already!" I heard skittering again and flinched away from the unseen scorpions.

"Let us go back inside, Miriam."

"I'm not moving." I opened my eyes. I was still stuck in this dream. I hugged myself and rocked back and forth, back and forth. *Please, no more scorpions.*

Serakh withdrew a few paces. Despite my own words, I inched away from the dizzying heights and steadied myself against the wall barely inside the cave. I refused to sit.

"Allow me to start again with Joseph." Serakh hummed softly. She stroked the end of her braid. "You have heard of Joseph?"

Joseph? It was Danny who haunted me. Just thinking his name made me afraid that he would appear. Danny—who was born under the sign of Scorpio and who died under that sign. I shuddered and rocked, and rocked… *Oh, please, not another nightmare.*

Serakh wrapped her arms around me. "Shhh, sweet Miriam, all will be well. I promise. I will protect you from harm." She guided me to the floor and cradled me in her arms.

And slowly, gradually, I relaxed into the strength of my imagined Serakh. Danny stayed in my mind, but he was no longer fearsome. He was the Danny I once adored. I counted to ten under my breath.

"Let us start again. Surely you know of Joseph."

It was nine years since Danny died, nine years since I stopped going to Religious School. But I did remember the basic stories. "Do you mean Joseph from the Bible?"

"From Thabible? No, Miriam, this Joseph and his brothers come from Canaan."

"Don't tease me," I said, even though she looked puzzled. "The Bible. Adam and Eve. Noah's Ark. Moses and the Ten Commandments."

"Do you mean Moshe who brought us the law?"

"Moshe? I guess so."

Serakh's look of confusion vanished. "Moses, yes—he is also called Moses. I know him well. Perhaps you will see him tomorrow."

"How can I see Moses? He died thousands of years ago."

"All the tribes of Israel are here with Moshe in the land of the Moabites, the children of Lot. The River Jordan is less than an hour's march. We have camped for many weeks, waiting."

The land of the Moabites? I never learned that in Religious School. I clasped the front of my prayer shawl, stroking its soft wool with my thumb. The shawl felt solid in my hands, as if attesting to the truth of Serakh's words. I'd traveled half-way around the world and thousands of years into the past. *It isn't possible…and yet…*

Serakh continued in her slow, even, lullaby voice. "The One guides me as I have been guided since the time of Joseph. Rarely am I mistaken."

"The One?"

"Miriam, surely you must know this. The One. It is a name we say in place of the name we cannot utter. We also speak of *Elohim*, and sometimes we say *El Elyon*."

I shook my head.

"Do you know *Eloheinu*—our *Elohim*? Or *Adonai*?"

Adonai Eloheinu. The words snapped something into place—part of a Hebrew prayer I recited during one of the rare times I went to services. I didn't know what *Adonai Eloheinu* meant exactly, and the words weren't quite as my congregation pronounced them, but the English translation of that prayer ended with "the Lord is One." The One.

"Yes," I whispered, feeling light-headed. "I do know that name."

Serakh stood in silence as the meaning of her words sank in. That prayer—the *Shema*, they called it—was something I recited without thinking. I was expected to say the words, and I did. And now where had those words led me?

"No, this can't be happening." I rubbed my forehead, try-ing to erase my confusion and a rising sense of fear. "Serakh, if this is from the Bible, which it isn't, but if it is, how can you be alive at the time of Moses and at the time of Joseph? You said yourself that Joseph died a long time ago." Perhaps logic would put an end to this strange imprint on my imagination.

"I am eighteen," she said. "I have been eighteen for more than four hundred years. To some, time means everything. To others, nothing."

"That's ridiculous."

Serakh turned toward me. "I know," she said softly. "Even Tirtzah looks at my smooth face and cannot believe that the wisdom of many years has grown inside my heart. Except for the color of my hair, I have not aged one hour since the day I told Grandfather Jacob that Uncle Joseph was alive and in Egypt. Grandfather Jacob prayed that I receive an abundance of years. I cannot explain this, Miriam. It is the will of The One."

"How old is Tirtzah?"

"Sixteen, she tells me. She grows as a regular person. They all do—her sisters, Moshe, everyone. They grow and they will die, like my beloved Miryam the prophetess and sister of Moshe. Maybe one day I will die, too."

The Serakh I met at Temple Beth Israel had looked so human hobbling on her high-button shoes. *And now?*

"Are you an angel?" I asked, as if that might explain everything. Maybe this was more like a visitation than a dream. *Do visitations happen to Jews?*

Her hazel eyes caught mine. "Are you?"

"Am I what? An angel? Of course not. No matter what you tell Tirtzah and her sisters, I'm just me."

"I, too, am just me. Come, it is time to return."

"Yes, definitely!" *Let this dream end.* I was eager to return to reality.

Serakh helped me to change into my 1912 clothes. She wrapped us in my shawl and twined the corner fringe with the blue thread around her fingers.

"Put your hand on mine."

I did. The blue glow spread across my fingers. That warm feeling started again. I closed my eyes and braced myself for the pulling—the crushing—the blue lightning—and the darkness.

Ten

SERAKH SQUATTED BESIDE ME. SHE WAS wearing the same clothes she had worn in my dream, but we were no longer in a cave. I was sprawled on my kitchen floor.

"You will adjust," she said. "It will be easier on your body next time, and on your mind."

I struggled to open my mouth. "Next time?"

"Yes, you told Tirtzah you will return, remember? Now you must think of ways to inspire her to take a brave step."

My teeth itched and my head felt like rubber. "Pardon?"

"She and her sisters must go before Moshe and the elders and ask for their father's land. Tirtzah knows this in her heart, but she is afraid." Serakh patted my hand. "Would you like me to seat you by the table, Miriam? That is the custom in Port Land."

I managed a half-smile. "I'll rest here for a few minutes."

She lifted my head, popped a licorice nib in my mouth before I could refuse, and then took one for herself. "Let us bring these next time. Makhlah will like them. Poor child, she is so young and so frightened."

Serakh gently returned my head to the floor. "Close your eyes against the flash."

I was so weary. As I closed my eyes, I felt her cover me with the shawl. Lightning streaked inside my eyelids. The grandfather clock ticked in the hall. The clock chimed six. Did that licorice she gave me taste extra salty? Was it tainted?

The clock chimed seven.

Eight.

Nine.

"Miriam!" I shaded my eyes against the kitchen light. What was I doing on the floor?

Mama knelt beside me. "Oh, my baby, what's wrong? The house was dark. You gave me such a fright! What hurts? Did you faint?"

I sat up. The room spun. I closed my eyes and opened them again. Better. I wiped a trickle of moisture from the corner of my lips. "Mama, I had the strangest dream. I must have...I was out for a walk and I stopped by a confectionery, and then..."

"Julius, she's in here!" Mama called.

My prayer shawl had slipped to the floor—my magic carpet prayer shawl. I wondered what Uncle Hermann would say about my dream. Or was it a visitation?

Struggling, I scrambled to my feet. "Mama, no! He can't come in yet!"

Uncle Hermann had warned me about not letting Papa see my shawl.

Too late. There he was at the kitchen door. "You should have turned on the front hall light, young lady."

I grabbed my shawl.

"We came home and...*Gott in Himmel!*" Papa shouted. *God in heaven.* What a stupid expression for a man who said he believed in neither!

I clutched the shawl to my chest and lowered myself into a chair by the kitchen table. I tried not to look at the embroidered bag resting on the far corner of the table, so close to Papa.

No good. Papa's eyes grew enormous. He snatched the bag and crushed it in his fist. Then he sat down across from me and held out his hand.

"That rag you are holding, that cursed rag, give it to me, child."

I wrapped my arms around the shawl. "It's not a rag, Papa," I managed to whisper. "It's one of the most beautiful—"

"Did my foolish brother give it to you?"

I bobbed my head yes.

"Did he tell you who wore it last and what happened to her?"

I nodded again and hunched over.

"Did he give you permission to wear it?" Papa slammed his fist on the table. "Did he?"

"Uncle Hermann said the shawl belongs to me," I said, my voice weak and raspy.

Mama rushed to Papa's side. She smoothed his thinning hair. "Please, Julius, you'll work yourself into a heart attack."

Papa brushed her away. "Silence! This has nothing to do with you."

She retreated a few steps and glared at me. Mama—the very same person who, moments ago, was practically cradling me in her arms like the Serakh in my dreams.

I breathed in the shawl's warm woolen smell. This couldn't be happening.

And then it hit me: maybe it wasn't.

The first part—that Bible part—had to be a dream. So, if I hadn't flown to some far-off cave in some far-off time, I wouldn't really have been sleeping on the kitchen floor. This craziness with Papa was still in my imagination.

I have to bring myself back to reality. I have to wake up. Wake up, Miriam!

I curled my right hand into a fist. I closed my eyes and bit down on the knuckle of my right index finger. I bit down hard.

I heard Mama say, "Miriam, get your hand out of your mouth."

I bit my knuckle harder. It throbbed with pain. Real pain. I released my knuckle and stared at the red flesh. I studied my teeth marks.

This part—this part in the kitchen—this part was no dream.

"Julius, I'm calling the doctor," Mama said. "Something isn't right."

"Sit!" Papa ordered. "We don't need a doctor."

And if I wasn't dreaming about the kitchen part... *Impossible!*

"Give me the shawl, Miriam." Papa's voice rumbled with menace. "It does not belong to you. It brings only evil and death. I should have destroyed it years ago."

Destroyed? I had to save my shawl. "No, Papa. It's mine," I said, my voice growing stronger, despite my confusion.

"You are toying with fire, child."

Toying with fire? My brain felt like it was stuffed with cotton. I rubbed my injured knuckle with one of the embroidered flowers on the shawl. It felt better. Yes, definitely better. *Toying with fire.* That wasn't right.

"Playing," I said. "The expression is 'playing with fire,' Papa."

"Julius, no!"

I looked up. Papa was leaning across the table. The palm of his hand hovered inches from my face. I covered my head with my arm and turned away. I felt a tug at my chest. *My shawl!*

I managed to catch one corner of the shawl, but my grip was too weak. He yanked hard and my shawl swept across the table, tipping over our saltcellar and crock of honey.

I reached across the table. Papa slapped my hand hard. He crushed my soiled shawl under his arm. My heart raced in my throat.

"You have no right!" I shouted. "It belongs to *me*."

Papa stood. "Lillian, you take your daughter and you put her to bed. Do not wait up for me. I have to call Hermann." He ground his foot into the embroidered bag that had fallen to the floor, and stormed out of the kitchen.

Mama turned to me, her eyes narrow, her cheeks flushed with anger. "You should never treat your father that way. Now look what you've done—spoiling a perfectly delightful evening for your father and me over a silly shawl. I hope you're satisfied."

I glared back. "Satisfied?" My voice rang in my ears and my temples throbbed. I rested my head on my fingertips.

"Yes, satisfied," Mama hissed. "And now look what you've done to your hand. Your hair is a mess, your dress has a smudge on it. And your fingernails—filthy! Miriam, whatever did you do tonight? What has come over you?"

I stared at my hands. Mama was right. Tan and black spots had wedged themselves under several of my fingernails.

I shuddered. *This can't be!*

Sand.

The grandfather clock chimed, "Sand...sand...sand..."

Mama put her hands on her hips and frowned. "Well, what do you have to say for yourself?"

I ran past her and rushed up the stairs to my room. Gasping for breath and near tears, I slammed my door, collapsed on my bed, and stared at my fingers. Sand was still there, sand from fetching twigs with Tirtzah, sand from Serakh's cave, sand from the dream that wasn't a dream.

I unbuckled my shoes and yanked off my cotton stockings. There, under my toenails. *Sand.*

I dragged myself to the window, wishing I could find answers—reason, some measure of sanity—in that lunatic moonlight. The day shattered into a million fragments that floated across my mind.

Mr. Olsen greets me at the temple. Charity recites bread and roses, bread and roses. Kirsten tells me about Papa's VOTE NO *card. Serakh sits on my kitchen floor, eating pink fish and licorice. My shawl. The flash!*

Serakh tells me do not feel troubled, we are not lost. Tirtzah says that she will not let her sisters be taken into servitude. Adonai Eloheinu. *Thabible? Serakh tells me that Joseph and his brothers come from Canaan. Papa takes my shawl. Mama lets him. My shawl. My shawl. My shawl...*

I closed my eyes.

The fragments faded into the fog now smothering my brain. Somehow none of it was a dream, not one moment. *I should be more frightened than this. Shouldn't I?*

Bringing my hands to my lips, I kissed each sandy fingertip good night. *Now I am the one dividing my own life into* shoulds *and* should nots, *taking over Mama's job. I am so tired, so tired.* A strange peacefulness overcame me as I drew in one breath and then another. Then I surrendered to the familiar darkness of my bedroom.

Eleven

HOURS LATER, MAMA PULLED ME FROM sleep. "You'll have to make do with porridge and coffee," she said, setting the breakfast tray on my desk. "Your father is going to the Club today, and he expects you to stay at home. How are you feeling this morning?"

How am I feeling? I glanced at Mama, looking for an opening, a way to explain my odd mixture of certainty and confusion. But Mama wore her Dinner Party Look—a mask of blandness with a hint of upturned lips and unreadable eyes.

"Fine," I said.

She frowned and shook her head. "I trust you will say nothing of last night's misadventure to Mrs. Jenkins when she comes in this afternoon. It's none of her business."

Misadventure? I picked at a frayed seam in the nightgown I must have put on at some point during the night.

"Where did Papa put my prayer shawl?"

Her mask slipped. "Don't you mention that shawl again, you hear me? You've stirred up a hornet's nest, Miriam. When I went to bed, your father was still on the telephone with Uncle Hermann. Speaking in German, no less."

I winced at the thought of Uncle Hermann getting an

earful on the other end of the line. "It's mine. He has no right to keep it from me."

"I have no notion where your father put that silly shawl, and I'll thank you to stay upstairs until he leaves for the Club."

Mama turned and left. I studied my hands. There was still sand under my fingernails. Something *had* happened. I curled up in bed and grabbed my feet. My toenails were still sandy, too. And my toes seemed pinker than usual. I peered into the small mirror at my bedside. A slightly pink nose stared back. My face could have gotten a bit of sun at the rally, but not my feet. I had been wearing shoes then. I had worn sandals…later.

My stomach cramped and I rubbed my side. Yesterday was not a dream. As fantastical as my "misadventure" had been, it had to be true. I felt it in my bones. Everything that happened to me on Saturday really did happen.

If only Serakh were here to tell me what to do. Serakh from the time of the Bible. I stared out the window. The Bible—why not start there?

I grabbed Uncle Hermann's copy of the King James Bible. Genesis, Exodus, Leviticus, Numbers, Deuteronomy. I'd read part of Numbers the last time, when I was looking for Zelophehad's daughters.

This time I'd look for Serakh. But where? I had no idea where to begin, so I did the easiest thing: I started at the beginning.

Genesis, chapter one:

1 In the beginning God created the heaven and the earth.

I raced through the early chapters. Adam and Eve. Noah and the flood. How did it go? Abraham, Isaac, and Jacob, then Joseph. Serakh had said she was Joseph's niece, so she was a part of his story. She had to be in Genesis.

Mama interrupted me in the middle of Genesis, chapter nineteen. "You should eat something."

I nodded. Mama likes to have the last word, and this time I let her. She left. Hungry for answers, I resumed my search.

Jacob married Rachel. Rachel gave birth to Joseph. Serakh's story had to be coming up soon. I skimmed page after page until, in chapter thirty-one, I read:

> I cannot rise up before thee; for the custom of women is
> upon me.

What? I read that part again and an earlier part that said Rachel stole her father's idols.

> Now Rachel had taken the images, and put them in the
> camel's furniture, and sat upon them.

Rachel—that sweet Rachel we learned about in Religious School—told her father she could not get up because of her monthly flow. Whoever thought *that* would be in the Bible?

I stood and stretched, then returned to Genesis. Joseph popped up in chapter thirty-seven when he was seventeen. He died in chapter fifty. No mention of Serakh. This couldn't be right. I worked the crick out of my neck and went back to chapter thirty-seven. This time I read every word. Chapters thirty-eight, thirty-nine, forty, forty-one, forty-two—nothing. Chapters forty-three, forty-four, forty-five—nothing.

Chapter forty-six had another list of unpronounceable names. I read line after line. The sons of Reuben. The sons of Levi. The sons of Gad. Sons and more sons. Until…

17 And the sons of Asher; Jimnah, and Ishuah, and Isui, and Beriah, and Serah their sister;

Yes! There she was, the daughter of Asher. My Serakh. Not spelled the way she pronounced it, but still the same person. Genesis, chapter forty-six, verse seventeen—it was like a birth certificate.

Does the Bible have her obituary as well? And if she lived and died in biblical times, how could she have shown up in 1912? How could time fold in on itself that way?

Mama knocked and then immediately opened my door.

I closed the Bible. "You could have waited for me to answer before you barged in."

She studied me top to bottom and noticed my untouched breakfast. "Are you sure you are feeling all right, Miriam?"

"I'll be down in a little while."

"At least have some coffee." She put the breakfast tray in front of me. She eyed the Bible and shook her head, watching me while I ate. The coffee was cold and the porridge tasted like paste. Still, I hadn't realized how hungry I was.

"You should scrub those fingernails and get dressed now," she said. "And come downstairs for lunch. There are fewer salmon cakes left than I thought. Did you eat any while we were away?"

Everything was slipping into place. Everything really had happened, from the moment I first saw Serakh in my kitchen. *A fish that is pink! Yum!* I felt my shoulders relax and a grin creep across my face.

Mama wrinkled her brow in confusion. "Plus there was a half-empty cone of licorice nibs on the kitchen table," she said. "You didn't buy it at our regular confectionery, did you? No? Miriam, you shouldn't wander into strange places and buy unwrapped candy."

Perfect. I had my excuse, and she'd be satisfied that what happened last night was due to the licorice—which it wasn't. I managed to look contrite. "Yes, Mama, and I felt awful afterwards."

"I threw out the rest of that licorice just in case it was tainted," Mama continued. She frowned and fussed, then finally took the breakfast tray and left me in peace.

I opened the window and leaned out, wishing Serakh might come flying in like Peter Pan. I was the perfect messenger for Tirtzah, she said. Suppose I was my own perfect messenger. What would I tell myself? What would I do now? I had to compose my own line of reasoning, or at least a start at reason. But most of all I had to rescue my shawl.

Determination escorted me to dinner that evening. I smiled like a lady as I passed the tureen of potato soup to the man of the house. I sat with perfect posture and refrained from the childish habit of twirling a lock of hair while my parents babbled at the table—I was, after all, sixteen. I took a petite piece of mince pie and commenced to eat without my usual enthusiasm.

"Papa," I said, between bites, trying to keep my voice steady. "Let us resolve our unfortunate dispute with regard to my prayer shawl."

He wiped his lips on his napkin. "I do not like your tone of voice, young lady."

My mince pie turned to mud.

"Miriam, please," Mama implored.

Stupid me. I should have kept my mouth shut, at least until after Tuesday, when I went to the print shop. Now was it too late? I looked at Papa, keeping my eyes soft, my tone pleasant but confident. "I am not trying to argue. But Uncle Hermann made it quite clear that—"

"Uncle Hermann is not in charge of what goes on in this house."

My left hand, the one I'd been trained to keep in my lap during a meal, curled into a fist. "You are perfectly right, Papa. But that shawl is my personal property."

Papa threw his napkin on the table. "Enough nonsense! You have ruined my meal. Lillian, I will take coffee in the parlor."

After he left, Mama shot me another disapproving look. "You'll never get what you want from him this way."

"Papa has no right," I told her. "This is the United States of America in the twentieth century, not some faraway land back long ago. Women should be equal to men."

"He has every right. He's your father."

"I need my shawl, Mama. It belongs to me."

"I'll buy you another one, something not so woefully out of fashion. Shall we shop for it at that French *boutique* Mrs. Steinbacher raves about?"

"You're missing the point."

"Think, Miriam," she said. "Perhaps you are the one missing the point. You should listen to me more. You have a lot to learn about men in general and your father in particular."

I was quiet a minute, while I collected my thoughts. "You don't know anything…special…about my shawl, do you? Papa never told you. Neither did Uncle Hermann."

Mama put her hands on her hips. "Men are entitled to their little secrets. They feel more important that way. And heaven knows women have their little secrets, too."

I stifled a snort. My secret was hardly little. An image of Tirtzah flashed through my mind. "Mama, can women inherit land?"

"That's an odd question."

"Well, can they?"

"Yes, I suppose they can. I have a small fund Grandma and Grandpa Goldstein left me. Your father sold their house for me after they died, and he's invested the proceeds."

"In your name? I mean, is it all yours?"

"I should think so."

"But you don't know for sure?"

"Miriam, what is all this nonsense? I trust your father's business judgments completely. He came here with just the shirt on his back and a younger brother no older than you. Now he says you and I can afford to spend a whole month at the Algonquin Hotel when we go to New York in December. Believe you me, I intend to see that you are married to a man who can provide for you as well as your father has for me."

She bustled out of the dining room, leaving me to devour a second helping of pie, which tasted better without parents. In my room that night, I wrote to Florrie.

> *I went to a suffrage rally yesterday with Charity and Prudence—yes, me, your friend who planned to avoid the campaign. Kirsten was there from Papa's shop, and her fiancé Nils told everyone about an anti-suffrage card Papa printed in 1906. Oh, Florrie, it was so embarrassing! It made me furious, but it also made me glad that I had attended the rally after all, as if just being there would somehow help counteract Papa's actions.*
>
> *The strangest thing happened afterwards. At first I was sure it was a dream—a fantastical dream about a prayer shawl with a blue thread that Uncle Hermann gave me. I know you probably won't believe me if I tell you now—I scarcely believe myself, but Florrie, this changes everything!*
>
> *I know this must sound confusing. But I've realized something. Something important. I've been asking for the wrong thing! Not wrong, exactly, but too small. I've been*

asking Papa for a chance to prove myself in his print shop—
which I will do starting this Tuesday (yes, I finally worked
up my courage). And I've been moaning to you that Uncle
Hermann's boys will inherit Precision Printers one day.

Well, from now on I am going to ask for a bigger inheri-
tance—more than just a portion of the print shop. I want the
same rights that Papa has. The same rights Albert and Baby
Nathan will have when they become men. Why not? Women
should be citizens just as much as men are.

I so wish you were here in Portland! I wish you could click
your shoes and fly home like Dorothy from the Land of Oz. I
have so much to tell you.
In friendship forever,
Mim

I reread my words, and there they were, the three things I
had to do, my next three steps.

First, Papa's shop. I had to continue to do what I had
planned for weeks. I had to go to the print shop Tuesday
and somehow make Papa see the businesswoman I wanted
to become.

Next, the anti-suffrage card Papa printed. I had to speak
to Kirsten about it, find out more. I could do that on Tuesday,
too. I had to do something in this suffrage campaign to make
up for what Papa did, something more than making yellow
bows and going to suffrage rallies.

And then, most importantly, the blue thread. My dream
that wasn't a dream. What to do between now and Tuesday?
That was obvious: find my prayer shawl and keep it close, in
case Serakh returned at a moment's notice. Serakh. Tirtzah.
My stomach gave a lurch at the thought—an odd composite
of eagerness and fear.

I sat back and gazed at the grains of sand still under my

nails. Step One. Step Two. Step Three. They sounded easy, though I knew they wouldn't be. Still, they were what I had to do here in 1912 and what I needed to do to get back to… to there and then. My "misadventure" was going to be the greatest adventure of my life.

Twelve

WHEN I CAME DOWN TO BREAKFAST the next morning, Papa was already gone. Mama announced she had an appointment with Mrs. Steinbacher. "I'm sure you'll find a way to keep yourself busy," she said.

I cleared my throat, smiled, and took a sweet roll to the back porch. After I heard Mama leave, I searched the porch and potting shed for my shawl.

Mrs. Jenkins bustled outside with my coat. "You'll catch your death in this weather."

"Mrs. Jenkins, have you seen a white embroidered shawl with a bag to match?"

"Can't rightly say that I have."

"If you find them, you'll tell me, won't you, please? They belong to me."

She tut-tutted, but agreed to help. Our library, parlor, dining room, and front hall yielded nothing. The same with the attic, cellar, and the nook under the stairs.

Mrs. Sablovsky brought my newly hemmed gray skirt right before lunch. I tried it on with its matching jacket and the hat Charity had decorated for me. Mrs. Sablovsky and Mrs. Jenkins pronounced me perfectly professional—I was ready for the print shop. Mrs. Jenkins invited Mrs. Sablovsky to stay for leftover pot roast, and I joined them. Then it was back to my search.

The cedar chest in our upstairs guest room held nothing new. Mama's dressing room—nothing. My parents' bedroom was tidier than an empty coffin. Not a wrinkle in the bed sheets, not an object out of place. I hugged myself and thought of the trip to New York in December. My parents would be thrilled to marry me off to some wealthy aristocrat, a German Jew with a country home in the Hamptons or a summer cottage on the New Jersey shore. I placed Papa's left slipper where the right one should be and left Mama's pillow askew. A little disorder never hurt anyone.

There was only one place left to look. I paced in my room, rustling up as much courage as I could. *This is for Tirtzah*, I told myself. I trudged down the hall and forced myself to open Danny's door.

The air was musty and cold. Papa had insisted the room be redone into a sewing room for Mama and me, not that either of us sewed much. The wallpaper was similar to mine, ivory medallions on a pale yellow background. Mama's Singer sewing machine stood in one corner, a rocking chair and ottoman in the other. Between them—emptiness.

Danny's bed, books, and toys were gone. Only his big mahogany dresser remained, with nothing on top but a thin layer of dust. I opened the dresser drawers. Each was empty, except for the bottom one, which had something bundled in tissue half hidden in the back corner. I put the bundle on my lap and carefully unwrapped it. Danny's bear peeked out with his brass button eyes. One ear was discolored where I used to suck on it—because Baloo had been mine, too, when I was little.

I suddenly felt very little again. I buried my face in Baloo's matted fur and breathed in Mama's perfume—it was a wonder that Mama's scent had lasted this long. I remembered how good it felt to snuggle with Baloo on her lap while she read *The Jungle Book* to Danny and me. Danny had told me Baloo belonged to him first, so he got to name Baloo after the sloth bear in that book. I swore to him that I would never change the name.

And I remembered when Papa told Mama it was improper to bury a ten-year-old boy with a baby toy. Mama was crying.

"Baloo was his favorite," she moaned. "He'll be lonely."

Papa's voice grew softer. "Lillian, please. He is gone from us."

I wanted to run into their room and claim Baloo for my own. But I had stayed away. Mama and Papa had been so sad. Besides, Baloo had been Danny's bear first.

Now, back in Danny's old room, I hugged Baloo for another minute or two. Wrapped in sadness, I gently placed Baloo back inside the drawer and left, closing the door softly behind me.

Death pulled at my thoughts for the rest of the day—Danny's death and the stillborn baby boy who came four years later. I thought of Grandma and Grandpa Goldstein from Seattle. Dead. And Papa's parents, although I'd never met them. Papa's grandmother, his *savta*. And Papa's sister Raizl, who Uncle Hermann said had died in the shawl that was now mine.

§

THAT NIGHT A GIANT WINDOW HOVERED at the edge of my bed. A scorpion crawled across the glass. Then a bloody spike three feet high sprouted from the floor. Danny stood by the giant window. He was dressed like a tin soldier, and he wore my prayer shawl.

"No," I screamed. "Don't!"

But he didn't listen. Danny jumped through the window and landed on that spike. Blood spurted from his foot. He took off the prayer shawl and wrapped it around a girl who looked like Papa, only with a long dress and long black curls. They walked toward me, with tin soldier buttons where their eyes should be.

My voice exploded. "No! No! No! No!"

They came closer. Closer. They called my name. They doused me with Mama's perfume. Gasping for breath, I flung myself forward and opened my eyes.

"Shh…" Mama said. "Shh, Miss Marmalade. Everything will be all right. It's only a bad dream. You haven't had one in months, thank goodness."

I stared at Mama. Her little girl name for me pulled at the back of my eyes, and I mashed my lips together so they would stop quivering.

"Mama? I—there was blood everywhere, all over them. Even on my prayer shawl. And a huge spike and button eyes."

"Hush now," she said. "There's no blood. Go back to sleep now. Don't worry about that silly shawl. I took it to the laundry today. It will come back Friday perfectly clean."

I gulped in air and clutched my coverlet. "Wait! Mama, what did you say?"

Mama smoothed my hair. "Shh…go to sleep."

I grabbed her hand. "You have my shawl?"

"Do you have a fever? You haven't been yourself since you fainted in the kitchen. I'll be right back."

Fainted? I'd done no such thing. Still, how could I explain landing on the kitchen floor after traveling back from… then? My head fell against the pillow. I stared at the ceiling. Mama returned with a teaspoon and a medicine bottle. "Here, this will help you sleep."

"Where did you take my shawl? Please, I have to know."

"To the Han Lee Laundry. But that doesn't matter now. Drink this."

"I don't need any medicine."

"Yes, you do. This is as harmless as Lydia Pickham's Vegetable Compound. It will help you sleep."

I took the medicine—Mama can be very insistent in these matters. I turned on my side and felt her straighten the bed linens. *Han Lee*, I thought. *Remember Han Lee.*

§

THE NEXT THING I KNEW, MORNING sunlight was streaming through my window. The grandfather clock chimed ten. *Ten o'clock...no! The print shop!* I stormed into the kitchen.

"You look out of sorts this morning," Mama said.

"I have a dreadful headache. Plus, it's Tuesday. I was supposed to go to the print shop with Papa today. I've been planning this for days."

Mama shook her head. "You had a difficult night last night, as you might recall. That's the second time in three days. Surely you can go to the shop another time. I trust you'll be relaxing at home again today."

Mama glanced at Mrs. Jenkins, who was busily making poached eggs and toast. "There are worse things in life than staying in a comfortable house and having someone to look after you. I can't help it if you have a headache," Mama said.

"I told you I didn't need any medicine."

"You did? You were in no condition to decide anything for yourself."

Mrs. Jenkins shoved a dish of poached eggs on toast under my nose. "Eggs are good for what ails you."

Breakfast was delicious. So was the news that Mama had another appointment downtown. Angry as I was at missing my first real work day at Precision Printers, I could now concentrate on reclaiming my shawl. Two minutes after Mama left with Mrs. Steinbacher, I strode into Papa's study to examine the Portland City Directory. Han Lee Chinese Laundry was listed at the northeast corner of Second and Pine. I snatched a few coins from the rainy day sock I kept under my mattress and raced downstairs.

§

ALTHOUGH HAN LEE'S WAS ONLY A few blocks from Precision Printers, the two places were worlds apart. After I got off the streetcar, I walked past shops with bright red lanterns, exotic scrolls with bold black calligraphy, and exquisite painted fans. Smoked ducks hung in front of shops that smelled of spices and cabbage. *And the newspapers!* A compositor would go crazy setting Chinese type.

The woman behind the counter frowned when I asked about an embroidered shawl that she had received the previous day. "It was a mistake," I explained. "It should not have been brought here in the first place."

"Ticket?"

"For the laundry? My mother has it, I suppose. I'm not picking up any clean clothes, just the shawl she gave you by accident. She might accidentally have left an embroidered bag, too."

"Come back Friday."

"I'm sorry, but you don't understand. I need the shawl now."

The woman disappeared behind a curtain of green and orange beads. Soon a girl about nine years old came out front and asked me what I wanted. I explained about the shawl and added before I stopped to think, "Shouldn't you be in school?"

"I'm very sick today." She faked a cough. "Very con-ta-gious."

The girl was the picture of health, with a starched white top and a bright pink ribbon in her shiny black hair. "I'm not a truant officer," I assured her. "I'd just like my shawl. Here," I said, reaching into my coat pocket, "would you like this yellow bow as a gift? I didn't mean to scare you."

She grabbed my bow. "This is better than a sash." She disappeared behind the beads.

"What about my shawl?" I called after her.

The girl returned a moment later with a clipping from *The Morning Oregonian* and a bundle wrapped in brown paper. She jabbed her finger at a newspaper photograph of two white women and several fashionably dressed Chinese women and girls attending what the caption said was the Portland Suffrage Luncheon last April.

"See?" She pointed to a girl in the first row. "This is my cousin. She has two yellow sashes, but a bow is better. A bow you can put in your hair."

I smiled at her enthusiasm and admired the picture for a moment before getting out my change purse. "How much do I owe you?"

"You are a nice customer. No charge." At last she placed the bundle on the counter. "Your shawl and bag are still dirty."

"Here's a penny anyway. Buy some candy."

The girl pocketed the penny in half an instant.

I practically kissed the bundle as I left the laundry. A block away, I saw Mr. Jacobowitz, that serious-looking fellow who was Papa's office assistant. He was across the street and walking in my direction. He clutched a small bag, and I wondered what he had bought in this part of town. Tea? An herbal remedy? Curiosity almost got the better of me, but then I remembered my shawl. Suppose he told Papa he saw me? I put my head down and hurried away.

A few steps from the streetcar platform, I noticed the back of someone's head reflected in a shop window—someone with a long braid of the purest white. My eyes grew wide and my heart thudded in my throat.

It had to be Serakh. She must have waited until I had my blue thread back. Magical Serakh. She seemed to know my every move.

I whipped around. There was the braid again, bobbing along on a short person huddled under a dark blue coat and wobbling down the street. She'd found a gray dress when I first saw her—maybe this time she'd found a coat. The blue was almost the color of that magical thread.

"Serakh, wait!" I shouted. "I'm over here!"

An old Chinese man turned my way, his long white braid falling over one shoulder. I faced the shop window again to hide my embarrassment, and my fear that Serakh might never come back.

§

MRS. JENKINS EXPLAINED HOW TO WASH a woolen garment stained with salt and honey. I followed her instructions to a T—a Baskerville capital T to be exact—dissolving soap flakes in a stream of hot water in the bathtub, and then switching to cold water and easing the shawl into the tub to soak.

Sand lifted off the woolen shawl—desert sand. I saved a few grains in an envelope and reluctantly let the rest swirl down the drain. Then I spread the damp shawl and bag over my coverlet and opened my bedroom window to let in the late afternoon breeze. I sat on the edge of my bed and caressed the shawl's corner tassel with its blue thread. Nothing shimmered, nothing glowed.

I had no notion of what to tell Mama about the laundry. Still, I had until Friday to figure that out. The shawl was safe for now. It was time to get back on track with Precision Printers and that VOTE NO card.

I straightened my clothes, tamed my frizz with two tortoiseshell hair combs, draped the shawl and bag over hangers in my armoire where they wouldn't be seen, and presented myself at dinner. Papa studied my appearance and grunted approvingly. I apologized for oversleeping on a Tuesday morning, but he didn't seem to mind.

"You can oversleep without worry. I am here to take care of you and your mama."

"I'm fine, now, thank you. I'll be ready to start work tomorrow."

"We have you come on Tuesdays."

"Only Tuesdays?" I could scarcely hide my surprise.

"Of course," Papa replied. "You are not needed every day." It sounded like I was the cleaning woman, come to scrub the floors. Still, I didn't argue, lest I make matters worse. I had my shawl, and next week I would have my chance at Precision Printers. Patience wasn't my strongest quality, but I was almost seventeen after all and had to make an effort. Until then I could help Charity and Prudence with the suffrage campaign as long as I stayed behind the scenes.

Mama filled her wine glass and chatted about her plans to spend the next morning at Neighborhood House. "There are so many immigrant families in need," she said. "And since I've joined the Council of Jewish Women, don't you think I ought to support their projects, Julius?"

Papa grunted again. His body was at the table; his mind was not.

Mama barreled on. "Mrs. Steinbacher's chauffeur will motor us over and back. Miriam, let's bring treats for the kindergarten." She gave me The Don't Argue Look.

I dabbed the corners of my mouth and considered. It would be better to be on Mama's good side when I told her about the shawl. Plus one of the Jewish ladies might know more about prayer shawls for women.

"Certainly," I said.

Later I slipped into Danny's old room and put the prayer shawl in the dresser drawer next to Baloo. I figured no one went into that room, and Mama was forever coming into mine. And besides, it just felt right. Surely the shawl would be safe there.

Thirteen

BY THE TIME MRS. STEINBACHER'S PACKARD came on Wednesday morning, I had filled our picnic basket with a dozen apples. Her latest chauffeur ushered me into the front seat, while Mama and Mrs. Steinbacher sat in back—a perfect arrangement, as I rarely got to sit near handsome young men. He reminded me of Richard Broxburn.

The air felt crisp and clean. Mount Hood dominated the eastern sky, while the snow-capped dome of Mount Saint Helens held court further to the north. Both distant volcanoes stood as quiet as Mount Tabor on Portland's east side.

The Packard stopped in front of a three-story brick building at Second and Wood. The chauffeur offered me a hand down, which I gladly accepted. I climbed the steps to the main entrance, and Mrs. Steinbacher pointed me in the direction of the kindergarten. The teacher there set me to work slicing the apples I had brought. While the children munched, she pointed her chin toward a small boy sitting by himself. "How good is your Italian?"

"Awful," I admitted, as my Italian was limited to menus and two opera records.

"A pity. His family just arrived from Naples, and we're the only free kindergarten in the area. He'll wind up speaking

English with a Yiddish accent." She clapped her hands for attention. "Now children," she said, "let us say thank you to Miss Josefsohn for the apples."

They shouted something that sounded vaguely like "thank you." Most were poor Jewish children from Russia and Poland, and I felt as out of place as that Italian boy. When they left for recess, I took my empty basket and wandered down the hall. The walls echoed a sing-song English lesson from one of the classrooms. A woman stopped me near the main office. Unlike Mrs. Steinbacher and Mama, she wore a simple suit and had her hair pulled back in a no-nonsense bun.

"You must be Lillian's daughter, Miriam," she said. "I'm Gertrude Rosenfeld." She shook my hand with strong fingers and a warm grip. "If you are free, I could use a hand in the office. Can you type?"

"Not very well." I liked her right off.

"No matter, I'm sure you'll be fine." She cleared a place for me in front of an Underwood typewriter that was similar to the one in Papa's office. "We're sending a letter to everyone on this list, asking for contributions." She handed me an ink eraser. "This will take care of mistakes. Don't bother with carbon copies."

I sat on a rickety swivel chair, put a piece of stationery in the platen roller, and felt my shoulders relax. There's something solid and comfortable about typing words on a page. Almost as good as printing. A while later, Mrs. Rosenfeld brought me tea and a biscuit from the cooking class.

"You've slaved away for over an hour. Let's take a break. They sweetened the tea with raspberry jam. It's surprisingly good."

She was right about the tea. I stood and stretched. And that's when I noticed the yellow ink blotter lying on Mrs. Rosenfeld's desk. I wondered whether the suffragists had come to Neighborhood House on Blotter Day. Maybe Mrs. Rosenfeld was active in the campaign.

"I'm writing to my mother in Cleveland," she said, eyeing the piece of notepaper next to the blotter. "Thirty years in this country and she still doesn't read English. Do you know Yiddish?"

I shook my head. "My parents prefer French and German. My father is from the Bavarian part of Germany, and my mother's from Seattle. I don't know why she loves French."

"It's always good to know a second language." Mrs. Rosenfeld's eyes brightened, the way Sister Margaret's did when she was about to give a favorite lecture. "Here, let me show you." Mrs. Rosenfeld reached for the notepaper. "I'm writing in Yiddish, which uses Hebrew script."

"Um, this doesn't look like Hebrew lettering to me," I said, hoping I wouldn't have to admit I couldn't read Hebrew.

"Ah, right. You would know only the printed Hebrew from the prayer book. This is like cursive. But you know *mazel tov*, I'm sure. It means 'good luck,' but we use it like 'congratulations.' I'm congratulating my mother because she won two chickens in a raffle."

"Well then, *mazel tov*," I said, practically exhausting my knowledge of Yiddish or Hebrew. "Were they roasted chickens?"

"Live chickens, but that's another story. See the letter *mem* at the beginning of *mazel?* It looks very different from printed Hebrew. But other letters, like this *vet* at the end of *tov* looks almost like the printed letter."

"I should get back to my typing."

But Mrs. Rosenfeld was not through. "Yiddish has a lot of German in it, Miriam. Take the Yiddish word *tzvai*. Two. Like the German *zwei*. I'm asking my mother what she plans to do with two live chickens."

I stared at the squiggle next to Mrs. Rosenfeld's finger. "What's this letter?"

"*Tzadi.* It looks like a giant three, don't you think? A cursive *tzadi* doesn't resemble the printed *tzadi* at all." I examined Mrs. Rosenfeld's note more closely.

"Would you care for another biscuit? I'd be happy to teach you Yiddish if you'd like."

"Pardon? Oh, um…yes, please. To the biscuit, for now." That giant three looked like two of the marks embroidered on my prayer shawl. *They must be words. Are they magic?*

§

I DECLINED MAMA'S HALF-HEARTED OFFER TO spend the afternoon shopping with her and Mrs. Steinbacher. The moment I got home I rushed upstairs to Danny's room and studied my shawl. Some of the embroidered letters weren't exactly like those in Mrs. Rosenfeld's note, but this had to be Hebrew script. I tore a page from my copybook and wrote each letter as precisely as I could. One slip of my pen might make a huge difference, like turning an o into a q.

צדק צדק תרדף

I commenced to pace and plan. Mrs. Rosenfeld could translate the letters for me, but when would I see her next? Mama thought the shawl was still at the laundry, and I doubted she knew Hebrew anyway. Papa was out of the question.

That left Uncle Hermann. I strode into Papa's study and lifted the telephone receiver.

"This is the Western Electric operator. May I have the number, please?"

"Main 4786," I said, practically swallowing the mouthpiece. With luck he'd be home and still on speaking terms with me.

"One moment please," the operator said.

I licked my lips and slid a finger along the telephone's smooth candlestick base.

"Josefsohn residence."

"Uncle Hermann? I owe you a huge apology. Papa wasn't supposed to see the prayer shawl. It was all a big mistake."

"No doubt it was." His voice sounded cool and distant.

"I was wondering if I could stop by with something for you to translate. I think it's in Hebrew. Maybe Yiddish."

"A translation? I'm intrigued." Curiosity brought out the best in Uncle Hermann, like it did with me. "When would you like to come?"

"I'll be right over," I said, as I blinked at a flash of light in the hallway.

"Excellent. I'll see you soon."

"Bye," I murmured, returning the receiver to its cradle. I turned, and my pulse jumped and echoed in my ears. My stomach twisted.

Serakh had walked into Papa's study. "Peace be unto you, Miriam. As you see, I wear the garments of my place and time, because we must not tarry. Tirtzah needs you. Are you ready?"

Speechless, I stared at her and hugged myself. Heaven knows what she must have read on my face. Amazement. Excitement. Terror.

Serakh smiled. "Still no trust? Come, let us wrap ourselves in your fringes. You will use your eyes and heart to know what your mind struggles to accept."

Going once was an accident—I thought I had stepped into a dream. But going twice...even to see Tirtzah? Going when who knew what dangers might await me? And suppose something happened to the shawl? Could I still come back? Serakh touched my cheek. I studied her face. Open. Friendly. Placid. As if we were about to embark on a walk around the block rather than a fantastical flight that shattered all reason.

I took a great shuddering breath.

"This trip will be easier," she said confidently. "Each time will be easier."

Each time? I feel in my innermost self that this prayer shawl will change my life, but so soon?

"Miriam, if you are not ready…if this is too hard for you—"

"Wait! Don't leave me." I sucked in more air and tried to smile. "Please, just give me a minute."

"You will be gone and back before a minute passes in your Port Land." She squatted on the floor beside me and hummed a sing-songy tune I remembered from the last time. Then she looked at me expectantly.

"I'll get my shawl," I whispered.

She nodded and returned to her humming. I raced to Danny's room, fetched my shawl, and wrapped the embroidered bag around Baloo. "I'll be fine," I told the bear, needing to hear my own words out loud.

When I got back to Papa's study, Serakh was eyeing the telephone with suspicion. I sat next to her and pointed to the shawl's embroidered letters, hoping they might help me take the step I wanted to take but was afraid to. "These are words, aren't they?"

"Words? Yes. The letters are not of my place and time, but they speak of justice. Another Miriam once explained her needlecraft to me—Miriam, the daughter of Rashi. She wove the shawl anew after the old one burned in the synagogue fire at Isfahan. Only this single blue thread remains."

"So they are not magic words or anything like that?"

Serakh shook her head. "I do not believe in magic, Miriam, and I am not a conjurer. I believe in The One."

"How old was the old shawl, the one that burned?"

She patted my knee. "So many questions. You ask more than any of the others of your line who have traveled with me."

"How many others have there been?"

"Miriam, let us not tarry. This room smells of your father."

I needed a little more time to work up my courage. Clutching her hand, I pleaded with my eyes.

"There have been many others," she said. "Some lose their courage to come a second time. While I wait for you to decide, I will tell you about the old shawl, yes?"

I nodded.

"The old shawl. Who can say its age? I lose track of time. The Babylonians destroy the great temple in Jerusalem, and we are cast out, but the blue threads stay with us—hidden for the next generation and the next. The Romans destroy the second temple, and we are cast out, but the blue threads stay with us. Fewer threads. I watch a woman weave a shawl of fine white wool. She winds and knots a long blue thread for each corner to remember the words of The One so far from our homeland."

I still wasn't ready to go. *But will I ever be?*

"Thank you," I whispered. "I will pretend to be ready."

"Good. Now let us bring those pieces of dark sweetness for little Makhlah."

"The licorice? I don't have any more. No, wait. Mrs. Jenkins keeps a stash in the cupboard. I'll be right back."

I raced to the kitchen. Mrs. Jenkins was still out somewhere. I tore off a piece of waxed paper, reached behind the tin of baking powder, and grabbed a handful of licorice. There wasn't time to write my usual I.O.U. to her.

Serakh was staring out the window when I got back. Without another word, she draped my shawl across our shoulders.

Breathless, I reached for the blue thread and closed my eyes against the flash.

Fourteen

SERAKH'S CAVE SURROUNDED ME ONCE MORE. My body felt like pulled taffy.

"You are well, Miriam?"

I rolled onto my back. "Yes, I think so. Just achy."

She kissed my forehead. "This time I pray you will trust me as Tirtzah does. Remember that you and Tirtzah will always understand each other if you are touching her while you wear your blue thread. But only in this cave will you understand the others."

A young girl's voice echoed from somewhere nearby. "Peace unto you, Serakh."

"Peace unto you," she called back. "Find a comfortable spot where you are. I will join you shortly."

Serakh put Mrs. Jenkins's licorice nibs by my side. "Tirtzah's sisters will taste these and will think that you bring sustenance from The One. They will believe that you are wise. Your garments are a few paces behind you," she said. "When you are ready, come forward."

Then she walked away. I crawled to the back of the cave. Struggling against a rising panic, I changed clothes and draped my prayer shawl over my shoulders.

How could anyone think I was wise, when it seemed so hard just to think of myself as sane? This was all so strange, so beyond belief. I hugged myself and took another deep breath. *I. Can. Do. This.* Clutching the licorice nibs, I stepped toward the light.

Tirtzah and her four sisters had arranged themselves on the cave floor in a semicircle facing Serakh. They reminded me of Danny's tin soldiers, each carefully placed, awaiting instructions. Only Tirtzah looked at me directly. She smiled but didn't speak. I wondered if Serakh had instructed her to pretend we hadn't met before.

"We are blessed," Serakh announced. "Our messenger has brought you dark *mahn*."

The smallest girl eyed my licorice. "Do I have to eat it?" She seemed about as old as Albert, her sandaled feet covered in dirt, her face scrubbed clean. Another girl shushed her and looked at Serakh apologetically.

"Makhlah, you will like this *mahn*," Serakh murmured. "It is even sweeter than the *mahn* that The One has provided in our wanderings. I have partaken of it, and it is most delicious."

She motioned for me to sit by her side, leaned toward me, and whispered, "This *mahn* I think you call it manna."

Manna. The word was familiar. I doled out the licorice and slipped a nib into my mouth. Its sugary-salty taste felt good on my tongue. The sisters seemed to like the licorice too. As I watched them, I remembered the Passover story about food falling from heaven to feed the Israelites during their exodus from Egypt. Manna.

Tirtzah kissed the hem of my robe. "These are my sisters," she said. "Hoglah, Milcah, Noa, and Makhlah." One by one they kissed my hem. Like Tirtzah, they reminded me of the Indian women I sometimes saw downtown or by the docks:

exotic with their dark brown eyes, long straight black hair, high cheekbones.

Serakh began. "Most welcomed messenger, the father of these sisters was Zelophehad, of the line of Manasseh, a son of Joseph. He died in the wilderness, leaving no brothers or sons to provide for these who sit before you, his daughters."

Not knowing what else to do, I nodded and tried to look wise.

Tirtzah took up the story. "We are honored to have you before us," she said. She must have kept our first meeting a secret. I smiled at her. So had I. "What has happened to your mother?" I asked.

"She lives with us among the Manassites, the half-tribe of Joseph. But when the tribes cross into Canaan there will be no place for us there. The elders will give my father's share away. Our mother prays a man will find her pleasing and take her as a wife. But her new husband will not be required to provide for us. I fear he will take our goats as a bride price and then we will have nothing."

"Can't you and your sisters stay on this side of the river?"

Tirtzah shook her head. "That is forbidden unless we are taken into the household of a tribesman who remains here. When Gabi takes me as his wife, I will join the Reubenites on this side of the River Jordan. We hope to keep little Makhlah in our household, but he cannot provide for all of my sisters."

Tirtzah paused, waiting for me to reply. I put my palms together and let my eyes rest on her sandaled feet. I suddenly thought of Mama and the New York marriage market. Couldn't a woman be secure in her own right, without being attached to some man?

Serakh spread her arms wide. "Take courage, all of you.

Our messenger is also of the line of Joseph. In her place and time, women have the right to possess the land, is that not so?"

Miriam Josefsohn to the front of the class. I swallowed hard. I tried to imagine Sister Margaret giving me her most encouraging smile.

"Absolutely," I said, hoping I sounded confident. I had no notion whether Mama owned our house with Papa or had any stake in the print shop. She ought to, though. "Where I come from, women are very important."

The sisters sat there, silent. *Now what?* The first image to pop into my head was that statue in Washington Park.

"Where I come from, the people honor Sacajawea. She was about as old as Tirtzah. And she guided men across the mountains and deserts, hundreds and hundreds of miles, to discover a way to the Pacific Ocean."

Six sets of eyes stared at me. My face grew warm and my hands cold.

I decided to leave out the part about one of the men being Sacajawea's husband. "They listened to her, and she kept them safe."

Tirtzah looked the tiniest bit hopeful.

"Where I come from there are other women, too," I said. I wondered whether I should tell them about the suffrage banner with their name on it. *Would it be too confusing?*

"Go on," Serakh said.

"Um…there are sisters who have their own hat shop, the Osborne sisters. And there is another woman who is a leader of women and men, too. Some men, anyway. Her name is Anna Shaw. She makes speeches in many places and goes on marches to help women get their rights."

Milcah's eyes widened. "Are these women also of the tribe of Joseph?"

"Some are, I'm sure. Sacajawea was from the Shoshone tribe. And the Osborne sisters and Anna Shaw are of the tribe of, um…Jesus."

Hoglah frowned. "There are no such tribes."

"Not yet," I said. "But there will be." How could I explain the *olam* when I didn't understand it myself?

Serakh touched Hoglah's robe. "Listen to our messenger. She speaks the truth. Now that she is here, she will help you to ask for your father's share of land. You deserve your father's portion, and you must explain this to Moshe."

Hoglah yanked her robe away. "Our father taught us to obey, not to challenge our elders!"

"If the land is important to you, then you have to be brave, like Sacajawea," I said. "And you have to speak up for what's right, like Anna Shaw."

Milcah frowned.

Noa shook her head. "How can we ask for something that is not of our tradition?"

"Someone has to be the first," I said. "Surely women should have the right to own land. How else could they survive?" I figured that married women owned land in Oregon, but what about unmarried women? Did the Osbornes really own their store? I didn't remember. Portland seemed as far away as the other side of the moon.

"Do not stare in horror, Hoglah," Serakh said. "Our messenger sets you on the right path. Tomorrow all of you must bathe at first light and dress in your best garments. Meet us in my cave. Then we will go before Moshe and the elders at the Tent of Meeting."

Hoglah scowled and said nothing. Serakh stood. We did likewise. One by one the sisters bowed and walked toward the entrance. Makhlah turned to look at me once, but Noa pulled her away.

§

"Suppose they don't come back," I said, as we got ready for the night. My blanket was itchy, and I missed my feather pillow, smooth sheets, and quilted coverlet.

"They will come now that they have heard wise words from a messenger. Tomorrow you will tell them of the women of your time who gather in great numbers to claim their right to own land. Do not talk of newspapers, they would not understand. But tell the sisters that they have been remembered. My encouragement is not enough."

"Yes, I read that article. And I saw the banner that said, 'Like the daughters of Zelophehad, we ask for our inheritance.' Is that what you mean?"

"The very one. I found it on your Hallowe'en, in your year 1908. It is easier to travel on this day. Many wear strange garments then, and I am overlooked. I waited until you and Tirtzah were ready."

"But that banner was carried by the suffragists. It's not about owning land."

She settled herself on her blanket. "Suf-ra-jists? I have heard that word, but I do not know its meaning."

I sat beside her as the darkness deepened. "Suffragists. They are people who campaign for a woman's right to vote."

"Vote? What is this?"

"Vote." I took a breath and tried again. "Hmm... Voting is how we elect government officials and make laws. People raise their hand or cast a secret ballot. In most places it's just the men, but in some states, the women are allowed to vote, too."

Serakh cocked her head. "Do you also vote?"

"No, I'm too young. I think you have to be twenty-one in most places, and I'm only sixteen. Besides, women can't vote in my state. Not yet anyway. I'm trying to change that."

"You are a suffra…a suffered…?"

"Suffragist." Two beetles crawled along a crack in the wall. "It's complicated," I said, sounding annoyingly like Mama. "My father is against women voting. He and my uncle own a print shop, and I want Papa to take me into the business. I was supposed to start last Tuesday."

"That banner is not about women inheriting land?"

"No."

She rubbed a callus on her thumb. "Forgive me," she said. "I have traveled the *olam*, but it is rare that I come to your place and time. Still, I trust in the blue thread, which has led me to you. You can speak with Tirtzah outside my cave. You are of the line of Joseph. You are named for the sister of Moshe—for Miryam, who guided us, and rejoiced with us, and who died in the wilderness of Zin. She was a great prophetess. If she were here to inspire Tirtzah, perhaps it would help, but she is not."

I hugged my knees and hoped she couldn't see my face in the fading light. "You're wrong, Serakh. I'm named for a woman who died in Bavaria. I'm not anything like the Miryam in the Bi…in this place. I'm not wise, or…or…" The words stuck in my throat. I swallowed hard. "This is all a big mistake. I'm not at all special. I'm useless here. You're counting on the wrong person."

Fifteen

A GUST OF NIGHT AIR BROUGHT a sudden chill. Serakh crawled out of her blanket, walked toward the back of the cave, and reached into an earthen jar. She cupped something in her hands, stooped, and hollowed out a darkened area on the sandy floor. She blew into her hands. They glowed slightly, not blue this time, but a reddish-yellow.

"Help me build a fire." Serakh nodded toward a pile of animal hair and kindling.

I was at her side in an instant, glad for a small task I could manage. I put kindling in the fire pit and watched her coax an ember from a brownish-black clump into flame. The clump smelled of animal dung. The fire was meager and smoky.

"Serakh—"

She cut me off with a wave of her hand. Then she squatted beside me and tilted my chin toward her face. "The prayer shawl rests on your shoulders, Miriam. The blue thread brought you here with me. Tirtzah and her sisters need you. I need you."

I brushed her hand away. "All I've done so far is hand out candy."

She responded in that lullaby voice of hers. "You give sustenance—sweet sustenance and hope. You bring Tirtzah the fresh air that fans her spark into fire. When she gathers that strength from you, she and her sisters will do what is right."

I focused on the tiny flame. "That can't be enough."

Serakh put her hands on my shoulders. "It is more than enough, Miriam. I might have been mistaken about the picture from the newspaper, as you say. But I am not mistaken about you. You are named for my Miryam, as was your great-grandmother. You are the perfect messenger."

The perfect messenger? Me? What does Serakh know?

I tried to straighten out my brain, but it was no use. My eyelids drooped, and I curled up on the blanket. *Maybe I am the perfect messenger, at least in this wherever-I-am, so far from Portland. Who am I to say otherwise?*

I fell asleep with that thought and awoke the next morning with only a moment's confusion. I watched Serakh lift a square cloth with a hole cut in the center. She fingered the blue thread from my prayer shawl and compared it with an identically colored tassel at each corner of her cloth.

"The threads are the same blue," I said.

Serakh tensed. It felt good to take her by surprise. For a moment, she seemed more human.

"Good morning," she said, leaning back on her heels. "When we cross into Canaan, we will make again Joseph's dye and have blue fringes for our garments. Moshe has told us that everyone must wear *tzitzit*. Men and women. The fringes remind us to follow the teachings of The One. I see in your place and time that this law is not obeyed."

I blinked the sleepiness out of my eyes and stretched. "Men still wear prayer shawls at my temple."

Serakh frowned. "The teachings belong also to women."

"Well... um..." I thought of Charity, pinning that suffrage bow on my coat, the one I took off as soon as Mama and

I had left her hat shop. Blue threads and yellow ribbons—reminders to do the right thing. "Yes," I said. "They do."

I braided my hair, which was decidedly straighter in the dry desert air and fell to the middle of my back. We breakfasted on a kind of sour cottage cheese and flat bread. I longed for a cup of coffee and a sweet roll.

Serakh scoured our bowls with sand to clean them. "Today you must be ready to return at any moment. Wear the garments of your Port Land underneath the garments I have given you. You must look like one of the multitude."

"With my shoes on?"

Serakh saw my point. "How can we hide them?"

I scratched the back of my neck. "I'll loop the ribbons on my petticoat through my shoe buckles. Thank goodness I wasn't wearing a corset when we…when we crossed."

"Corset? What is this?"

"Corsets pinch your waist, push up your bosom, and push out your…*derrière*," I said, pointing to mine. "I don't know how Mama can stand them."

"Worse than your shoes." Serakh wiggled her hips and winked.

Laughing, I slipped into my 1912 clothes, hiking my skirt up slightly so the hemline wouldn't show at the bottom of the shift and robe. When Serakh wasn't looking, I wiped my breakfast bowl with my cotton stocking, in case I had to eat another meal in the cave. Then I draped my prayer shawl around my shoulders and covered everything with the ochre shift and robe. Had it been the Arctic, or the dead of night in this desert, I might have been comfortable.

Tirtzah appeared at the cave's entrance as I was trying to lick the scum off my teeth and wishing I had a toothbrush or peppermint. Her hair was still wet and her feet looked thoroughly scrubbed. Her sisters trooped in one by one, in order of height and, I supposed, age. Hoglah stared straight ahead, clenching her jaw. Milcah wiped a tear from her cheek. Noa studied the cave floor. Makhlah bit her fingernails. Their robes were the color of ivory stationery, and all of them except Makhlah wore headscarves to match. They looked grim.

Finally Tirtzah spoke. "We are ready to present ourselves to Moshe and the elders. But we beg you to speak for us. You are wise and we are not. We do not know what to say."

Serakh shook her head. "I cannot do this for you. Neither can our messenger. It is you who will lose your father's inheritance. So it is you who must prove that you are wise enough to claim it."

Hoglah snorted in disgust. She turned to Tirtzah. "I told you they would say no. Now see what you have brought upon us? You will be safe with the Reubenites, but we live by the goodness of the Manassites. If you anger them by asking for our father's share, we will lose what little we have left."

Tirtzah's face reddened with embarrassment. "I am doing this for your sake. Don't be so stiff-necked!"

"Stop it!" Milcah looked at her two older sisters. Then she looked at the floor and muttered, "They will laugh at us. Mother will be ashamed."

"No one will be ashamed," Serakh said soothingly. She turned to Makhlah, who had tears forming in her eyes. "Little Lamb, there's no need to cry."

Noa stroked Makhlah's hair. "Our little sister is afraid to go before the elders."

Tirtzah shook her head. "Is she not also frightened of becoming a servant in a stranger's household?"

Makhlah let out a wail. "Hush now," Serakh said, patting Makhlah's back. "Come. It is time." She leaned over to smooth Makhlah's robe.

Tirtzah stepped closer to me. "My father was a good man, Miriam," she whispered. "I do not wish to soil his name."

I wondered whether he was as stodgy and controlling as Papa. "Did he treat you well?"

"He gave heed to my words. He was kind. And he longed for his share of the land. Now his share will be gone forever."

Tirtzah's father seemed so different from Papa. *He listened to her!* "Tell them what you've told me," I whispered. "Tell them that this is not about you and your sisters. It's about your father's hope for his land."

She creased her forehead and bit her lip. Then her face relaxed and her eyes sparkled. "Yes, you are my perfect messenger."

Serakh urged the sisters toward the mouth of the cave. "Tirtzah, wait with your sisters at the entrance. Our messenger and I will meet you there."

I watched Tirtzah walk toward the exit with the others. She stood straighter than the rest of them, although I knew she must be as frightened as they were—maybe more so. Dear Tirtzah. She wasn't a friend like Charity, or even Florrie. She claimed a deeper part of me somehow. She trusted me. She made me want to set things right.

Serakh led me further into the cave. She gave me a long ochre scarf with crimson stripes. "You must not attract attention," she said. "Cover your head completely, stay close to me, cast your eyes downward, and say nothing."

"Aren't we walking with Tirtzah and her sisters?"

"We will remain some steps behind. As I do not show my age, some amongst my people grow suspicious. And you are a stranger. It is better for Tirtzah to be on her own."

§

ON THE TREK TOWARD THE ENCAMPMENT, the sun toasted my head and made the rest of me soggy. At first I saw little of the alien world around me except the sand under my feet. I suffocated in an extra layer of clothes, my chemise thoroughly wet and itchy against my chest. Clutching at my headscarf to keep it on straight, I longed for the silk fan that Mama had bought for me in Chinatown.

Mama and Papa must be frantic by now. Why hadn't I thought of that before? I touched Serakh's sleeve. "My parents were away the first time I came here. But this time I've been gone overnight."

She shook her head. "Time has not moved in your Port Land. Your world will remain as you left it—only you will have changed."

"Are you sure?"

"If we cross carefully, I am sure."

"I see," I said, although I didn't really. I felt even more anxious than before.

Soon there were people all around us, speaking in a language filled with strange rhythms and sounds. The sisters slipped from view as more and more people pressed up against us, their clothes smelling of campfires, animals, and exertion. Serakh placed her hand on my elbow. She guided me through crowds as densely packed and excited as revelers by the Willamette River on the Fourth of July.

And suddenly there we were, standing near a magnificent tent so large it could have swallowed half my house. Animal skins and yards and yards of purple, crimson, and blue material covered the sides. Wooden posts topped with beaten silver, gold, and copper reminded me of Temple Beth Israel's two tall, gilt-topped towers. I gasped in wonder. Anxiety gave way to awe.

"The Tent of Meeting," Serakh whispered. "Inside is the holiest of holy places."

Tirtzah appeared at Serakh's side and mumbled something to her. Hoglah and the three younger ones huddled a few feet away, a knot of robes, headscarves, and nervous tension.

Tirtzah grabbed my hand. "Peace be unto you, sister of the heart," she said.

Sister of the heart. Yes. That's what she was to me. I brought her forehead to my lips. "I'll be close by," I whispered. "I won't let you down."

She joined her real sisters and led them toward that spectacular tent. I started to follow them. Serakh grabbed my sleeve and shook her head.

"But I have to see Moses," I told her. Moses. That was about as fantastical as you can get. In my wildest dreams… *But this is no dream.*

"I will not deny you, but we must be very careful. Stay well away. They must not see you." She pointed to several dozen men who stood or sat near the entrance. Two of them carried spears.

Ignoring the spears, I edged closer.

Sixteen

HIS HAIR AND BEARD WERE AUBURN. His robes were mostly a blue that nearly matched the thread on my prayer shawl, and there were other threads woven into patterns of crimson, purple, and gold. His chest was covered by a thick square made of cloth and metal with twelve brilliantly colored stones. A blue and gold turban crowned his head. He looked like he belonged inside that magnificent tent. He looked like a king.

"Moses," I murmured to Serakh, who was keeping a watchful eye on the crowd.

She shook her head. "Eleazar *ben* Aharon," she whispered.

I frowned. The name meant nothing to me.

"Eleazar the priest, the son of Aharon the priest, the brother of Moshe and Miryam. Moshe is over *there*."

I looked where Serakh was pointing, but didn't see anyone dressed like a king. Then I watched Tirtzah kneel and kiss the hem of an old man's robes. They were dyed the same ochre as mine, with crimson stripes similar to my headscarf. The man sat on animal skins, under a huge palm tree that looked twenty times larger than the potted one in our parlor.

I gave Serakh a questioning look. She nodded. Moses. Except for his darker skin and his robes, he could have been my great-grandfather. His beard was white, his face deeply lined. Several men stood at attention by his side. Tirtzah stayed on her knees. She seemed to quake in his presence.

Keeping her head bowed, Tirtzah talked softly to Moses for a moment or two. Then Moses gestured toward her sisters. Tirtzah stood, bowed again, and retreated a few feet. Milcah slowly came out of the crowd to stand just behind Tirtzah. Noa followed, with Makhlah clinging to her side. Hoglah inched toward her sisters. Milcah reached out and took her hand.

Tirtzah touched the gold ring in her nose and glanced in my direction. Her mouth was drawn and tight, her eyes pleading for help. She seemed to be losing confidence by the second. She began to speak more loudly, her voice strained and quavering. Moses leaned forward. The crowd fell silent.

Tirtzah said something again. She pointed to her sisters. First little Makhlah shuffled forward, mumbled gibberish to Moses, and retreated behind Noa's robes. Noa and Milcah each bowed their heads, recited a string of words, and then stepped back. Hoglah mumbled worse than Makhlah, and said even less. Finally it seemed to be Tirtzah's turn again.

I longed to stand beside her and touch her, so that I could understand what she was saying. Once I heard what sounded like "Zelophehad," and I knew she was speaking about her father. I whispered to Serakh, "What is Tirtzah saying?"

Serakh's lips brushed my ear. "Tirtzah explains the plight of her sisters. She tells Moshe that her father was an honorable man. She asks why her father's share of the land should be divided within the tribe as is the tradition when a man has no sons. She says her father's name would be lost forever. Our Tirtzah is wise. She asks in the name of her father, not herself."

Yes! For that one brief moment I did feel like her perfect messenger. Tirtzah had taken my advice. *Perfect!*

Tirtzah hesitated and then began again. She placed her hand on her heart. She gestured toward the ground. I wished I could see her face, half hidden by her headscarf, but I dared not move.

Moses stroked his beard. Eleazar frowned. An older man, who also wore a fancy turban, shook his head and muttered something.

Serakh continued. "Tirtzah asks that she and her sisters be allowed to claim their father's portion of the land, the portion that the elders intend to divide among her father's brothers."

I nodded. With Moses, everything was supposed to go well. *Isn't that what they teach you in Religious School?*

Tirtzah said nothing more then. She bowed again to Moses and to several other men. People in the crowd began to move. There was a low murmur. Then a man with a curly black beard yelled in anger and pushed through the crowd toward the five sisters. Another man raised his fist and followed. A third one joined them.

"Serakh, what's wrong? Those men look ready to explode. We have to do something!"

"Shhhhh!" she hissed. "You are talking too loudly in a language they have never heard."

The three men spat at Tirtzah's feet. She flinched as if she had been struck. Finally she took a step back. Hoglah fell to her knees and clasped her hands toward the men. She seemed to be begging.

I tugged at Serakh. "We have to do something! The daughters need that land. Look at Hoglah, she's ready to give up now. Tirtzah won't last long."

Serakh shook her head and said nothing.

The three men circled the sisters and shouted at them. Milcah covered her head in her hands. Makhlah started to cry. Noa's eyes were filled with terror. Tirtzah bowed her head. Hoglah huddled on the ground.

I let go of Serakh and took a step forward.

She reached for my arm. "Miriam, you do not know our ways. You must not interfere."

I jerked away and took two long strides. "I can't let this happen," I said—too loudly. "She needs me!"

A little boy tugged at my robe and said something to me, his eyes wide with wonderment. An older girl suddenly jerked him away.

I heard Serakh call after me, "Stop!" I turned and saw a man grab her arms. Part of me wanted to return to her side, to apologize, to explain, to make sure she would be all right.

But how could I? Someone had to speak up for justice. I had to save Tirtzah.

I took another stride and then another. The man with the curly beard looked at me. He motioned to the others, and all three turned toward me. The man growled at me—ugly words that must have been filled with hate. I felt my face burn, but I kept my gaze steady. Tirtzah's perfect messenger did not turn away. I had to do what was right for my sister of the heart, especially when her real sisters thought she was wrong.

I could feel Serakh watching my back. "Do not move any closer," she said. "Look down, and I will come get you."

The man with the curly beard grabbed Tirtzah and threw her into the dust. His eyes locked on mine.

"No!" I shouted.

Someone grabbed me. I yanked free and raced to Tirtzah. She scrambled to her feet. We hugged.

"Go back," she said. "My father's kin are furious. You are in grave danger."

"Moses will understand," I assured her, hoping that was so. "I've got to explain. It's your only chance."

I pulled myself away from her, squared my shoulders, and marched into the empty space between the sisters and Moses. The three men seemed struck dumb. I heard nothing but my own rasping breath. I stood face-to-face with the man everyone said was the most important leader of the Jewish people. *My people.*

I looked back toward the sisters. My headscarf fell to my shoulders.

The crowded hissed and shouted. Hoglah and Milcah grabbed Tirtzah. Tirtzah called to me, but this time I understood not one syllable. Noa stared at me and touched her hand to her headscarf. Realizing what was wrong, I covered my head and turned back toward Moses. He looked puzzled, but not angry. My mouth went dry.

"Come away!" Serakh pleaded with me as she struggled to free herself from a man who held her wrists.

No. I stood my ground. Tirtzah depended on me. All of her sisters depended on me, even Hoglah, though she wouldn't admit it. I took a deep breath. I bowed as I had seen Tirtzah bow, and I faced the one man who really mattered.

"I am here to speak on behalf of the daughters of Zelophehad," I said, trying to sound important. He had to understand me. Serakh and I could communicate, and she was hardly mentioned in the Bible. But the Bible said that Moses spoke with God. And Moses did other amazing things I couldn't remember. Surely he could do what Serakh could.

I put my hand over my heart. "I come from another time and place. I am Miriam of the line of Joseph, and I beg you to honor their request for their inheritance." At that one crazy moment I thought of Mama and her favorite motto: It pays to be polite. "Please."

His eyes were deep brown, almost welcoming. "Miryam?"

"Yes! Miriam. You understand me. I knew you'd be able to, I just knew it."

"No!" Serakh shouted. "Moshe understands nothing but his sister's name. And you are wearing her robes. Be silent, bow, and step away. Walk back to me, before he thinks you are a conjurer and orders you to be put to death!"

Seventeen

Miryam's clothes? I suddenly itched all over. No wonder the robes Moses wore looked like mine. As I turned toward Serakh, I saw a woman eyeing me with such horror that I thought devil's horns must have sprouted from my head. A chorus of menacing voices surrounded me, and the two men with spears who stood near the entrance of the tent began to move toward me.

"Serakh, I need your power to speak to him."

"I do not have such power to give you. Come away. Now." She switched to a language that I couldn't understand, the language of these people. The Hebrew they spoke—if it was Hebrew at all—sounded like a distant dialect of the Hebrew I heard back home.

Moses stroked his beard and frowned. I searched his face in vain for some sign of hope. My head pounded. My ears buzzed, and I felt dizzy and sick.

"Please, Your Honor...Your Holiness...Serakh brought me here. You've got to listen."

Moses said nothing. The man with the curly black beard picked up a large round stone. Makhlah shrieked and raced to me. She hugged my legs and buried her face in my robes.

"Get away from me," I urged, hoping she'd understand. She didn't budge.

Then Tirtzah was at my side, her hand on my waist. "We stand together," she whispered to me, her eyes fierce. She took Makhlah's hand and called to the sisters behind us. Milcah and Noa took a step forward. Hoglah stayed put.

Serakh's voice rose above the din. "Miriam, speak to them of The One, of Our *Elohim*. Remember the words and say them now."

Our *Elohim*? I closed my eyes and struggled to think straight. I focused on my time alone with Serakh in her cave and on the Yom Kippur service where we had met. Our *Elohim. Eloheinu.* I cleared my throat, filled my lungs with the hot desert air, and chanted the only Hebrew prayer I knew by heart. "*Shema Yisroel Adonoi Eloheinu Adonoi echod.*"

Would Moses understand the kind of Hebrew I recited so many centuries after his death?

I no longer felt Tirtzah's hand on my waist. The noise of the crowd began to die away. Still I kept my eyes shut, afraid of what I might see if I opened them.

"Hear, O Israel," I whispered to myself, remembering the translation in the prayer book, "the Lord is our God, the Lord is One."

Silence.

Then someone pressed my shoulder, and I heard Serakh's voice, strong and steady. "You have done well, my Miriam sweet and strong. You speak of The One who brought them out of Egypt. You are still a stranger to them but no longer an enemy."

I dared to open my eyes. Serakh was beaming. Noa—and even Hoglah—stood near us. Tirtzah held Makhlah in her arms. The two men with spears had returned to the entrance of the tent.

Moses beckoned me to approach.

My heart beat in my throat. Serakh squeezed my hand. She and I stepped forward. As Serakh spoke, Moses shifted his gaze to me. He brushed a fly from his cheek. A pleasant odor rose from his clothes, spicy and sweet, like cinnamon and mulled wine. He smiled at me once, and I noticed two teeth were missing.

Serakh touched my shoulder. "Can you show Moshe your blue thread without removing Miryam's garments?" Serakh asked. "Make sure your headscarf does not fall again. You must maintain your modesty."

I slipped my arm into my sleeve and touched the shoes I'd tied to my petticoat loops—shoes in the wrong time and place. I felt for my prayer shawl and ran my fingers over the corner fringes. A faint tingle told me when I'd touched the right one. I pinched it gently and pulled my arm through the sleeve. The blue thread emerged. I bent toward Moses.

"*Eloheinu,*" I said, as he touched what I held in my hand. I longed to say so much more, yet there didn't seem to be a need. Perhaps I'd already said it all.

Moses turned to Serakh. They spoke again, and I knew everything would be all right.

"Bow your head," Serakh told me. As I did, Moses placed his hands on my shoulders and recited words that sounded vaguely familiar. His grip felt firm and comforting. My eyes filled with tears.

Moses spoke to the crowd. Afterward, a hundred conversations erupted around me. When I looked up, I saw the back of his robes as he walked into the Tent of Meeting.

"Moshe has declared that he must speak with The One about the daughters," Serakh said. "We will wait and watch over them until he returns. Certainly he will not emerge before the noonday meal."

"But Moses will do what's right, won't he, Serakh? He'll give them their land."

She turned her palms upward and cocked her head. "He will do what can be done. The daughters are safe for now, as are you. Moshe has given you his blessing."

His blessing. If we have such things as souls, then surely mine was radiating light. Yet even knowing the magnitude of what had just happened, I felt strangely calm.

"We shall wait for the decision of Moshe in the hospitality of your mother's tent," Serakh announced to the sisters. "Tirtzah, you have spoken wisely in the name of your father." Milcah nodded. Noa fussed over Makhlah, who still seemed upset. Hoglah grabbed Tirtzah's arm and hissed something that sounded not at all like a compliment.

My eyes met Tirtzah's. I crossed my fingers and gave her a hopeful look. She frowned in confusion.

Doesn't she know that good luck sign? "Tirtzah," I said, and smiled the biggest smile I could muster. She did the same.

The crowd parted in our presence, as if we were royalty or diseased. But a muscular young man stepped forward to stand by Tirtzah, a hair's breadth away from touching her.

"Oh, my!" I murmured before I could stop myself. He looked like Richard Broxburn, the bookstore clerk whose charm and good looks had tantalized Florrie and me in Portland.

"This is Gabi the Reubenite, who wishes to marry Tirtzah," Serakh whispered to me. "You must not stare at him. She will wonder at such boldness."

I pretended to adjust my robe until my embarrassment faded.

I kept my head down and followed Serakh through the camp. The sun grew hotter. My head throbbed. The walk seemed endless—tent after tent, many filled with women's voices, goats tethered to stakes or roaming free, a circle of men squatting together and talking loudly, children laughing, squabbling, or racing past, the littlest ones naked from the waist down.

Serakh stopped sometime later. It could have been ten minutes or an hour. "Tell your mother we are coming, Tirtzah. Our messenger and I will rest for a moment under this tree."

She guided me to a shady spot. Grateful, I sat beside her, and wiggled my hips until the shoes around my waist didn't bother me. I took off my sandals and rubbed my feet.

"Do not uncover the soles of your feet in public." Serakh flicked her robe across them and rolled her eyes.

But our messenger's feet hurt, I thought, putting on my sandals. *Our messenger has a headache, and our messenger would like a large glass of lemonade, several sweet rolls, and a long soak in the bathtub.* Seeing this Gabi version of Richard, I suddenly longed for home.

I brushed sand from the robes that made Moses think I was his dead sister. "Why didn't you tell me I was wearing Miryam's clothes?"

"Why didn't you stay by my side?" Serakh sounded like Florrie, not someone who was over four hundred years old.

"We're even-steven," I said, now that the danger was past.

"Even what?"

I smiled. "I mean you had your reasons and I had mine. Tell me about Miryam, Serakh. The sister of Moses. Was she your best friend?"

Serakh rubbed the callus on her hand. "Miryam is more than that. Her wisdom still inspires me. I have watched her grow up and grow old. Her death tears at my heart." Serakh wiped her nose with the back of her hand. She called to a boy who looked about the age Danny was when he died.

He nodded and scampered away, arms pumping the air, legs flying.

I sifted sand through my fingers. "My brother's death was like that," I told her, suddenly feeling the need to tell Serakh all about Danny. "Tearing at my heart, I mean. We had a favorite game—Steadfast Tin Soldier."

"You played war?"

"*The Steadfast Tin Soldier* is a story our mother read to us when we were little. It's about a toy soldier who loved a paper ballerina. When Danny got bigger, he used to jump from our kitchen window, like the tin soldier did. He'd go on adventures and tell me about them."

The boy returned with a handful of what looked like huge, smooth raisins the color of caramel. He dropped them in Serakh's lap.

"Dates," she explained. "The fruit of this tree. Eat them carefully, there is a hard seed inside." She scooped out a shallow hole in the sand.

I filled my mouth with warm, sticky fruit, sweet as honey. My headache dissolved.

"How did your brother die?"

I put the date pit on the ground next to me. "Danny must have jumped from that window a hundred times. But one time he landed on a roofer's nail, and it punctured his foot. My mother cleaned the wound as best as she could. Four days later my father fetched the doctor. By then it was too late." I bit my lip and reached for another date.

Serakh waited quietly.

"Danny played Steadfast Tin Soldier because of me. I liked to watch him jump from the window. I didn't know he could get hurt. I didn't know he could die."

She touched my hand. "This game. How old were you the last time you played it?"

"Seven. Danny was ten."

"You were a child, no more than the age of Makhlah. It was not your fault." She leaned forward and spat the date pit into the hole. "Now you try. Chew the fruit and spit as I do. Did you ever spit seeds before? Try."

I rolled the pit on my tongue, puckered my mouth, and took aim at the hole in the sand. Bull's-eye.

"Here," she said, offering me another date. "Do that again."

I did. No one had ever encouraged me to spit seeds before, and I must admit I enjoyed it. Danny retreated back to the place I kept him, tucked away in my mind—safe.

"I am sorry I did not tell you about Miryam's clothes," Serakh said, sounding serious again. "I thought you would be safe if you stayed by my side. What you did today was brave, but also foolish and dangerous. I brought you here to inspire Tirtzah, not to act in her place. Save your interference for your own spot on the *olam*."

"But what happens here is so important!"

"In your Port Land is there nothing worth fighting for? You say women there gather to ask men for more rights. Would your elders punish you if you interfered to help this Annashaw?"

I took another date and chewed slowly. Tirtzah dared to do something because her father was dead. But mine was very much alive.

Serakh let the matter drop. "Moshe knows of my travels and has respect for me," she explained. "I told him that no harm must come to you and that you wear the blue thread."

"So we're safe now? Is that why that man is guarding us?"

"Who?"

I cocked my head toward a fierce-looking man some yards away—a large man with bushy hair, a scraggly beard, and a scar that started at his calf and disappeared mid-thigh under a torn and filthy tunic. He carried a long, thick pole, which I imagined he used to herd goats. Only there were no goats nearby.

Eighteen

SERAKH GRABBED MY HAND. "WE MUST go. That man is evil, Miriam. Do not look at him."

"Suppose he follows us?"

"We are under the protection of Moshe, at least for now." She linked arms with me, and we hurried away. I looked over my shoulder once—the man was gone. I felt my jaw relax.

"When we go to the tent of the sisters, they will offer you food," Serakh instructed. "Take only two bites, and then place your hand above the serving plate and smile. They will offer you water. Drink the whole cup, even if it tastes bitter. Do not spill any on the ground."

"Will I be able to understand them in the tent?"

"No."

"What about Tirtzah?"

"Speak with Tirtzah at her peril. If she appears to understand you while others do not, they might think she is a witch."

"That's ridiculous."

"But it is so. You have inspired Tirtzah, and now, for the safety of all, you must go back to your Port Land as soon as Moshe brings us his decision. Do not argue with me, Miriam.

This is the way it must be." Serakh got that fierce look again, and I didn't say a word.

Gabi stood outside the tent and bowed as we entered. I nearly gagged at the smell. In the sudden dimness, I could barely see Makhlah curled up asleep next to two small goats tethered in the corner. A woman sat cross-legged in the opposite corner, twirling fibers attached to a spindle. She rose to greet us, holding her palms out toward us and bending slightly at her waist. Serakh did the same and removed her headscarf. I copied her exactly.

"Peace unto you," Serakh said. "My companion has taken a vow of silence. Still she greets you with respect and thanks you for your hospitality."

The woman went back to her spinning. Her look reminded me of Mama when she has to entertain an unwanted guest.

Serakh motioned me to sit near the center of the tent. "Your wool is worthy of priestly garments," she told the woman. "Did your husband's kin give you this fleece?"

The woman nodded, adding what seemed to be a paragraph of explanation. As the two women conversed, I thought about home. What would I do in Portland to support suffrage for women? Give a *tonneau* speech—standing by the back door of an automobile and addressing the crowd? How many men would hear me, change their minds, and vote for women's suffrage? *Couldn't I do more?*

Milcah entered with a large earthen jug and a small bowl. Serakh explained my "vow of silence." Milcah frowned, but passed the water to Serakh, then to me. I drank the bowl dry, and thanked her with a nod. Noa arrived with a platter of small round cakes, fritters of some sort. Milcah said something to her, and Noa rolled her eyes. I took two cakes, as Serakh instructed, and nearly choked on the spices.

Makhlah woke up as Tirtzah and Hoglah entered, looking like they could use a nap, too. Milcah spoke to them, and Hoglah pursed her lips. Touching my sleeve, Tirtzah leaned toward Hoglah and muttered, "If you dare to say anything against our messenger I shall stick brambles in your hair." I stifled a laugh.

Hoglah glared at Tirtzah and spat out a reply that sounded not the least bit friendly. With so many of us in the tent, the air turned stuffy and rank. The goats bleated their discomfort. I longed to go outside, even though it meant another dose of hot sun.

When I thought I could stand it no longer, Gabi shouted something from outside the tent. Serakh thanked Tirtzah's mother for the hospitality and told her we had to gather at the Tent of Meeting. All of us except Tirtzah's mother and Makhlah had on headscarves. Tirtzah's mother continued her spinning, as if Tirtzah's hopes and plans had nothing to do with her. Just like Mama.

I wanted to tell Tirtzah that everything would turn out all right, although I dared not speak to her directly. I remembered that Sister Margaret said Roman emperors made the thumbs-up sign to spare the lives of Christian gladiators. Those gladiators were nearly two thousand years ago for me, but probably hundreds of years in the future for Tirtzah. I decided to keep my thumbs to myself and settled for what I hoped was an encouraging smile.

The sun shone ferociously on our way back. Again Tirtzah and her sisters stood alone before Moses and the others gathered in front of the Tent of Meeting. Serakh, Gabi, and I stayed near the front of the crowd. Eleazar raised his hand for silence. Moses spoke.

Queasy and anxious, I wanted to believe everything I had learned in Religious School about Moses. He gestured toward the cloudless sky and to Tirtzah, to the tent behind him and to the people. I remembered his touch on my shoulders, his blessing. I willed myself to stay in one spot and to keep quiet. Tirtzah and her sisters—even little Makhlah—stood impassively, seemingly focused on the ground a few feet ahead of them. Serakh's face told me nothing. I dared not look at Gabi.

Suddenly Makhlah's face crinkled into a grin. She let out a joyous whoop, then covered her mouth with both hands as Noa shushed her.

No translation needed. Tirtzah and her sisters would get their father's land. One word welled up silently inside me, a memory from Yom Kippur services: *Hallelujah!*

"Do not show your excitement," Serakh warned. I struggled to hide my joy.

One by one, the sisters bowed to Moses. They walked backward toward us, their heads down. Hoglah pushed her way into the crowd. Tirtzah started to follow her sister, but Serakh grabbed her sleeve.

"Let her be," Serakh said. Noa and Milcah seemed more confused than excited. Makhlah tugged on my robes. I kissed the top of her head. I yearned to talk to Tirtzah, but I dared not in this crowd.

As we left the assembly area, dozens of men shook their heads, grumbled, or spat on the ground. Four of them spoke to Gabi in a tone of disappointment that reminded me of Papa. One was the man with the scar and the filthy tunic, the goatherd with no goats.

"What's wrong?" I asked Serakh.

She drew me close and whispered, "Moshe has said that the case of the daughters is just. The portion of the land that would have gone to their father belongs to them. He also made a law for all the Israelites. If a man dies without leaving a son, his property goes to the man's daughters."

"But isn't that fabulous? That's more than I hoped for. It's not just an exception for Tirtzah and her sisters. No wonder the suffragists had a banner about them."

Serakh paused. She motioned for Gabi and the sisters to go ahead without us. "There is more, Miriam," she whispered. "Tirtzah's kinsmen tell Gabi and the others that Tirtzah and her sisters will cause a grave injustice if they marry men who are not of the line of their father."

"Why?"

"It is our tradition that land belongs to the tribe and whatever belongs to a wife belongs to her husband. Tirtzah and her sisters would take their portion of land with them to the tribe of the men they marry."

I folded my arms across my chest. "It's their father's land, not their husband's. The sisters should be able to do with it what they want. Otherwise it's not fair."

Serakh held out her hands, palms up. "We pursue justice, Miriam, but will we ever overtake it?"

I thought about that banner again. It said that the daughters of Zelophehad *asked* for their inheritance. But the banner didn't say whether or not they got it.

"But he's Moses!"

"In every place and time, who decides how much of fairness is enough?"

"*Ach!*" I said, sounding far too much like Papa. I wasn't ready to settle for half-measures, not here or in Portland, not if I could help it.

I strode ahead to catch up with the sisters. Tirtzah and Gabi stood close together, murmuring in a way that made me blush. Tirtzah caught my eye. She pointed to a brambly bush several yards away. We met there, the tips of her headscarf dancing in the desert wind. She enveloped me in her robes, shielding us from the others.

"I do not know how to repay you for all you have done today," she said, holding my hand.

"Me? You were the one who's been so brave. And now these men are demanding that you marry a Manassite if you want to keep your land. And Gabi is a Reubenite. Tirtzah, this is wrong. We can't let this happen."

"Moshe will not take back his words," she assured me. Then her voice grew shaky. "But the tribal leaders will get satisfaction, of this I am sure."

"Tell Serakh you won't settle for that." I said. "She'll know what to do. She'll bring me back."

Tirtzah glanced over her shoulder. "Serakh approaches now." She kissed my cheek. "I don't know who you are, but we are linked, yes?"

My eyes filled with tears. "Yes," I whispered. "We are linked."

Serakh assembled us under a date palm, all except Hoglah, who was nowhere to be seen. "It is time for our messenger to depart," she said with a certainty that stifled contradiction.

I rounded on her, suddenly angry about having to leave so soon. "We've got to go back to the cave, so I can tell them to fight for their land. Or at least I can say good-bye properly. What kind of messenger is deaf and dumb?"

"This is how it must be, Miriam. I cannot do otherwise."

I clenched my jaw. "Then you'd better tell them to fight. Tell them that thousands of years from now their names will be remembered. Tell them about the suffrage banner. Tell them they did the right thing. Tell them I miss them already."

Serakh smiled and nodded. I clutched my headscarf against a sudden wind. While Serakh spoke, Tirtzah dabbed at her eyes and Makhlah hugged my legs. Noa and Milcah held hands and stared at their sandals. Gabi kept turning his head, as if watching for someone. When Serakh was done, they all bowed and began to walk away.

"Tirtzah, wait!" I shouted. I ran to her and wrapped my arms around her. "I will never forget you."

I felt her hands on my back, her head on my shoulder. "Nor I you, sister of the heart," she murmured. "Thanks to The One who has sustained us and enabled us to reach this day."

I held on for one more moment. Then I let her go.

Serakh led me away. "Now we find a quiet spot on that hill, where you can see the River Jordan. Then we shall cross the *olam* to your place and time."

"Will I see ever you again? Serakh, I promise I'll listen to everything you say. I'll obey your every word."

She laughed. "Then you would not be the Miriam who stands before me, a Miriam worthy to travel the *olam*." She took my elbow. "Come. We can delay no longer."

"What should I tell everyone when we get back?"

"Say nothing, if you choose. If we cross carefully, they will not know that you left."

We climbed in silence for a few minutes. I followed her as slowly as I could, even pausing to show her a tiny flower. But it was no good.

"Do not tarry," she warned, with a worried tone. Still I lagged behind, hoping she would change her mind and let me stay longer. We stopped at a pile of flat rocks near the top of the hill.

Serakh embraced me. "My Miriam sweet and strong, it is time now."

I took off Miryam's clothes and set my 1912 shoes on the ground. The hot wind soon covered my prayer shawl with grains of fine sand.

Serakh pointed to my shoes, black leather pumps with

pointed toes and silver buckles. "Why do you bind your feet in this manner?"

"They do pinch," I said, glad for a moment of easy conversation. I handed my shawl to Serakh. "Please tell me about this. My uncle said my father was afraid of it. There's not a curse, is there?"

Serakh wrinkled her forehead. "A curse?"

"My father called my shawl a cursed rag. He exploded when he saw me with it. You know Danny died. Well, later, my baby brother was stillborn. It's not…connected in any way, is it?"

Serakh stroked the shawl. "Nonsense. Your father is foolish to keep from you what is rightly yours. This blessed garment is for the women of your line—for you. It works only for good."

Several small rocks skittered past our feet.

"My uncle says that his sister Raizl died wearing the shawl," I reminded her.

Serakh rubbed the embroidered flowers. "Ah, Raizl, poor child. She believed in the travel stories her *savta* unwisely described to her."

"Raizl's *savta* was my great-grandmother, Miriam Seligman, right?"

Serakh nodded. "Raizl was already in her last moments. Her neck had swelled. She could hardly breathe."

"Diphtheria?"

"Perhaps. I do not know the name of her ailment. That Miriam and I took Raizl through the *olam* to see King Solomon's temple. In all my years I had never done such a thing, but for that Miriam and her beloved Raizl, I did. She paid dearly for fulfilling Raizl's dying wish."

Another rock rolled against the side of my foot. I looked up.

Standing at the crest of the hill was the man with the dirty tunic and the scar. Two other men crouched behind him.

Serakh stepped in front of me. "Leave us," she commanded, sounding five times her size. "If you harm her in any way, I shall pray to The One to open the earth and swallow you whole!"

The man with the scar bent down, his eyes locked on mine, his hands searching for something on the ground. "*Meh-khah-shay-FAH!*"

Serakh crushed the shawl against me. "He calls you a conjurer. A witch. Quick, find your blue thread. Wrap it around your finger and hold tight to me."

I clutched my shawl and stared at that horrible man. My body froze. He closed his hand around a rock.

"Miriam," Serakh shouted, "Look away from him! You must find your thread."

I stared at my shawl. All I saw was crimson embroidery on a sea of white.

"It's gone!" I yelled. "My blue thread is gone!" *I'll never go home. I'm trapped here forever.*

"This cannot be. Look again."

Terrified, I thrust my useless shawl at Serakh. *Run!* But I couldn't move. *Then fight. Fight or die.* I scrambled for my shoes. *Aim for his eyes.* I hurled the first shoe at him. It grazed his shoulder and fell at his feet. A ray of sunlight hit the buckle. He dropped the rock and picked up my shoe. He shouted something to the other men.

I grabbed my other shoe and took aim. As I started to throw it, Serakh yanked my arm, pushing the tassels of the shawl into my hand. "Take your thread, Miriam. Here. The blue one. Miriam, listen to me."

The man reached into the air and caught my second shoe. He cocked his head, as if deciding his next move. The two other men stepped closer.

Serakh threw herself on top of me and we tumbled to the ground. "I must stay here to make sure you are safe. You must cross alone."

"No! I can't leave you. I don't know how to get home!"

Something sharp and heavy hit my leg.

"Go," she commanded. "Now!"

I grasped all four of the long fringes and stuck my fingers into the tangled threads. Blood trickled down my leg. I clutched Serakh against me. "I can't travel without you. I'm afraid!"

She pushed me away.

"No!" My hand glowed. The pulling and crushing gripped my body.

Blue lightning. I slammed my eyes shut.

A voice—mine—screamed, "Se-rakh!"

Nineteen

THE AIR TURNED COOLER. THE CRUSHING stopped. My right arm hit something hard and I collapsed against a smooth, soft surface. When I dared to open my eyes, I found that I was lying on the Oriental rug by the desk in Papa's office, the telephone cord coiled near my shoeless feet.

I rolled onto my side, stumbled to the commode, and retched. I collapsed on the floor. Some time later I managed to wash my face, clean the cut on my leg, and drag myself to my bed.

My lips quivered. I wrapped myself in my coverlet, but I couldn't stop shaking. Was Serakh safe? Was she still struggling with that man who attacked us? Would I ever see her again? Had he...did she... Was I the last of her Miriams now? All I knew for certain was that I was back and she was gone. *That man. That horrid man.*

The telephone rang. And rang.

I padded back to Papa's office. "Josefsohn residence." My voice sounded shaky.

"Hello, Miriam," Uncle Hermann said. "I thought you were coming over this afternoon."

"This afternoon?" I stared at my dirty stockings.

"Yes, you mentioned a Hebrew or Yiddish translation. You said you'd be right over. That was nearly an hour ago."

"Only that long? Oh, I mean…I don't know what I mean. I'm sorry, Uncle Hermann."

"Miriam, is there something wrong? You don't sound well."

I cleared my throat and took a deep breath. "I'm fine," I said, hoping I would be by the time I saw him. "I'd still like to come."

"Certainly." He chuckled. "It sounds as if the walk will do you good."

I padded back to my room, changed my clothes, found another pair of shoes, and sank into my chair. The grandfather clock chimed four. I stared out the window. *There's nothing you can do for her now.*

Heaving myself out of the chair, I collected the page where I'd copied with the letters from my shawl. Then I put my shawl inside its bag next to Baloo and stumbled downstairs. The fresh air steadied my nerves.

Aunt Sophie answered the door. She had more color in her cheeks than the last time I saw her, and she wore a pretty green and peach dressing gown that looked new. I heard Albert shout from upstairs: "Come see my castle!"

Nathan started crying, and Aunt Sophie rolled her eyes. "I just put the baby down for a nap. Whoever said two children are as easy to raise as one was dead wrong. There's cider in the kitchen, and shortbread. Help yourself." She headed for the nursery.

Here was a normal family having a normal day. I tried to act normal too. I met Uncle Hermann in his study and handed him my copybook page. He glanced at it, then eyed me over the tops of his spectacles, his face lined with concern. "Does your father know you're still interested in the *tallis* I gave to you?"

"Neither of my parents knows I have my prayer shawl right now, Uncle Hermann, and I need to keep it that way. I'm terribly sorry if I got you in trouble. I fell asleep in the kitchen."

"Why were you wearing it in the first place?"

I concentrated on a spot in the rug. He of all people might believe me.

"Miriam, is everything all right?"

No, I couldn't take the chance. "Oh, honestly, Uncle Hermann, I meant to hide the shawl as soon as I got it, but I couldn't resist wearing it once. It won't happen like that again, I promise you. Can you tell me about these words, please?"

He ran a finger across the page. "They are definitely Hebrew. I recognize the passage. It's written in a script that I think was used in Europe hundreds of years ago." He sat back and stared at the ceiling. "Yes, there's a chart in my Jewish encyclopedia somewhere." He got up from his desk and walked towards a crowded bookcase.

"Perhaps another time, Uncle Hermann," I said. "I'm in a bit of a hurry." I dared not tell him how exhausted I was. "If you could just translate these letters…"

He slowly returned to his desk, but he seemed determined to continue with his lesson. "See this *fey*—this final letter in the sequence going from right to left? We don't write it that way today. Hebrew lettering has changed over the years. Printers in the Middle Ages used a typeface they called Rashi script. We don't think Rashi ever wrote in Rashi script, though."

"Who was Rashi?" The name sounded familiar. Hadn't Serakh told me about him?

"Rabbi Shlomo Itzhaki. He was that extraordinary scholar who lived in France in the eleventh century. Surely they taught you about Rashi in Religious School."

I wondered what Papa would have expected me to learn if I had been a son rather than a daughter. Surely I would have learned Hebrew and studied the Torah. Danny would have done that. Then I remembered what Serakh had said about my shawl.

"Didn't Rashi have a daughter named Miriam?"

Uncle Hermann brightened. "So you do know about him after all. Yes, Miriam was his middle daughter. He had no sons. Rashi's three daughters were scholars in their own right. Mim, are you sure you're all right? You look a bit pale. Would you like a drink of water?"

I shook my head and turned to him with a smile. *Miriam, daughter of Rashi, just as Serakh told me.* The shawl Rashi's daughter had woven and embroidered was a thousand years old—another miracle, another piece of the unbelievable. She was of that line of Miriams, and I was among them. "I'm fine, Uncle Hermann. Really. More than fine. So these are words, right? What do they mean?"

Uncle Hermann tapped the copybook page. "See these three letters? They spell the Hebrew word *tzedek*, 'justice.' They are repeated here. Then these four letters spell *tirdof*, which Rabbi Leeser translates as 'pursue.' It's part of a biblical passage. *Tzedek, tzedek tirdof.* 'Justice, justice you shall pursue.' I'll get you the exact verse." This time I didn't stop him. He pulled a Bible from his collection.

Justice. My "magic" words were about justice. *It makes perfect sense.* Justice in Tirtzah's time. Justice in the time of Rashi's daughter. Justice now. I felt my cheeks grow warm. "Who said this?"

"Isaac Leeser. He was a German Jew who lived in Philadelphia. He wrote this translation just before the Civil War."

"I mean who said this in the Bible?"

"Moses, I assume, when he speaks of God's commandments." He riffled through the pages. "Ah, yes, it's in Deuteronomy. Here. Chapter sixteen."

I leaned over and read the verse he pointed to.

> 20 Justice, only justice shalt thou pursue; in order that thou
> mayest live, and retain possession of the land which the
> LORD thy God giveth thee.

"Scholars argue about whether 'follow' or 'pursue' is better. The King James Bible you borrowed uses 'follow,' as I recall, but I think 'pursue' makes more sense, don't you?"

I stared at my hands. Justice in my time.

"Mim? Pursue or follow. What do you think?"

"Pardon? Oh…um…like in 'life, liberty, and the pursuit of happiness'?"

"Justice and happiness—they're not always compatible. I'll have to think about that." Uncle Hermann smiled and rubbed his chin. "Did you ever find that story about the daughters of Zelophehad?"

I've done more than read the story. I lived it about an hour ago. "Yes, I did," I said, trying to put my thoughts in order. "Moses made a law that daughters could inherit their father's property if there were no sons. Tirtzah and her sisters were overjoyed, but a lot of men grumbled to Gabi the Reubenite."

"Gabi the Reubenite? I don't remember reading that name in the Bible."

I bit my lip and shrugged. "I must be mistaken. Thank you for the translation," I said, standing to leave.

Uncle Hermann touched my shoulder. "Wait a minute and I'll walk you home." I told him it wasn't necessary, but he insisted.

Two blocks from my house, I could hold out no longer. I had to tell someone, and, except for Sister Margaret and Rabbi Wise, Uncle Hermann was the most religious person I knew. Besides, he told me he heard that someone would ask about my blue thread some day. Maybe he believed in miracles. Maybe the ancient lettering on my shawl was just the evidence he needed. Maybe he wouldn't think I was insane.

Twenty

UNCLE HERMANN PAUSED AT THE CURB to offer me his arm. Before I took it, I picked up a particularly beautiful red and yellow leaf. "You've told me that our Torah was inspired by God, but that it was written down over centuries and shouldn't be taken literally." I focused on the veins in the leaf. "Some parts could be true, though, don't you think?"

Uncle Hermann escorted me across the street. "It's possible, especially in the later biblical books on kings and prophets."

I kept holding his arm, although I avoided looking at his face. "Well, Uncle Hermann, I am certain that the story about the daughters of Zelophehad is true." My voice shook. "Because the prayer shawl you gave me is magical."

"Magical? How is it magical?" He sounded encouraging.

"It…um…I know you won't believe this, and it does seem incredible. But that shawl transported me back to the time, across the *olam*. It was made by Rashi's daughter Miriam, that's why I know about her, although I didn't meet her. I met Moses, the real Moses, and a woman named Serakh who's hardly mentioned in the Bible, and Tirtzah and her sisters—the daughters of Zelophehad. That's how I know about Gabi."

"I see." Uncle Hermann replied in a way that meant he didn't see at all.

"It's true. I was there. You have got to believe me! Serakh took me there with the blue thread in that shawl. She was the woman your mother and *savta* told you about. She's four hundred years old—or she was back then. Please believe me, Uncle Hermann."

"Miriam. Mim. Oh, my dear, Mim."

"Listen to me! The blue thread is from Joseph's coat of many colors. We traveled through the *olam*, and I stood before Moses and said that *Shema* prayer we say at services. I went there after I called you on the telephone—well, that was the second time really. That's why I was late this afternoon. Uncle Hermann, this has been the most amazing experience in my whole life!"

He cleared his throat.

I let go of his arm and tore my leaf in two. And in two again. And again. Ragged fragments clung to my skirt.

Half a block later, he finally responded. "Sometimes our visions, or dreams, or whatever you want to call them... sometimes they can seem very real."

"It wasn't a dream, Uncle Hermann, I swear it was real!" I pleaded.

"Perhaps I was mistaken in giving you that shawl. I didn't mean to upset you this way. Please listen to me, Mim. The mind plays tricks on us. Dr. Sigmund Freud says so, and he's an expert on dreams."

"It wasn't a trick."

Uncle Hermann put his arm around my shoulder and kept it there until I'd unlocked the front door. "Get some rest," he said.

I pushed him away and went inside, completely defeated. I thought that he, of all people, would believe me. I was wrong.

"Dinner is at seven," I heard Mama call after me. "Oh, Hermann, how nice to see you."

I shut her out. I shut them both out. I went to my room, closed the door, and curled up in bed. Alone. Lonely.

§

By dinnertime, it had been decided that I was to go with Mama to her bridge game at Mrs. Steinbacher's the next day. I wondered if Uncle Hermann and Mama had talked about me after I went upstairs—she never invited me to play bridge.

I was sorely tempted to tell them how much I loathed the idea. Still, I wanted Mama to be in a good mood when I told her I had the prayer shawl. And I wanted Papa to see me as mature and sensible—an asset in the print shop. Most of all, I didn't want either of them to think I was going insane.

"I'd be delighted," I mumbled. "Please pass the salt."

The next afternoon I chose a brown and ecru outfit to go with my brown shoes, the only pair that wouldn't make Mama wonder what had happened to the black shoes I usually wore. Mrs. Steinbacher seemed overjoyed to see me. She hugged Mama, then me, engulfing me in her perfume. "It's so good of you to join us."

Mama's nose twitched. "Guerlain's new *L'Heure Bleue*, if I'm not mistaken. Lovely."

"Isn't it divine? Leave your hats and coats here with Martha, and we'll introduce Miriam around." Mrs. Steinbacher released me, then grabbed my hand and dragged me to a tallish, thin woman with curly red hair. "Estelle, I'd like you to meet Lillian's daughter, Miriam. She's here to learn bridge. Miriam, this is Mrs. Lowenthal."

"Very pleased to meet you," I lied in that proper sort of way.

"And you know Mrs. Baum."

"Good to see you," I lied again.

Mrs. Steinbacher steered me to the sideboard and poured me a glass of Chablis. "Try these Belgian chocolates," she said. "They're positively luscious. Here, come sit beside me. I'm playing East, partnering with your mother. Oh, it's such a treat to have you! I miss my Florence so. Don't you? Ladies, after we've filled our glasses and plates, are we ready?"

Mrs. Steinbacher studied her cards. "I'll begin the bidding at one diamond." She leaned over and pointed to the card in her hand. "See why, Miriam?"

I nodded, figuring I'd get the hang of it later. The card designs looked like little advertisements for the jack of spades or the ten of clubs. I wondered whether Precision Printers ever made playing cards.

"Try these." Mrs. Baum thrust a porcelain bowl of chocolates under my nose. I blinked and thanked her, took a coconut-covered one, and passed the bowl to Mrs. Lowenthal. As the chocolate melted in my mouth, I stared out the window and imagined telling Makhlah this was dark manna with white slivers on top.

"…a gypsy fortuneteller. What do you think, Miriam?"

"Pardon?"

Mama looked annoyed. "Mrs. Baum asked if you're planning to be a gypsy fortune teller again at this year's Hallowe'en masquerade dance."

"At the Concordia Club?"

Mama frowned. "Of course at the Concordia."

Mrs. Lowenthal leaned toward Mama. "Miriam has a point, Lillian," she said. "The other social clubs haven't changed their unfortunate membership policy toward Jews, but our own Neighborhood House is having a party this year. As members of the Council of Jewish Women, we ought to support their activities. Although I must say I am going to the Concordia, too."

I silently thanked Mrs. Lowenthal for making me look like less of an idiot.

"My costume might be biblical," I said. "Sandals, robes, maybe something with fringes."

"What a lovely idea for next spring's Purim Party at the temple," Mama said. "Miriam's been reading my brother-in-law's Bible recently. His wife just had their second son, Nathan. Very colicky, poor dear."

Mrs. Baum reached for another chocolate. "Too bad. A touch of sugar water helps."

"Or a touch of brandy for the mother," Mrs. Lowenthal said. "When I have children, I'll go for the brandy. And chocolate. Lots of chocolate." They all laughed.

"I thought I might go as Mary Pickford, the darling of the cinema," Mama said.

"But, Lillian, with your blonde hair you always look like Mary Pickford," Mrs. Baum replied. "An Oriental look would be more alluring."

Mrs. Lowenthal fluffed her red curls and bid two clubs. "I'm going as a suffragist, which is hardly in costume. I'll hand out VOTES FOR WOMEN *boutonnières* to all the men at the Concordia. Oregon women had better get the right to vote this year—or else."

Mrs. Steinbacher caressed her brooch nervously, and Mrs. Baum reached for more chocolate. Mama rearranged her cards. Were these playing cards the size of that horrid VOTE NO card that Papa had printed? I sipped my wine and said, "What happened in the 1906 election, Mrs. Lowenthal? Wasn't there a big campaign against suffrage? An anti-suffrage card?"

She nodded. "I did hear about some scandalous material."

Mama didn't bat an eyelash.

I took another sip. "What did the card look like?"

"Well, I never actually saw one, Miriam. Seriously, ladies, it's about time we got the vote. Abigail Scott Duniway fought this battle for decades and now she's taken to her bed with rheumatism. Poor Abigail deserves to get the vote in her lifetime."

Mrs. Baum dabbed her lips with a napkin. "Estelle, dear, Oregon does a lot for its women without all this fuss over suffrage. We have that law that protects female employees from working more than ten hours a day. Our lawyers defended it all the way to the Supreme Court, and we won."

Mrs. Lowenthal shook her head. "That's all well and good, Lucille, but women should have a voice in these matters, too. We're not children, you know, or imbeciles."

"We can have a voice without the vote," Mama added.

I looked at Mama. "But why can't we have—"

Mama glared at me.

Mrs. Steinbacher chimed in. "Ladies, ladies, let's have a quiet afternoon of bridge, shall we? I bid two no-trump."

The game dragged on. My head started to ache from Mrs. Steinbacher's perfume, which was much more floral than Mama's. I leaned back, closed my eyes, and remembered Mama's scent on Baloo.

No, wait. Danny died years ago, and Mama started wearing that perfume only last summer. My stomach knotted before my brain managed to compose a thought: *How could you have been so stupid? She hid Baloo on purpose. She must cuddle with him when no one is looking. I might as well have left my prayer shawl by the hat rack in the front hall.*

"Miriam, your wine!" Mama shot me The Appalled Look as she rushed to blot Mrs. Steinbacher's rug with her napkin.

"Oh, Mrs. Steinbacher, I'm so sorry," I said. "It must have slipped out of my hands."

Mrs. Steinbacher called for the maid and gave me a reassuring smile. "No harm done. See? The glass didn't break and it's white wine. Martha will fix everything good as new."

"Something has gotten into you," Mama declared as we walked down Nineteenth toward our house. "You are not yourself, Miriam. And you haven't been entirely truthful."

"Mama, I don't want to talk right now," I said. *Where else can I hide the shawl? Who knows what she'll do if she finds it?* "I've had too much Chablis."

To my surprise, she didn't pry. When we got home, she went into the kitchen to speak with Mrs. Jenkins. I made a beeline for the bottom dresser drawer in Danny's old room.

Baloo was still there. My prayer shawl was not.

Twenty-One

Damnation! Mama had spent the whole day with me and had said not one word about my shawl. She knew how much it meant to me. How could she?

I paced Danny's room and collected my thoughts. At least it was just the two of us—Papa would have had my head by now if he knew I took the shawl from Han Lee's. Well, Mama was going to have to deal with me now. *Two can play this game*, I thought to myself, as I composed a plan.

I took Baloo and wrapped him in a piece of oilcloth from the pantry. By the time I faced my parents at the dinner table, Baloo was snug and safe inside an extra planter in the potting shed. Bridge games, draperies for the parlor, and the best restaurants in New York City were the main topics of conversation. Not one whisper about the shawl.

I kept a civil tongue. I nodded, smiled, sipped, cut, chewed, and swallowed. I dabbed the corners of my mouth with the corners of my napkin. I imagined the look of surprise—no, horror—on Mama's face when she discovered Baloo was gone. She would be miserable, and I didn't care. She'd know I took him. I felt a bit mean-spirited, since the bear was so obviously a comfort to her. Still, if I wanted my shawl back, I was going to need all the leverage I could get.

I devoured a double portion of dessert.

Sitting at my dressing table before bed, I felt so alone. I'd lost the shawl again. How would I ever know if Serakh was all right? If Tirtzah and her sisters got everything they deserved? I commenced to force one hundred brush strokes through my hair. I looked in the mirror…*four, five, six, seven*… and wished Serakh's reflection were there…*sixteen, seventeen, eighteen.* Or Tirtzah's. *You're the bravest girl I'll ever know,* I thought…*thirty-one, thirty-two, thirty-three, thirty-four. You stood before Moses…fifty-nine, sixty…and so did I…sixty-six, sixty-seven…and he changed the law, because you made him see what's right. Seventy-three, seventy-four…*

I leaned over my knees to give the back of my head a thorough brushing. "Serakh told me one step, and then another." I explained to the floor…*seventy-eight, seventy-nine…*"and to interfere in my own time and place…*eighty-nine, ninety, ninety-one, ninety-two…*"which is just what I mean to do…" …*ninety-nine…* Done. I piled my hair on top of my head and admired the result. I could be twenty with a hairstyle like that. Old enough to run a printing business, like the Osbornes ran their hat shop. Or help to run the business, anyway. Even at sixteen I was certainly old enough to help women get the vote. *And I'll find my shawl again. I'll show Serakh how I made a difference in my own time and place. I won't forget what Tirtzah taught me.*

§

WHEN I CAME DOWNSTAIRS LATE THE next morning Mrs. Jenkins was humming to herself, and I was in an equally good mood. I hugged her good morning for the first time since she came into Papa's employ.

She grinned. "Bless you, child. You make me feel as welcome as a laying hen right before Easter. Your mother should be back late this afternoon. Here, let me fry up some sardines for your breakfast. I won't take no for an answer."

By the time I left the kitchen, I was *farcie* as Mama would say—stuffed. Next order of business: Mrs. Lowenthal. The Portland City Directory had only one listing for Lowenthal, which was lucky. The operator connected me right away. I introduced myself again and got to the point. "Are you still planning to distribute suffrage sashes and *boutonnières* at Concordia's masquerade dance?"

"Definitely. It's time we stirred up some trouble."

"I agree. The new millinery shop at Seventeenth and Marshall has a large supply of yellow ribbon. The Osborne sisters run the store, and they are suffragists through and through. I'm going over there today. Perhaps I can give them your order."

"Thank you for your offer, dear, but I wouldn't want to get you in trouble with your mother."

"Or with my father," I said. Mrs. Lowenthal's laugh was hearty and infectious. Maybe I'd be like her one day.

When I arrived at Osborne Milliners half an hour later, Mrs. Lowenthal had already called. Prudence thanked me for the business, and Charity treated me like a long lost relative.

"We haven't seen you since Dr. Shaw's rally," Charity said. "I was just telling Prudence that we ought to pay a visit, even though we're not in the same social circles. We've got lots of suffrage bows to make and distribute if you're of a mind to help. No one else in the city is making bows for the campaign. Prudence says it's a good way to help the cause and to bring in business."

Raising a finger and thumb about an inch apart, she explained, "Miriam, we are *this* close. Prudence thinks the voting amendment will be defeated again this time, and she's rarely wrong. But I'm optimistic. So is Dr. Lovejoy. Esther Pohl Lovejoy? She got Dr. Shaw to come to Portland, remember?"

"I think so." That suffrage rally seemed eons ago, although it had only been last Saturday. Talking to Charity made me think of Tirtzah, my…*what did she call me? My sister of the heart.*

"Dr. Shaw was a huge success, you know. Of course we didn't have the money for the banquet at the Multnomah Hotel on Tuesday. Did you go?"

I shook my head.

"Prudence and I heard Dr. Shaw's talk at the First Congregational Church on Sunday and at the library on Monday. Oh, Miriam, she is so inspirational!"

Charity slipped her arm around my waist and led me to the back room to work on suffrage bows. "And here's the best news. Dr. Lovejoy just started the Everybody's Equal Suffrage League. You'll join, won't you? Dues are only a quarter, and everyone who joins is a vice-president. May I sign you up? We have the forms behind the counter. The next meeting is tomorrow night."

I felt suspended between two worlds—out in the middle of no place—talking to Moses and then to Charity. "A quarter for justice?"

"Ooh, that's a great slogan. Yes, for the price of a pound of pork loin you can be a member for life. It's a bargain. The Portland Equal Suffrage League costs a dollar a year. If you don't have a quarter, I can lend you one from the till. Only you'll have to return it to me by tomorrow or Prudence will have a fit. Miriam?… Miriam?"

I jerked back to here and now. "Sorry. I haven't been myself these last few days." I fetched a quarter from my purse. "Oh, and I need a new bow; I gave the other one away."

Charity handed me scissors and several spools of ribbon, and I settled into the rhythm of handcrafting bows. Four dozen bows later, Prudence put me to work cutting pictures of hat styles from the newspaper to put in her samples album. "It's easier to show women a variety of styles than to try to describe everything," she said. "And we don't have the money to keep a large inventory."

It felt good to be doing something, to feel like I was making a difference, however small. It also felt good to keep my hands and mind busy. By mid-afternoon, I was getting hungry again. "Do you close the shop for lunch?" I asked Charity. "We could stop by Hanneman's for a quick sandwich."

Charity looked at Prudence, and Prudence looked at the cash register.

"Not today," Prudence said. "We don't usually close, in case there are lunch hour customers. Frankly, we don't usually eat lunch. But I can make you a cup of tea."

I bit my lip. I felt ridiculous; I should have realized they were counting their pennies. "No thanks. But I do have a hankering for a sarsaparilla soda, and Hanneman's has the best. Let's share a bottle."

I brought back three bottles, a small loaf of sourdough bread, and five ounces of liverwurst. Prudence produced a tarnished butter knife for the liverwurst, and we toasted the birth of the Everybody's Equal Suffrage League.

A handful of customers came to Osborne Milliners in the six hours I was there. Only two of them bought hats, but Prudence and Charity seemed satisfied. I pinned a new yellow bow to my coat and started for home. I remembered Papa's reaction to the suffragists about Blotter Day. Only three more days until Tuesday, until my first day at work. *How can I make myself an asset at Precision Printers?* What I needed was to invent a whole new job.

That's when I thought of that album of hat styles, the one that Prudence and Charity showed to their customers. By the time I waltzed into dinner I was practically whistling.

Twenty-Two

As I passed the pickled beets to Papa that night, I cleared my throat and tried to look as competent and mature as possible.

"I have a new idea for Precision Printers," I told him. "It's sure to increase sales."

Papa speared a beet. "I have enough of business at the office," he said. "At home I want to hear news from the ladies. What is playing at the theatre, how our new nephew is doing, who is going on vacation where. Or I listen to a concerto from my lovely wife." Papa reached across the table and took Mama's hand.

"Certainly, Papa, but I've been thinking a lot about Precision Printers, and I'd like to discuss my ideas with you. It won't take long."

He smiled, as if I were the evening's live entertainment. "You have never composed even one line of type and already you have new ways to run my business."

It wasn't my fault that I had no experience. My typography book said nothing about how to operate the presses, and the closest Papa let me get to printing was an inking pad and a set of wooden blocks with raised letters. He had never let Danny or me on the production floor.

"I didn't mean it that way," I said. "I have a plan for how I can be useful at the office starting next week. I'd like to work on an album of our most popular products, a samples album."

Mama concentrated so hard on deboning her halibut that you'd think she was a surgeon. Papa sipped his wine. "I do not talk business at the dinner table."

"Then let's talk in the library. Five minutes, Papa."

He shook his head and speared another beet. "Not to-night, child."

I excused myself directly after dessert and marched around the block to blow off steam. Wasn't I worth five minutes of his time?

I wasn't worth his time on Saturday either—what little time he had at home after going to the office in the morning and the Club in the afternoon. Mama seemed to welcome his absence. After her usual piano practice in the morning, she practically pushed me out the door.

"It's such a lovely day," she chirped. "Don't you want to take a long walk? Or go to the library? I don't mind your go-ing downtown for a bit of shopping on your own, so long as you come home before dark."

"I thought young ladies don't go gallivanting around Portland unescorted."

"I'm making an exception today," she said, arching her eyebrows.

The exception, I realized, was so she could search for Baloo while Papa and I were away. I would have none of it. "I feel like staying home today."

Mama tried a few more ploys to lure me away. I refused to budge. When Papa returned later that afternoon, Mama announced a change in plans. "I'm so sorry, Julius," she said, "but I have a headache. Let's dine in tonight. Mrs. Jenkins is making stuffed cabbage, just the way you like it. We'll go to the theatre another time."

The stuffed cabbage was tolerable. My parents were not. Mama pretended everything was perfect "*chez* Josefsohn." Papa droned on about how the new cheap cigarettes were no substitute for a good, hand-rolled Havana cigar.

Mrs. Jenkins served chocolate cake for dessert. I took a bite and let the flavor explode on my tongue. *I'm going to have my cake and eat it, too*, I thought, despite Mama's motto to the contrary. I'm going to work with Papa, who's against women voting, and when I'm not in the print shop, I'm going to work on the suffrage campaign.

Sunday probably dawned gray and rainy. At least that's how it was when I opened one eye and heard the grandfather clock chime ten. There was a familiar, annoying warmth between my legs.

Oh, damnation! I shuffled to the bathroom for my menstrual belt and cloths. It felt like a cat was clawing at my insides. A spoonful of Bayer's aspirin powder with a dollop of honey and a glass of seltzer calmed the cat—barely. A sweet roll helped. So did a hot water bottle.

I curled up with *The Art & Practice of Typography*, my favorite fountain pen, and my copybook. I practiced writing "bread and roses" in several typefaces. I block-lettered "VOTES FOR WOMEN." I wrote "Tirtzah" a dozen times, then "Serakh." I linked her "k" with her "h," turning them into an elegant ligature.

I wondered if Serakh was in the Exodus part of the Bible. The time and place she had taken me to on the *olam* was the end of those forty the Israelites left Egypt. It was worth a look.

Exodus, chapter one:

1 Now these are the names of the children of Israel, which came into Egypt with Jacob; every man and his household came with Jacob.

I ran my finger down the columns, skimming the verses. The story was familiar from Religious School and from the Passover Seders we had at Aunt Sophie and Uncle Hermann's house. Chapter five: Moses and Aaron telling Pharaoh "let my people go." And then the ten plagues that happened in Egypt because Pharaoh wouldn't listen—until that last plague, in chapter twelve: the slaying of the firstborn.

The spring after Danny died, Uncle Hermann had skipped the ten plagues part when he read the Passover story at our Seder. But I had just turned eight. I could read. Those words rose up from the page and frightened me. I hated Passover ever since.

The first part of Exodus was about the exodus from Egypt. That made sense. There was nothing about Serakh, though. Chapter twenty listed the Ten Commandments. Chapter twenty-one had a whole passel of other laws. So did chapter twenty-two, down to this one:

18 Thou shalt not suffer a witch to live.

My stomach lurched. *Meh-khah-shay-fah.* Witch. That's what the man with the scar shouted at us on the hill. Had he thought that Serakh was a witch when I disappeared? *Horrid man. Stupid law!*

When I dragged myself down the stairs later, Mrs. Jenkins was just starting Sunday dinner. "I have another Bible question," I told her. "Do you remember reading about someone named Serakh?"

"I can't rightly say if I've heard that name before."

"So she wasn't mentioned as a witch or anything?"

"No." Mrs. Jenkins aligned the pepper mill and saltcellar. "But there are witches in the Bible. King Saul consulted the witch of Endor. It's in First Samuel, I believe."

"I thought God told Moses that witches had to be killed. It's part of a long list of laws in Exodus."

Mrs. Jenkins eyed me with interest. "You've been studying Scripture, I see. Walk in the path of the righteous, I always say. Let's talk about the prophecy of the new covenant one day real soon."

"Your cherry cobbler smells wonderful," I said, hoping to steer the conversation elsewhere.

She grinned. "The way to a man's heart is through his stomach."

I doubted Papa would suddenly take me into the business even if I prepared his favorite meal: sauerbraten, braised red cabbage, and apple strudel.

Still, I got lucky on Monday morning. The telephone rang and I heard Mama answer. A few minutes later she handed me a sheaf of papers.

"That was Mr. Jacobowitz from the shop. Your father left these contracts here by mistake, and he needs them for a meeting this afternoon. Would you mind taking them to him, Miriam? I'm terribly busy."

I momentarily forgot the urgency of guarding Baloo's hiding place in my eagerness to get to the shop earlier than Tuesday, even if it was just to drop something off. And while I was downtown, I could replace my black shoes. Surely Meier & Frank would have the same pair. I took four dollars from my rainy day fund—a serious depletion, but it couldn't be helped. Then I bundled up against a stiff breeze, tucked Papa's papers under my arm, raced to the streetcar, and breathed in the bustle of downtown.

Newsies hawked *The Morning Oregonian* and *Oregon Journal*. Some of the boys looked no older than the Chinese girl at Han Lee's laundry. Many were not nearly as well dressed or healthy looking. Why were they working instead of in school? Where were their parents? Why hadn't I noticed before?

Four women walked toward me, each wearing a yellow sash. "I see you support votes for women," one of them said, eyeing the suffrage bow pinned to my coat and the papers under my arms. "Tell your boss to vote 'yes' on the fifth of November for Amendment One."

"I don't have a boss," I said, flattered at being mistaken for a clerk or secretary. "But I do have a father. Same thing, I guess."

Precision Printers filled a large brick structure—two store-fronts wide—next to the new Wells Fargo Building at Sixth and Stark. It was the perfect location. You could see Wells Fargo's twelve-story skyscraper from everywhere in the city, so everyone could find our shop. The plaque on Precision Printers' front door read "J. and H. Josefsohn, proprietors." The brass doorknob was polished to a high gloss and the windows sparkled—Papa was as fastidious at work as he was at home.

I waved to Kirsten through the window, and she rushed to meet me at the door. "You'd better get rid of that bow before he sees it."

I slipped off my coat instead. "I'm starting work here tomorrow," I told her. "Isn't that terrific?"

"What about school?"

"They're not letting me go this fall. It's a long story. Anyway, will you show me that VOTE NO card you mentioned at the rally? One of my mother's friends was talking about it."

She shook her head. "It will only get you upset. What's done is done. There's nothing you can do about it now."

"You must have kept one. I promise I won't get you in trouble."

"Forget the whole thing, Miriam. Suppose you had one. What would you do? Show it to your father? Give it to the Osborne sisters? Why raise a ruckus? Women might think it's awful, but it's their husbands and fathers and brothers who will vote in a few weeks."

"First I have to see that card," I persisted. "Then I'll figure out what to do."

"I'll think about it." Kirsten glanced at Papa's office. "I'd better get back to work."

The tangy, floral smell of kerosene and inks tickled my nose and the *ka-chunk ka-chunk* of the presses lifted my spirits. I exchanged hellos with several of the men and even greeted Mr. Jacobowitz. He was only in his early twenties, but he behaved like someone twice his age. Stodgier than Papa, if that's possible.

"What a pleasant surprise to see you, Miss Josefsohn," he said softly, in his Polish-Russian accent. "Thank you for bringing those contracts. I trust I have not inconvenienced you."

"Not in the least," I answered politely. As Mr. Jacobowitz reached for the contracts, I took a step back and clasped them to my chest. "I'll take these into my father personally."

As usual, he didn't argue. I wondered if Mr. Jacobowitz ever argued with anyone. And I wondered what he had been doing when I saw him across from Han Lee's laundry.

I knocked on Papa's partially opened door and stepped inside. "Good morning. I brought you the papers you needed."

Papa looked up from his accounting ledger and stretched out his hand for the contracts. "Your mama is too busy again?"

"I think she had a prior engagement. Besides, I like coming to the shop."

"You like to visit with Miss Svenson," he said, reading the papers I had given him.

"No, I really love this place, Papa."

He grunted. "I'm glad it brings you pleasure."

"Where is Uncle Hermann?"

"Not here where he should be. Now, I will call your mama to tell her you are on your way home." He gave the operator our number while I looked around the office. "Last night's dinner was delicious, Mrs. Jenkins," I heard him say. "Yes, I am coming home at six. I am sending Miriam home now."

"Ask her if she needs anything from the shops while I'm downtown."

Papa put his hand over the speaker and glared. "You interrupt me to tell me how to treat my own employee?"

"Sorry, Papa," I managed through clenched teeth. He said good-bye to Mrs. Jenkins and hung up.

I put on my coat and turned to leave.

That's when he noticed the yellow bow. "Miriam, you let foolish women pin their politics on you, poisoning your mind. Take that off your coat!"

I straightened my hat. I focused on the starched collar guarding Papa's sagging neck.

"Miriam, if you wish to work here tomorrow, you must follow the rules for every employee of Precision Printers. No politics."

"I see." I walked toward his office door. "But I'm not working in the shop today, right?"

"Correct. You do not work here today. You may come in tomorrow, as we agreed."

"Then today I'll keep my bow on, Papa." I ushered myself out, and I didn't look back.

Twenty-Three

MEIER & FRANK HAD A PAIR of black shoes with a slightly different buckle. I also bought a pair of cotton stockings similar to the ones I ruined…back then. With luck Mama wouldn't notice the difference. People see what they expect to see—or, with Papa and my suffrage bow, what they never expect to see. The bow sat on my desk while I worked on a letter to Florrie.

The most amazing things have happened since I wrote
last. I am afraid you'll think I'm crazy as a bedbug if I tell
you in a letter, so my secrets will have to wait until we see
each other. Thank goodness you'll be back soon.
*   One month to go before the election and everybody's talk-*
ing about suffrage for women here, even a woman I met
at your mother's house—Mrs. Lowenthal. Do you know
her? She's buying yards and yards of suffrage ribbons from
Charity and Prudence Osborne, thanks to me. Think of what
women voters might do in Oregon—and across the nation
someday. I'd wager we'd make laws that protected children
from having to sell newspapers or work in factories. I'd wa-
ger most of the poor people I see at Neighborhood House make
do with less food in a week than Mrs. Jenkins makes for me
every day!

§

Getting up early had never been a problem for me. Usually I met Mrs. Jenkins when she came to the house at half past six, and we chatted in the kitchen until I heard the plumbing in the upstairs commode. But Monday night, I was sure I'd oversleep. I spent half the night lying in bed awake, listening to the grandfather clock chime the hours downstairs and staring at my wear-to-work gray outfit by the armoire.

At a minute before a quarter after eight on Tuesday morning I stood in the front hall with my hat, coat, and gloves on, and an extra dollar in my handbag for lunch. Papa nodded approvingly and escorted me to the streetcar. "I take the Oldsmobile only when it rains," he said. "And when I deliver items to my customers."

"I should like to learn to drive," I said with as much assurance as I could muster.

Papa looked at me like I was a two-headed calf. "There is no need, not in the city. Your mama does not know how to drive. She is wanting to hire the Steinbachers' chauffeur when the Steinbachers go to Paris next spring."

"Have you ever met their chauffeur, Papa?"

"There is no need. The hiring of help is your mama's department."

"He's very...um...capable. Perhaps he can teach me."

Papa didn't say absolutely positively no. I suppressed a smile.

Uncle Hermann hadn't yet arrived by the time Papa gave instructions on the day's jobs to Kirsten, Mr. Jacobowitz, and his six other employees. "My daughter will be working in the office today, not on the production floor," he said. "She is not to be around the presses or the cutter."

"I plan to look through all the samples of previous jobs, Miss Svenson," I said. "Where are they kept?"

Before Kirsten could answer, Mr. Jacobowitz said, "In the storage room." He smoothed his mustard-colored mustache, which he had waxed at the tips. "I would be most happy to get them for you, Miss Josefsohn. Where would you like them?"

"On the table in my father's office, thank you," I answered in a professional tone.

Papa gave me a look I couldn't read. Annoyance? Admiration? Surprise? Probably annoyance. He insisted that I remain in the office and not accompany Mr. Jacobowitz, who made a great show of presenting me with five large boxes. I set to work.

1897. Our first job was a handbill that announced the opening of a new bank. I wrote "commercial announcements" at the top of a blank page and left the handbill in the chronological file. A mediocre print job, not worth putting in a samples album. By the time I got to 1903, the category list had grown to include invitations, party menus, birth announcements, visiting cards, informal notepaper, and stationery.

For most of the morning, Papa busied himself with telephone calls and accounts. He never asked about my progress.

Uncle Hermann arrived at a quarter after eleven. "Well, look who's here! Miriam, what a happy surprise. What are you doing with all these boxes?"

"It's nearly noon," Papa said.

Uncle Hermann hung his coat on the rack by the office door. "The doctor examined Sophie and the baby this morning. Just routine. Everything is fine, thank goodness. Tell me about these boxes, Mim."

"I'm going through everything we've printed to see which kinds of jobs have been the most popular and to pick out samples of our best work."

"Your idea, Julius?"

Papa shook his head, reached for his letter opener, and slipped the thin blade under the first of a stack of sealed envelopes.

"My idea," I said, trying to sound confident. "I'm putting together an album to show customers. A samples album will help them decide what they want and encourage them to order other items from us."

"Fifteen years' worth of printing jobs? That's hundreds of samples. An ambitious undertaking."

"And definitely worth it, Uncle Hermann, definitely. If I work here the rest of the week, the album will be done in no time. Then we can place an advertisement in newspapers to encourage new customers in time for the Thanksgiving and Christmas seasons."

"And who pays for these advertisements?" Papa punctuated the air with his letter opener.

I swallowed hard and faced him. "It might lead to increased sales, Papa. Sometimes you have to spend money to make money. It's worth a try."

"So, let us say a new customer comes to the shop. What does he see? You. The owner's daughter. The customer thinks: Ha! This printer is not successful. His womenfolk work here, too. He cannot provide for them. Better I take my business somewhere else."

"I'd tell the customer that I want to work here, that I'm learning the business. Or suppose the customer is a woman, and she would like a woman's advice."

"Nonsense." Papa jabbed the next envelope with such force that he slit the letter inside. "Where do you get such foolish notions, from that typography book my brother gave you? I know my inventory. A customer comes in, he tells me what he wants. I bring out one sample—maybe two. I tell him what works best, and he trusts my judgment."

"But, Papa." My voice cracked with anger.

Uncle Hermann closed the office door and put his hand on my shoulder. "I admire your innovation. This album is worth a try. Let's discuss advertisements another time. If we set up a larger table along the back wall of the production floor, you'll have more room to work."

Papa slammed the letter opener against his desk. "And have all my men staring at her instead of concentrating on their work? This is my daughter, Hermann, not yours. Miriam, you may try your little project here in the office today and next Tuesday. I will not have you underfoot all week."

Underfoot! I clenched my jaw and willed myself not to cry. "The samples album will take forever then. It deserves a fair chance." *So do I.* "At least let me work at Precision Printers the rest of this week until I'm done with sorting these boxes. Then I'll take home our best samples and put them in an album there."

I strode to the wall calendar. "Papa, it's the eighth of October. We're already starting the busy season. The new album will be very useful now."

"She's being perfectly reasonable, Julius," Uncle Hermann said.

Papa muttered something in German. Uncle Hermann answered in German. The office felt sticky and close.

Papa ran his fingers through what little was left of his hair. "Tomorrow I am very busy. Miriam, you will come here on Thursday, but that is all for this week. Do I make myself clear?"

"Yes, Papa."

"You have persistence," he said, not unkindly. "I give you that."

Two days this week. Maybe three days next week. It was a start. I declined to dine at a restaurant with Papa and Uncle Hermann for lunch, saying I'd pick up a sandwich at the café down the street. Mr. Jacobowitz looked as if he wanted to escort me to the café, but he must have lost his nerve. He tipped his hat to me and left on his own.

As soon as those three were out the door, I headed for Kirsten. She kept nodding her approval while I told her about my samples album. "Now about that VOTE NO card," I said.

"You're not going to like it."

"Of course I'm not going to like it. Let's go out to lunch, you can show me then."

Kirsten took off her apron. "I brought my lunch, but I wouldn't mind a break."

We walked to the bench by the library. Dark clouds rolled in from the east, threatening another shower, but the bench was dry and Precision Printers was only a block or so away.

Kirsten fiddled with a coat button. Someone had mended a tear near the buttonhole, and my mind conjured up Serakh when I first met her, in her out-of-fashion dress and lace-up shoes.

"Don't say I didn't warn you," Kirsten said. She opened her handbag and put the VOTE NO card on my lap. "Here's the face." She flipped the card. "And here's the reverse."

"My father printed this?" I turned the card over and over, as if the image on the front and back might change for the better.

It was the shape of a playing card, the kind that men can hide in their pockets, take out in the palm of their hands and snicker at. On the face of the card:

VOTE FOR GOVERNMENT?

And on the face, an image of a flouncing petticoat. On the other side, that same petticoat and:

My mouth turned sour. "It's…it's disgusting! How could he? Petticoat government! That's so degrading."

Kirsten grabbed at her hat, which threatened to take flight in the wind. "They wanted to show a woman in a corset," she said. "Mr. Josefsohn told them no. I wasn't supposed to do the job, but then the compositor got sick and they needed me."

"This is bad enough. It's an under muslin; it's intimate apparel. Doesn't my father think women have any brains at all? How many of these cards did you print?"

"The order was for five thousand. No one noticed an overrun of a half dozen I kept for myself."

"Five thousand! How many votes did the suffrage amendment lose by?"

"I don't know."

"Me neither," I said. "Not by much, I'd wager. Oh, Kirsten, I never thought he'd print such…such…"

Kirsten nodded. "I agree it's a scandalous picture. But I must say, in fairness to your father, it does get the point across."

"You bet it does. Women aren't playthings in petticoats. Is he printing one again this year?"

"I don't think so."

I clutched at my coat and commenced to pace in front of the bench.

"How long did it take to print these cards?"

"A few hours, as I recall."

"That's all? So we could do the same this year. We've got almost a whole month before the elections."

Kirsten frowned. "We could what?"

"This time Precision Printers will print a VOTE YES card. I refuse to let men like my father ruin this election for us, like they did the others."

"Your father would never agree to that."

I shoved my hands in my coat pockets and felt a defiant smirk spread across my face. "Who says he has to know?"

Kirsten stood and shook her head. "That's practically impossible. Even if you did manage to print them behind his back, he'd find out eventually. Don't you realize how angry he would be? He could make your life miserable."

I stared at the sidewalk. "He's doing that already."

She snorted. "Oh, no, you have no notion what miserable means. What if he threw you out on the street? Not that he would, but Miriam, suppose he did."

"I'll be seventeen come January. I'll find a job. You did." Squaring my shoulders, I turned to walk away.

Kirsten grabbed my arm. "You have no idea what it's like being a woman on your own, with no resources. Please, you mustn't print something your father wouldn't like. It's too dangerous."

I said nothing, but I wasn't ready to give up. Tirtzah had been on her own with fewer resources than Kirsten could have ever imagined, and look what she had accomplished.

Kirsten returned the card to her handbag and started for the shop. "We'd better get back, Miriam. I have to finish that job for Mrs. Ladd."

"A VOTE YES card is only fitting, don't you see?" I argued, striding by her side. "I'll watch what you do and learn how to operate the presses myself."

"It's not that easy."

"But you'll help, won't you? It's for a good cause, Kirsten. You know that. I saw you at the rally. Even Nils believes in suffrage for women."

"Nils also believes in socialism and Eugene Debs for president." Kirsten adjusted her coat collar and looked at her gloves. "And if I say no?"

"I'll find a way to print those cards regardless."

"Then I guess I'll have to do what I can," she said, with the beginnings of a smile.

When you're taller than most women, it's easy to sweep them off their feet with an overenthusiastic hug. Kirsten tolerated my exuberance.

By the time we reached Precision Printers, I knew I couldn't face Papa and still keep a civil tongue in my mouth. And now, surely, was not the time to lose my temper—and my chances to work at the shop.

Mr. Jacobowitz planted himself in front of me before I reached Papa's office door. "They are both still away. May I offer you my assistance?"

"Oh, yes, please," I said. "Would you kindly put that first box of samples back in the storage room? And tell my father I'm leaving work early."

He cleared his throat. "I'd be happy to escort you home, Miss Josefsohn. With your father and uncle absent for the moment, it stands to reason—"

I laid my hand on his arm, the way Mama would, and I smiled at him. Not a fetching smile, just one of the formal kind. "Thank you for looking after my well-being, Mr. Jacobowitz, but I should enjoy some solitude and the weather is cooperating. Perhaps another time."

He went away looking happy. I tried not to think about whether I had encouraged his attentions. As I started for home, an east wind grabbed me with sudden ferocity. I clutched my hat with one hand and clamped my coat collar closed with the other. Newspaper pages flew past. A gust caught at my skirt and petticoat, causing them to flare far out above my ankles. I hunched over, let go of my coat collar and grabbed at my skirt for modesty's sake. Papa would have been scandalized if he had seen how much of my petticoat and legs had been exposed in the wind. Yet he had no trouble printing a petticoat on both sides of his VOTE NO card.

I vowed that this election would be different. We women of Portland would distribute a suffrage card to make up for that disgusting one. A VOTE YES card. Designed by me. Printed by Kirsten and me on Papa's very own presses. Yes, it was only fair. It was right. It was Miriam Josefsohn in pursuit of justice.

I barely noticed the rain. My mind was elsewhere. How many cards would we need? When could we use the presses? Who would sell us supplies and not tell Papa? How could we smuggle that much paper into the office? How would we distribute the cards?

My thoughts churned as relentlessly as a sternwheeler. I stepped into the street.

I heard Mr. Jacobowitz yell, "Watch out! Somebody stop her!"

I looked up. Three huge white horses galloped toward me at a furious pace. I stood there, stuck to the cobblestones.

Twenty-Four

I SMELLED TOBACCO. A PAIR OF massive arms grabbed my waist. I dangled in the air as the fire engine sped by, its brass boiler spewing steam and smoke. Two firemen eyed me with what was either alarm or anger—it was hard to tell which. Probably both.

A workman in a heavy cotton shirt and vest settled me on the sidewalk. He took longer than he should have to let me go.

Mr. Jacobowitz rushed toward us, his face a composite of immense relief—presumably for my safety—and irritation at the man still touching my waist. "Thank you, sir," he said, stepping so close to me I could smell his pomade. He had one hand on an umbrella and another by his side. "I will take care of her now."

The man backed away from me and hitched up his pants. "You tell your missus here that there are all manner of cars and horses and wagons on these streets. She'd best be more careful."

"She will, sir," Mr. Jacobowitz said, blushing. "I'll see to it she does."

The man raised his hand to the brim of his cap, bowed slightly to Mr. Jacobowitz, clucked at me in a disapproving manner, and went on his way.

Furious, I straightened my hat and coat. "Your missus! How dare you let that man think that I belong to you, that you are in charge of my every move!"

He took two steps back and handed me the umbrella. "I…I saw it was raining. You had no umbrella. I rushed after you, thank God. Miss Josefsohn, I assure you—"

He looked at my angry face and fumbled the rest of his words. He sighed and offered me his umbrella. I took it and opened it, covering the both of us, as it was pouring now. Mr. Jacobowitz seemed to shrink into himself, and suddenly I felt foolish.

"I'm sorry," I said. "You meant well. And you did keep me from getting hurt."

He cleared his throat. He was forever clearing his throat in front of me. "I'd…ah…I'd…with the rain and all this excitement, if I might renew my offer to escort you home…"

"Here's the streetcar," I said. "I'll be careful. Thank you for the loan of your umbrella."

I tried not to be annoyed as he watched me board the streetcar. He gave me the sweetest little wave, which I couldn't help but return. I assigned a piece of my brain to watch where I put my body as I headed home. I greeted Mrs. Jenkins, counted myself lucky that Mama was out, and carried a tray of sweet rolls and coffee to my room. I moved Uncle Hermann's Bible to make space on my desk. If only Serakh and Tirtzah could see me now, pursuing justice. I longed for the prayer shawl that Rashi's daughter had made.

Suddenly my mind designed the perfect VOTE FOR JUSTICE card. I got out my copybook, my typography book, and my best fountain pen, and commenced to put it on paper.

Heavy cardstock, high gloss ivory
Vary typefaces between Bodoni Poster Compress and
Bodoni Book Italic

Front text:
"JUSTICE, JUSTICE SHALT THOU PURSUE" [blue ink]
—DEUT. 16:20 [blue ink]
VOTE YES ON AMENDMENT 1 [red ink]

Front image:
Roses (for Bread and Roses poem) [red ink]

Reverse side text:
GOVERNMENT OF THE PEOPLE,
BY THE PEOPLE, FOR THE PEOPLE [blue ink]
VOTE YES ON AMENDMENT 1 [red ink]

Yes, this will do nicely. I wanted to print six thousand, which was a thousand more than Papa had. The Osbornes could help with distribution.

I could hardly wait to show my design idea to Kirsten on Thursday. I propped my head in my hands and stared out the window. Kirsten was right, though—if Papa found out that I designed and printed these VOTE FOR JUSTICE cards, he'd be furious. Maybe he'd never let me back in the shop again.

A pair of geese headed south, escaping to make a new life in another place more to their liking. But what do you do when the life you want is only a streetcar ride away, within reach, if only they thought you were good enough to invite you inside?

I sat at dinner later, concentrating on my food, my head pounding. "You are quiet this evening," Papa said.

I put down my knife and fork and settled on a simple, "I'm fine."

Relaxing in the bath that night, I thought even more kindly of Mr. Jacobowitz's actions. *Richard had been so exciting, but he'd never been...sweet.* I slathered rosewater lotion on my arms and legs, remembering Tirtzah staring at my feet that first time in Serakh's cave. "I am going to make a difference here, Serakh," I muttered to myself. "I promise you."

§

MAMA WAS WAITING IN THE KITCHEN for me the next morning when I came downstairs. "Mrs. Lowenthal lent me the perfect costume for you for the masquerade dance. Marie Antoinette! After your breakfast let's go up to my dressing room and try it on. You'll be the hit of the Concordia Club."

Hallowe'en was the last thing on my mind. I leaned against the kitchen wall and put my arms across my chest. "Why should I dress up as the queen who got her head cut off in the French Revolution?"

"Because she was beautiful, and you'll look beautiful, too. Mrs. Lowenthal went out of her way to lend this to you. The least you can do is see how it fits."

"At least Mrs. Lowenthal is going as a suffragist. Are any of your friends besides her working on the suffrage campaign?"

Mama smelled of the perfume that lingered on Baloo. "I don't get involved with politics, Miriam. You should know that by now."

"Why?"

Mama put her hands on her hips. "Do you like playing croquet?"

"No."

"There you have it. I don't like politics. Now, I'll be in the parlor practicing for the benefit concert. Tell me when you're ready to try on the costume."

An hour later we trooped upstairs. I had to admit the dress was stunning. Yards and yards of green and gold brocade, with a low, tight bodice that showed off what passed for my bosom. But I refused to wear the wig.

"It looks ridiculous, Mama. And it probably has fleas."

She stood behind me as I sat at her dressing table and looked in the mirror. She piled my hair on top of my head, leaving a few curls to fall down the side of my neck and onto my bare collarbone.

"No wig then. We'll get fancy feathers and ribbons from the Osborne sisters for your hair. Hmm…and we'll have to add some lace to hide your alluring *décolletage* or your father will have a seizure."

She fetched a strand of pearls. "Here, let's put these on… oh, my, yes, they do look lovely, don't you think? Miriam, you've hardly cracked a smile."

"I'm fine, Mama."

"All you say these days is 'I'm fine' when clearly you are not. Are you worried about our train ride to New York? You shouldn't be. The travel agent assured me that the rails are clear of snow, even in December. At least we're not going overseas. The *Titanic* was such a shock. I can't imagine how the Steinbachers have the courage to make the crossing next spring."

Mama put her hands on my shoulders. "There's something else that's bothering you. You should know it hurts us both when you keep secrets. You can unburden yourself with me."

I kept my eyes on the mirror. I had let her play dress-up with me. And I hadn't groused about that ridiculous trip to

New York City. Mama was in a good mood. Maybe she was ready to listen to reason about my prayer shawl.

"You know, Mama, I'm not the only one in this family who's hiding something."

Mama toyed with her earrings. "Life is full of compromises, Miriam. You can't always have what you want."

"Not even if it belongs to me?"

She arched her eyebrows.

"You don't have to do everything he says, Mama. You have as much right to make decisions as he does." I wanted her to understand so badly.

She left the room.

Twenty-Five

Waiting in the front hall the next morning, I wondered what Papa's face would look like when he saw me in the Marie Antoinette costume with my hair up and my shoulders bare. I commenced to pace and mutter to myself about giving him a taste of his own medicine and showing him some petticoat—the flouncing kind that was on his VOTE NO card.

"Miriam, I expect a proper good morning when I see you."

I jerked my head toward Papa's voice. How long had he been standing in the hall? I smoothed my skirt and avoided his gaze. "Good morning, Papa. I'm sorry, my mind was elsewhere."

He put on his coat and gloves. As I handed him his bowler hat and umbrella, he shook his head and scowled. How could Mama ever have imagined him as her German Prince Charming?

After the employees' morning instructions, I tried to return the umbrella to Mr. Jacobowitz, but he insisted I keep it in the shop as a spare. When I asked Kirsten for help with buying the samples album, Papa interrupted with, "Miss Svenson, you are to finish the first inking of the menu for

Miss Failing, and then you may accompany my daughter. Tell me as soon as you pull the printer's proof."

Kirsten lowered her gaze. "Yes, Mr. Josefsohn."

When Papa disappeared into his office, I leaned toward her. "I want to tell the Osbornes about our...plans, after we shop for the album. Shall we meet them around noon where Burnside Street meets the North Park Blocks?"

She nodded, and I headed for Mr. Jacobowitz. Or, more precisely, I headed for the telephone on Mr. Jacobowitz's desk.

"You wouldn't mind if I made one short call from your telephone, would you?" I asked. "I don't want to trouble my father with using the telephone on his desk."

"By all means, Miss Josefsohn," he said, gazing up at me with a smile. He busied himself by the front counter—to give me privacy, I suppose. I called Osborne Milliners, and arranged to meet with Prudence. When I was through, I smiled at him—polite but not inviting—and scooted toward the office door.

At half past ten, Kirsten told Papa the first inking was done. I collected my umbrella and shopping sack, and we were on our way. The sun shone through the clouds as we walked toward the stationers on Alder Street, but the sky had turned gray over the West Hills. October in Portland— sunny one minute, rainy the next.

Kirsten walked as fast as I did. She chattered happily about going to a dance with Nils and about her plans for their wedding, but when we got to the stationers, she was all business.

"This is Miss Josefsohn from Precision Printers," Kirsten told the woman behind the counter. "She is interested in your albums."

The woman turned to me. "Are you looking for a more traditional album, with green or beige pages, or one with the new black pages?"

"Black. With white photo corners," I said confidently. "And an album that opens flat. Something in leather, with an insert for our company name. Put the purchase on my father's account, please."

We looked at six styles and agreed on one with maroon leather and a thin silver strip around the edge. The woman wrapped up the album, a small box of photo corners, and a dozen extra pages. "Photographs look particularly good with white ink titles on black," she said.

"We're using the album to show customers samples of our work," I explained. "That way they can pick the design features they like best. And with the photo corners, customers can take out the samples to see the reverse side and to feel the weight and texture of the stock." She seemed to approve.

"You have the makings of a businesswoman," Kirsten said, after we left—music to my ears. We waited for Prudence on a park bench under a large elm tree.

"Precision Printers at your service," I called out when I saw her coming up the path.

Kirsten shushed me. Prudence looked puzzled. "What's this all about? Charity said you told her something about suffrage cards."

I modulated my voice. "Do you remember how Kirsten had to print VOTE NO cards in 1906? Well, wouldn't the suffrage campaign like VOTE YES cards this time around?"

From the look on Prudence's face, you would have thought I had given her the keys to the city. "Definitely! The more information, the better our chances. The suffrage leagues here are using posters, broadsides, handbills, newspaper ads, anything and everything. We've even designed a cartoon to project at the cinema. How many cards could you print?"

I looked at Kirsten. "Maybe six thousand." I said. She didn't object.

"That's quite a handsome amount. But isn't your father against suffrage for women?"

"We have to be careful, that's all."

Prudence shook her head. "I couldn't let you do that. If he ever found out..."

"That's what I've tried to tell her," Kirsten said. "But she's not listening."

I barreled on. "You'd have to buy the cardstock, Prudence. My father would know if that much paper went missing from our supplies, and we shouldn't use his account at the stationers. What about ink, Kirsten?"

"We have enough in-house," she said. "I'll use a popular color; no one will notice."

Prudence and Kirsten eyed each other. "I have to do this," I said.

Prudence clasped my right hand in both of hers. "In that case, I won't stand in your way. We'll raise the money for whatever supplies you need. How soon can you print these cards?"

"It depends on when we can get the presses," Kirsten said.

"Any time up to Election Day—November 5th. But the sooner the better."

Kirsten frowned. "And another thing, Miriam. If your father ever sees this VOTE YES card, he'll know it came from his shop. He knows the printing quirks of our machines. Even if he's not certain, he's bound to guess you're the one behind this—and me."

"Are you sure?"

"Absolutely."

I wasn't about to give up my suffrage cards, but I didn't want to get Kirsten in trouble with Papa. Who knew what he might do?

I fiddled with my gloves and watched two squirrels chase each other up the elm. "Well, a vote is a vote and this is a statewide election. We don't have to distribute them in Portland. Couldn't we ship the cards out of the city?"

I watched my idea catch hold. "Certainly," Prudence said. "We'll batch them and send them in hatboxes to our pro-suffrage customers. And we'll get them to suffrage leagues in Eugene, Salem, and Pendleton—maybe even Astoria, Hood River, and La Grande."

"It's settled then." I practically floated back to work.

Papa examined my supplies. "Navy and silver for a cover would have been better, but maroon and silver will do. Let us see what it looks like with the samples."

"You made a good choice," Uncle Hermann said. "I like the black paper."

"Me, too," I replied, choosing to ignore Papa. "I should finish selecting samples by early next week. Monday or Tuesday."

"Tuesday," Papa said. "You do not come to the office Mondays."

Not yet. But one day.

§

FRIDAY I WAS BACK AT OSBORNE Milliners, which was beginning to feel more like home than home did. I pretty much ignored the hats, but I was becoming an expert at making yellow bows. Charity showed me an article she'd cut out about the Duniway festival.

"It says two senators will speak at Mrs. Duniway's birthday because Rabbi Stephen Wise can't attend. He's a great supporter of suffrage for women. Doesn't your temple have a Rabbi Wise, Miriam? His wife bought a hat from us last week."

I nodded. "Stephen Wise used to be our rabbi, but the one we have now is Jonah Wise. I don't think they're related. When is Mrs. Duniway's birthday?"

"October 22nd. We're staging a big rally for all the work she has done. By the by, Mrs. Lowenthal called again. She'll pay us extra to make up *boutonnières* for the Concordia Club masquerade dance. Thanks to Mrs. Lowenthal, we managed to pay our rent this week."

"Why don't you buy the shop? Don't you plan to stay in Portland?"

Prudence put her hands on her hips. "We're renting because we haven't the means to buy," she said, as if that were obvious. "It's hard enough for a married woman to get a bank loan, but an unmarried woman…that's practically impossible."

Charity put the kettle on for tea. "Are you going to this dance, too, Miriam?"

"My parents insist. Mrs. Lowenthal lent me her Marie Antoinette costume. Yards and yards of silk brocade—and all for a costume. Ridiculous."

"Maybe next year we'll pull a bit of a party together. When times are not quite so tight. What do you think, Pru?"

Prudence brushed a strand of hair from her face. "That would be lovely."

Stupid me. "Would you like to come to the Concordia Club? I'm sure I could arrange it," I said, although I doubted I could. I was technically coming as Papa's guest.

"That's kind of you," Prudence said, wearing a close resemblance to Mama's Dinner Party Look. Maybe she thought I was a spoiled brat. I hoped not.

I pressed a yellow bow to my chest. "Can you imagine Mrs. Lowenthal sticking *boutonnières* on all those men?"

Prudence laughed. A genuine laugh. Still, at dinner that night, I wondered whether Charity and Prudence ever went to bed hungry.

§

Saturday I got a letter from Florrie—finally! She was on cloud nine, writing paragraph after paragraph about Anna Head Boarding and Day School, which, I admit, made me envious. Then she added:

> *You would love Berkeley as much as I do. We're just a ferry ride across the bay from San Francisco. Imagine being so close to the home of Ghirardelli chocolates! You can stay at my aunt's with me—she has rooms to spare. Everyone talks about San Francisco rising from the ashes after that earthquake and fire, and it's true. You must visit me. I miss you terribly.*
>
> *Next weekend Jeremy and I are going to the moving pictures. I wrote to you about him, didn't I? He's even nicer than Harold. Are you still swearing off fellows since Richard headed for Los Angeles? That was months ago, Mim. Forget about him.*
>
> *I don't think I'm coming up to Portland for Thanksgiving. Sorry. I haven't told Mama yet, but it's so much lovelier down here. I hope you'll understand.*
> *In friendship forever,*
> *Florrie*

Had Florrie gotten my last letter, she would have asked about the suffrage campaign and my prayer shawl. Berkeley felt as far away as the South Pole.

Florrie was a friend by birth, our mothers being close friends before we were born, two months apart. I never knew a world without Florence Steinbacher. Sometimes I thought she merely tolerated me, although she wouldn't dream of saying so. But I didn't ask for much, and Florrie trusted me to keep her secrets. She kept mine as well, including my enchantment with Richard Broxburn. I started a letter back to her:

Nobody interests me the way Richard did, so there's
nothing romantic to report. How could I ever have gotten
so sweet on him? Well, you know how! I wonder if he ever
made it to Los Angeles and if we'll ever see him in the cin-
ema. Thinking about him still gives me goose bumps.

Papa's clerk, Mr. Jacobowitz, is making eyes at me—can
you believe it? Maybe he means well. Maybe he's watching
out for me for Papa's sake—or on Papa's orders. I'm not sure
what to think.

I told Florrie everything about the petticoat card and my
VOTE FOR JUSTICE card. And I assured her that we weren't
distributing the cards in Portland, lest Papa find out.

Each time I used Charity's yellow blotter to set the ink on
my letter, I yearned to get started on my cards. I had more
questions for Kirsten than there are letters in the alphabet.
How hard is it to set up a job with two typefaces? How long
must the first inking dry before you do a second? How often
do you have to stop the press to clean and re-ink it? I wedged
my fingernail between my teeth. It would take weeks to figure this all out, and we didn't have that much time. I had to
learn faster than Kirsten expected.

Sunday dragged along as usual, pouring down rain. Dutiful
and bored, I sat in the library listening to records on the
Grafonola and reading *The Morning Oregonian*. Papa took
the front section and gave the rest to Mama and me. The
society page had a spread on advice to women from Sarah
Bernhardt.

"Madame Bernhardt says women should have the right to
vote," I told them.

"Madame Bernhardt is an actress," Papa said, as if actresses
were no wiser than Cousin Albert. He took my part of the paper, thumbed through pages, and thrust another article at me.

"This is written by a real journalist," he said. The headline read FIVE STATES WILL VOTE ON WOMAN SUFFRAGE IN NOVEMBER. Underneath a picture of Anna Shaw, the caption read: COMMANDER IN CHIEF OF THE AMAZON FORCES.

Amazon forces? What kind of journalist would write such a stupid thing?

Papa turned to another page. "And here is an editorial for you to consider." The headline read: SUPERFLUOUS WOMEN HAVE BECOME THE PROBLEM IN ALL COUNTRIES WHERE CIVILIZATION FLOURISHES.

This was too much. I glared at Papa. "How can women be unnecessary? That's completely insane!"

"It simply means there's a shortage of husbands," Mama said, cranking the Grafonola. "Don't worry, Mim. There will be plenty of men eager to marry you."

"Mama, that's not the point. Independent women aren't the end of civilization."

"Do not raise your voice," Papa grumbled. "Come, tell your mama what you would like for dessert tonight. Mrs. Jenkins is a good cook, *ja?*"

"I'm not interested in dessert, Papa."

He chuckled. "You? This I cannot believe."

Twenty-Six

THE RAINS CONTINUED INTO MONDAY MORNING. By the time the grandfather clock chimed eight, I was downstairs, fully dressed, and ready to get started on the VOTE FOR JUSTICE cards. A minute before a quarter after the hour, I strode into the front hall and picked up Papa's umbrella and bowler hat.

"You are up early for no reason today," he said with a trace of confusion when he met me in the hall a few seconds later.

I tried to sound confident. "It's good practice, don't you think? Perhaps I might join you at the print shop three days this week instead of two. The sooner I finish the samples album, the sooner we can show it to our customers."

He opened his pocket watch. "Tuesday and Thursday, Miriam. That is the plan."

Undeterred, I tried to hide the seriousness of my question behind a sweet smile. "Oh, and one more thing," I said, handing him his hat. "I'm curious. How much cardstock would you need to make six thousand cards?"

"Why are you asking about cards?"

My face felt warm. I took a sudden interest in the umbrella still in my possession. "Just wondering," I lied. "It would be less than three thousand sheets, wouldn't it?"

I braced for a lecture about asking foolish questions when a man had to get to the office on time and earn a living for his family. Instead, he asked, "How large a card?"

"Average size. Bigger than a playing card, smaller than a handbill."

"There are technical terms, but for you I give the simple answer. I rarely use American standard letter-sized cardstock because we have a variety of jobs. I would cut in quarters a larger sheet—ledger-tabloid—which is eleven inches by seventeen inches. That gives a rectangle a bit bigger than five by eight and uses only fifteen hundred sheets. I allow ten percent for waste on printer adjustments for pressure and ink levels and so forth. I would order seventeen hundred sheets to be safe."

He pinched my cheek. "Now leave such matters to me, or you get worry lines on your face. Mama is still sleeping this morning and is not to be disturbed. My umbrella, Miriam?"

As soon as Papa left, I told Mrs. Jenkins I had to run an errand. The Osborne sisters found me huddled in the doorway to their store when they came downstairs to open for the day. I told them we'd need at least seventeen hundred sheets of ledger-tabloid cardstock. "We can use any supplier except the one on Alder," I said. "My father has an account there, and the clerk knows me."

Prudence looked through the city directory. "How about Haverford's? It's right off the streetcar line."

An hour later, Charity and I stowed our bundle in the back room of Osborne Milliners. Charity decided to buy extra, and I had no notion that two thousand sheets of large cardstock could be so heavy.

I looked out the window and saw something behind the store that could serve as a peace offering. "Mind if I cut some lavender to take home?" Charity was delighted to oblige.

"Papa said not to wake you," I explained to Mama later, handing her the lavender.

"You were at the Osbornes again? You should spend more time perfecting your French for our trip to New York, not lollygagging at a millinery shop. You don't even like hats."

I rubbed the lavender and sniffed my hands—a refreshing antidote to Mama's remarks. She didn't bother to tell me her plans for the day, nor did she ask about mine.

That afternoon, I rummaged through my armoire to find my fullest skirt, one that I could wear with two petticoats. I basted a wide hem in part of the bottom petticoat and slipped the VOTE FOR JUSTICE design page inside. It seemed only fair to spirit the plans for my card into Precision Printers in the very garment Papa chose for his VOTE NO campaign.

We drove to work Tuesday, owing to an appointment Papa had in the afternoon. A few minutes after we arrived, Uncle Hermann burst in the front door. His eyes were wide and his face pale. He waved a newspaper and shouted, "Colonel Roosevelt has been shot!"

My stomach cramped. "Is he dead?"

Someone shouted, "Good Lord, no!"

Mr. Jacobowitz rushed over. Uncle Hermann unfolded the newspaper. "The bullet hit Roosevelt in the chest, but he survived, and even finished his campaign speech." He read aloud: "It takes more than one shot to kill Bull Moose." Uncle Hermann looked at Papa. "Teddy Roosevelt deserves a third term as president. He can do a lot for this country."

Papa harrumphed. "I do not wish the man ill, but his ideas are preposterous. Votes for women. A new national health service for everyone—that would bankrupt us. Better now he should drop out of the race."

Uncle Hermann sputtered, "If you had your way, that bullet would have killed him." Then he said something in German.

Papa turned positively livid and marched into his office. Uncle Hermann followed him. He slammed the door. I—and likely everyone else in Precision Printers—could hear their muffled argument.

I zipped over to Kirsten. "Quick. Let's go to the storage room. I have something for you."

Once we were out of sight, I ripped the basted hem of my petticoat and showed her my VOTE FOR JUSTICE design. "What do you think? Charity and Prudence already bought two thousand sheets of ledger-tabloid cardstock that we'll cut in quarters."

"Hmm…that would be considerably larger than the VOTE NO card."

I grinned. "Precisely!"

She studied my design. "What kind of cardstock did they buy?"

"I don't remember the weight exactly."

"What was the rag content?"

"I didn't check."

Kirsten frowned. "Does the paper have a glossy finish? I have to know what the paper is like so I can figure out which ink to use and how long the ink will take to dry."

"I don't think it's glossy. Sorry. I'll see if I can show you a sheet of it today."

Papa stormed out of the office just as Kirsten and I left the storage room. Kirsten slipped the design page into her apron pocket and high-tailed it back to her station.

"Today I leave Uncle Hermann in charge," Papa told me. "I let him see what business is like for most of us."

"But, Papa—"

His eyes narrowed. "No nonsense, Miriam."

I took a deep breath. "Yes, Papa."

"Good. I will drive you home. Tell your mother I will

spend the rest of the day at the Club, and I should like veal schnitzel for dinner."

Mama shook her head when I told her Papa's demands. "What did you do this time?"

"Nothing! Why do you think it's always my fault? Uncle Hermann told Papa that Colonel Roosevelt got shot, and they started shouting at each other."

"Teddy Roosevelt died? Don't roll your eyes at me, Miriam. I've had more important things to attend to this morning than reading the newspaper."

"He's not dead. They say he'll recover and continue the campaign."

"Your father will ruin my evening here if Mrs. Jenkins can't get schnitzel." She hurried into the kitchen. I trudged upstairs, slouched into my wicker chair, and stared at the rain streaking my bedroom window.

What if it had been a real fight at the shop? What if Papa got so angry he had a fit? What if he and Uncle Hermann had a duel and killed each other? October 15, 1912—Day of Death.

And what if the only person left to run Precision Printers was Julius Josefsohn's grieving but competent daughter, Miriam? I let my mind wander. *Mr. Jacobowitz could stay, I suppose, and I would promote Kirsten. I'd make Precision Printers the best print shop on the West Coast. I'd take care of Aunt Sophie and her children. Mama would be fun to be with, the way she used to be, and—*

A tree branch thwacked the window. I shuddered at the sudden noise. *Am I crazy? Killing off Papa and Uncle Hermann so I could own a print shop?* I closed my eyes and imagined Serakh shaking her head in disappointment.

"This is the way you pursue justice?" she would say. "Elders make mistakes, but is this how you honor your mother and father?

My bedroom seemed to close in on me. I fled to the kitchen. Mama was conferring with Mrs. Jenkins.

"Treats," Mrs. Jenkins said, holding up small box tied with a tiny satin ribbon. "On my way back from the butcher shop, I stopped for caramels. Wrapped, of course, from your favorite store, Mrs. Josefsohn."

"You are a gem," I said, reaching for a caramel. Not as tasty as licorice; but Mrs. Jenkins knew better than to offer me licorice in Mama's presence.

"Mrs. Steinbacher has a touch of lumbago," Mama said, her code for the monthly curse. "We're not going to Neighborhood House tomorrow, Miriam, so I thought I'd visit her for a light luncheon. Would you care to join us?" Mama's mouth said one thing; the expression on her face said another.

"I think I'll visit with the Osbornes."

"Again?"

"They have what you need for my costume. By the by, Mrs. Lowenthal ordered sixty yards of yellow ribbon from them, did she tell you?"

Mrs. Jenkins stirred her tea and looked puzzled.

Mama laughed. "It's for a silly suffragette costume, Mrs. Jenkins."

"Lordy," Mrs. Jenkins said, "What is the world coming to?"

I shook my head. It was no use trying to talk sense into either of them about votes for women.

The next morning, before Mama came down to breakfast, I told Mrs. Jenkins I'd be at Osborne Milliners for most of the day. I filled a picnic basket with cheese sandwiches, apples, and the few remaining caramels, and headed for freedom. The air carried a faint smell of rotting fish and garbage from the docks along the river. There was a metallic taste on my tongue from the foundry. Still, it felt great to stride along the new cement sidewalk and admire the cedars, firs, maples, and madrones growing in this part of the city.

Prudence took my food basket with nary a thank you.

"You look like you haven't slept all night," I told her, in a fit of honesty.

"You're right," she said, thankfully not offended. "It's Colonel Roosevelt. We finally got him to support suffrage for women, and now this. Were you at his rally here a few weeks ago?"

"I read about it in the newspaper."

Prudence offered a weak smile. "Of course, you started helping us mostly because you're friends with Charity, and Lord knows she needs a friend."

Honesty stings when it's flung back at you. "I read that Colonel Roosevelt walked on a carpet of roses from the railroad depot to his automobile," I said in my defense.

"Yes, and we showered him with rose petals later on. Did you know that Jane Addams seconded his nominating speech at the Progressive Party convention?"

I took off my hat and gloves, unbuttoned my coat, and wondered where Charity was. "The woman who started Hull House in Chicago?"

"The very same. She is the first woman ever to give a speech like that. She's on the Party's platform committee, guiding Colonel Roosevelt every step of the way, and she wants justice for everyone. She even helped start the National Association for the Advancement of Colored People."

Charity ambled in from the back room. "You must be talking about Saint Jane."

Prudence looked annoyed, and Charity held up her hands in mock surrender. "I'm only joking. Stop worrying, Pru. Colonel Roosevelt will be fine."

Prudence tightened a loose comb by her bun. "He won't win. He'll never get another chance as president. This country's not ready."

I retrieved a caramel from the basket and gave it to Prudence, who clearly needed cheering up. "You know, Portland has a settlement house, too, like Hull House, only smaller. It's called Neighborhood House, and it runs the same kind of programs for immigrants and poor families. I…um…volunteer there."

Prudence looked at me with interest—and, I thought, more respect. Charity beamed.

"Prudence, please go upstairs and get some rest," I told her, acting like an older sister to someone nearly twice my age. "Charity and I will mind the shop today." To my surprise, she listened.

I stayed with Charity until closing time, helping her with the few customers who showed up and making more yellow bows and sashes than I could count. Before I left, I put a sheet of cardstock in my basket to show Kirsten.

Mama and I avoided getting in each other's hair when I got home. She was her usual chatty self at dinner. Papa asked her to bring his coffee into the library, as they had plans to discuss. After he left the table, Mama whispered, quite unexpectedly, "So, Miriam. How is Baloo?"

Twenty-Seven

I NEARLY DROPPED MY NAPKIN INTO my half-filled water glass. Mama studied her fingernails. It took me a moment to realize my relief that we were talking about what mattered to us both.

"I assure you that Baloo is perfectly safe, Mama," I answered gently. I was feeling a bit ashamed ever since I heard Serakh's voice in my head the other night, admonishing my behavior toward my parents. Here was the chance to undo what I'd done.

Still, I was not giving up my side of the fight. "And how is my prayer shawl?"

"Safe."

"Then let's come to some sort of agreement."

"It's complicated, Miriam. One thing has nothing to do with the other." Mama's face closed down, replaced by The Dinner Party Look—end of conversation.

Two could play this game as well. I folded my arms across my chest. "I'm sorry to hear that. When you put the two things together, let me know."

While my parents were in the library, I grabbed an extra suffrage bow from my coat pocket and strode to the potting shed. "Here's a reminder to do what's right, Baloo," I said. "Sit tight, my friend. You might be here for quite some time." I tucked the bow beside him. Danny would have approved.

The next day at work, Uncle Hermann and Papa acted like bosom buddies. Apparently they both preferred the Boston Red Sox to the New York Giants. They congratulated each other on backing the team that won the World Series.

After the morning meeting, Kirsten and I went to "look at the supplies" in the storage room. I handed her a sheet of the cardstock Charity and I had bought. She rubbed it between her thumb and forefinger, and raised it to the light.

"It's going to soak up more ink than a better grade of paper, but it will have to do." She leaned against a shelf and smiled at me the way someone smiles before delivering bad news.

"What's wrong, Kirsten?"

"Miriam, I admire your design for the VOTE FOR JUSTICE card, I really do, but it's much too complicated. It's going to take hours to make six thousand cards, even on the new Chandler & Price. So, anyway, I've made a few changes."

She handed me the page from my copybook.

VOTE FOR JUSTICE card:
Heavy cardstock, ~~high gloss~~ ivory *Matte finish*
~~Vary typefaces between Bodoni Poster Compress and~~
~~Bodoni Book Italic~~
Whatever typeface is available at press time

Front text:
"JUSTICE, JUSTICE SHALT THOU PURSUE" [blue ink] *black*
—DEUT. 16:20 [blue ink] *black*
VOTE YES ON AMENDMENT 1 [red ink] *black*

Front image:
Roses (for Bread and Roses poem) [red ink] *black*

~~Reverse side text:~~
~~GOVERNMENT OF THE PEOPLE,~~
~~BY THE PEOPLE, FOR THE PEOPLE [blue ink]~~
~~VOTE YES ON AMENDMENT 1 [red ink]~~

"That's it?"

Kirsten put her hands on her hips. "It takes more than twice as long to print in two colors, considering how much you have to clean the press in between. And a two-sided card is unnecessary. Plus, we can't be picky about the typeface."

"It's so…boring. And a black rose? It reminds me of Hallowe'en. Or someone's funeral."

"Only one ink, Miriam, remember? Besides, if women don't get the right to vote this time, it will feel like a funeral, believe you me."

Mr. Jacobowitz opened the storage room door. "A funeral? Oh, I am so sorry for your loss. Who has passed on?"

Kirsten turned around and glared at him. "You, if you don't leave us alone."

His eyes widened, and then he vanished.

Kirsten smiled at me. "I'm twice the compositor Mr. Jacobowitz is, although I daresay he tries hard. Plus, we have an understanding."

"About what?"

She smoothed her apron. "Well, Nils goes to these meetings of the Socialist Party—you know they are supporting Eugene Debs for president."

"And?"

"And a couple of times he's seen Mr. Jacobowitz there. So I

mentioned it to Mr. Jacobowitz one day, and he pleaded with me not to tell your father."

"He should stand up for his rights, like Nils does."

"Oh, Mr. Jacobowitz is nice enough. He just can't afford to be fired, and your father isn't the easiest man to work for."

I brushed what passed for bangs off my forehead. "He's not the easiest man to live with either. Kirsten, if we have to use only one ink, let's print it in blue—to match a…a certain garment that I own. I know that sounds silly, but it would mean a great deal to me, really."

"Let's see what I can do." A moment later she returned with a can labeled Cerulean. "I opened this for another job. No one will notice if we use more."

I looked inside; it was a little dark and didn't quite shine the same way, but it was a rich, strong color. "It's close enough. When can we get started?"

"Today, if you get me the cardstock. I should have time to cut it to the right size."

I straightened the little navy bow at my collar and headed for the door. "I'll call Charity and tell her to bring it over."

"Wait a minute. What are you going to tell your father?"

"Listen in; you'll have a good laugh."

I used the telephone on Mr. Jacobowitz's desk again. "Osborne Milliners," I told the operator, "Seventeenth and Marshall."

Prudence answered. "Miss Osborne," I said loudly enough for Papa to hear if he came out of his office. "This is Miss Josefsohn at Precision Printers. I understand you have your own cardstock and are looking to print a variety of handbills and advertisements for your new store. If you can bring your supply to our shop, we would be happy to show you samples of our work."

Prudence didn't miss a beat. "What time would you like us to come?"

"At your earliest convenience."

Three-quarters of an hour later, Charity heaved two thousand sheets of cardstock onto the counter. Papa came out of his office, and I told him Osborne Milliners had an unexpected supply of cardstock and was interested in printing a simple postcard. "Isn't that right, Miss Osborne?"

Charity nodded and looked at me to continue.

"Miss Osborne would like design ideas. Since my album isn't ready yet, I thought we could lend her several samples. In the meantime, we could cut the cardstock to size."

Papa creased his forehead. "This is quite irregular."

"Won't you excuse us a minute, Miss Osborne?" Charity took a few steps back. "Papa," I whispered, "Mrs. Steinbacher buys her hats from these women. Soon they'll be the most popular milliners in Portland. It won't take long to cut their cardstock for them, and they might get us other customers."

Papa rubbed his chin and looked at me as if he thought for the first time that I might have a bit of a brain in my head. "You do have a point, Miriam. But I don't want you near the machines. Give the job to Miss Svenson."

"Certainly." I turned away so he couldn't see me grinning from ear to ear. I gave Charity three samples of postcards from our inventory and told her to leave the cardstock for us to cut.

Kirsten hid her smile behind an invoice pad. "Nice to have met you, Miss Osborne." The two shook hands, and Charity left.

"Show me how to cut this cardstock," I said, ignoring Papa now that he was in his office.

Kirsten rolled her eyes, but obliged. She refused to let me try the big cutter, so we lugged the cardstock back to the smaller cutting machine, the one that reminded me of a guillotine. Kirsten placed about forty sheets on a grid, lined up the restraining brackets, and screwed a heavy metal plate on top of the pile. She placed one hand on a special knob and reached for a razor-sharp slicer with the other. "Lesson number one: Watch your fingers."

The slicing mechanism was harder to operate than I thought. I tried it only a few times, lest Papa come looking for me. Then I went back to the inventory boxes in the office. If I didn't take my samples album seriously, neither would Papa.

By the end of the day, I had finished going through our inventory and had selected samples. Kirsten had assembled a pile of six thousand blank cards, with five hundred sheets of cardstock left over. As Papa had driven us to work that morning, he agreed to bring home the samples and the album for me to complete over the weekend.

"Tell Mr. Jacobowitz to help you put them in the back seat." Then he added, "And do not encourage him, Miriam. He is not the caliber of husband we have in mind for you."

Oh, for pity's sake. Marriage is the last thing on my mind. "Yes, Papa," was all I said.

Twenty-seven piles grew on my bedroom carpet Friday. I divided each of the nine categories of samples into "definitely use," "possibly use," and "don't use." The choices were harder than I first thought.

Mama knocked and came right in anyway. "I pinned that lace you brought to the bodice of your costume. Come try it on." She didn't even nod in the direction of my samples.

I arched my back and stretched. "In a minute, Mama. I'm sorting samples for the customer album." I pointed to six different baby announcements spread out near her feet. "Which three of these do you like best?"

Her eyes flickered toward the floor. "They're all nice. Your costume is by my dressing table. Tell me when you are ready to try it on."

The costume waited while I got back to work. By dinner the album looked stunning, with three samples for most categories and four for our business stationery and birth announcements. I included the 1910 program for the confirmation class service at Temple Beth Israel because of a particularly elegant font—and because Florrie's name was listed.

If it weren't for my samples album, Mrs. Jenkins's cooking, and the purchase of more licorice nibs, Saturday would have been a complete loss. No mail from Florrie. A dull evening at La Ballet Classique. Not a single notion about how to print the VOTE FOR JUSTICE cards under Papa's nose.

§

I AWOKE SUNDAY MORNING TO A flash of blue.

Serakh sat on the edge of my bed, my old black shoes in her lap. "Moshe will speak to the people again, and Tirtzah is worried. She wants you by her side."

I scrambled across the coverlet and squeezed her against me. "You're alive! I was afraid they killed you as a witch. It says in the Bible…oh, never mind. It's so good to see you! How is Tirtzah? Has she married Gabi? What's her land like?"

She eased away from me and smiled. My shoes fell on the floor. "I will answer all these questions after we cross. Fetch your prayer shawl."

My stomach sank to my knees. My mouth turned sour. "I can't."

"You cannot what?"

"I don't have my prayer shawl. My father saw me wearing it and snatched it away. I found it, but then my mother stole it."

"Does she know of the blue thread?"

"No, I don't think so. I tried to explain about…everything…to Uncle Hermann, but he wouldn't believe me."

"Miriam," she said softly, "you cannot cross the *olam* without your blue thread. I must leave now."

I grabbed her hand. "Don't go," I pleaded. "Wait right here and I'll—I'll get you a salmon cake. Two. And a cucumber. Have you ever eaten a pickle? We have sour gherkins in the icebox. Serakh, please! Stay and talk to me."

She kissed the top of my forehead. "I cannot linger, even for such delicious sustenance. But I will tell Tirtzah that one day you will come again."

I refused to listen. "Nibs! I just got some yesterday. Give them to Makhlah; she'll love them. Two minutes, Serakh. I'll be right back." I raced to my bedroom door and opened it.

There was a flash of blue behind me.

And in front of me, by the door to his upstairs study, stood Papa, already arrayed in his business suit. He stared past me into my bedroom, his face contorted with utter and absolute fear.

Twenty-Eight

I LOOKED BEHIND ME. SERAKH WAS gone—I knew she would be. When I turned to Papa, he was leaning against the wall by his study, his face a sickly white.

I rushed to his side. His hands felt damp and cold and he seemed to be staring off into space. For a moment I thought he was having an apoplectic fit. Grandpa Goldstein had died of apoplexy at fifty-seven, and Papa was fifty-three. I started to fetch Mama, but Papa grabbed my wrist.

"Savta!" he wheezed. "She comes back to haunt me. Flash—she vanishes. Flash—she returns." He clutched my arm, his breathing shallow and his voice raspy.

"No one is haunting you, Papa. We're all safe," I said softly, trying to calm him.

"You think I never saw? I did! Raizl wrapped in that cursed rag—dead! My dear Raizl. Even the rabbi said Savta was a heretic, a madwoman. And he was right! I fetched him myself. Who else could save us?"

"Come sit down," I urged, pointing to the study. He wouldn't move.

"Who else could save us from this evil, I ask you? Frida? She worried more about a stain on her best dress than about a blight on our family. Hermann was still in knee pants."

"I'd better get Mama."

"No!" He fixed his wide eyes on mine. "Are you crazy? Mama loves Savta. She won't believe me. Now that Savta lives with us, there is no escape. Mama says I have visions from the fumes I breathe at the print shop, but she is wrong. Wrong! I see. I know. I am not crazy. Mama refuses to listen to the rabbi. I have to save my family!"

"You did the right thing, Papa," I said, patting his hand, hoping to stop his raving. "It's me, Miriam. I meant my mother, not yours."

"Miriam?" he blinked at me and frowned. "You look so much like her."

Like who? I dared not ask.

"Lillian!" I shouted, lest I add to Papa's confusion. He seemed so helpless. He needed me. And I knew what it was like to feel reality slipping out from under you.

He finally let me guide him to the big chair behind his desk. His breathing relaxed. Color began to return to his cheeks.

"Miriam?"

"Yes, Papa. I'm here. Everything will be all right."

He reached for my hand. I thought the worst was over.

Then I watched his face harden into anger. He glared at me. "Miriam, where is that shawl?"

"I don't have it, Papa."

"*Gott in Himmel*, don't lie to me! I saw a flash of blue light in your room. Savta has returned. She's come to kill you!"

"What light?" I needed time to make up a story and make it good, or else I'd never get my shawl again.

He pulled me closer, grabbed my shoulders, and shook me. "Answer me!" he shouted.

Mama swooped into the room, her dressing gown half open, her curls in disarray. "Julius, what's wrong?"

"She's found that cursed rag again!"

"Shh…Julius, she couldn't have. The shawl is safely tucked away, I promise you."

He let me go and I retreated to the other side of his desk. "There was blue light in your room," Papa said, jabbing his finger at me. "Do not deny this, Miriam. I saw it with two eyes of my own."

My own two eyes, I thought, out of habit. I took a breath. "I was going to the kitchen to get a snack," I said, which was true enough. "I was looking at you, Papa. I didn't see anything in my bedroom."

He put his head in his hands. I still felt sorry for him. "The shawl is so beautiful, Papa," I explained. "Nothing wicked could have come from it. It has a quote from the Bible about pursuing justice. Your *savta* was a wise woman no matter what that rabbi said. It was all some sort of mistake."

I wiped my wet cheeks and imagined Raizl, Serakh, and Savta at King Solomon's Temple. Papa was so miserable and so wrong. *Isn't this the time to tell Papa the whole truth?*

"Mistake?" His eyes narrowed. A vein pulsed in his forehead. "How dare you tell me what is a mistake! Never!"

I backed away.

"Justice?" he shouted. "What do you know of justice, you foolish girl?"

My last shred of sympathy vanished.

Papa stood. He straightened his suit jacket and smoothed his hair. "I swore once long ago to destroy that shawl, but like an idiot I listened to Hermann. No more! Lillian, you will take that shawl and you will burn it!"

Mama caressed Papa's cheek. "But, Julius, dear—"

He pushed her hand away. "Burn it! Don't you dare to give it back to Hermann. Do you hear me? *Ach*, women! I am going to the Club, and I will be back for dinner."

He stormed off. A moment later, I heard the front door slam. I wanted to be grateful that he hadn't suffered a fit or spun off into insanity, but I couldn't. Not now.

Mama was rewrapping her dressing gown. "About my shawl," I ventured.

She shook her head. "We'll talk about it another time."

"But you won't burn it."

"Don't you threaten me, Miriam. I am not in the mood."

"I meant it as a question, that's all. A plea. Besides, I would never burn Baloo...I know how much he means to you. And I loved Danny every bit as much as you did." It slipped out before I could stop myself.

"Danny has nothing to do with this," Mama said. "Your father just wants to keep you safe. You're the only child we have left."

Her voice broke. Soon both of us were crying.

"I need my shawl, Mama. Papa's wrong about it being evil—it's no such thing. He's made a huge mistake."

She searched my face. "And what is so important about this shawl?"

Should I tell Mama? I stared at the very spot in the carpet where I had returned from my latest...trip. *Can I trust her?*

I licked my lips, which had suddenly felt dry. It would be my word against Papa's, I reasoned, and she always took Papa's side these days. Even Uncle Hermann didn't believe me.

"Tell me," she whispered.

"It's an heirloom." That was the best I could do. "Savta intended it for me because I'm named for her. Her prayer shawl can't hurt me, I promise."

Mama dismissed me with a wave of her hand. "You're only sixteen, you're in no position to make that promise. You should listen to your father. And to me. We've kept you clothed and fed and sheltered and safe. What can you possibly know about the real world?"

"The real world?" I remembered the grains of sand under my fingernails, and Tirtzah and her sisters standing before Moses. "I know that we have to take risks. We have to stand up for what's right. I know that Papa shouldn't have printed that disgusting VOTE NO card even if he is against suffrage for women. I know that Papa was wrong about Raizl and the shawl. I know that he was wrong to wait so long before calling the doctor about Danny."

A muffled cry rose in Mama's throat. Instantly I regretted what I had said about my brother. Mama raced to her room. I crawled back into bed.

Sunday was horrid.

§

MONDAY MORNING I LEANED AGAINST MY brass headboard and tried to put my thoughts in order. One idea kept pushing to the front: I had work to do. The suffrage campaign was here and now and important. If I focused on that I wouldn't have to think about Danny, or my parents, or my stupidity in hiding my shawl next to Baloo. I slipped out of the house while Mama practiced the piano.

The walk to Osborne Milliners did little to clear my mind, but at least I could make rosettes, bows, and sashes for Mrs. Duniway's birthday rally.

"I hear the mayor will be there tomorrow," Charity said, cutting another length of yellow ribbon. "Maybe the governor, too."

By mid-afternoon my head throbbed and Charity counted five cuts on my fingers. When I was finished for the day, I practically crawled home. Mrs. Jenkins made me chamomile tea with plenty of honey. Closeted in my room, I tried to concentrate on Mrs. Duniway's party and the suffrage campaign. No good. My mind kept wandering back to Serakh and my prayer shawl. Serakh had said something about Tirtzah and another decision Moses was going to announce. Or, rather, Moses had already announced it because that was thousands of years ago. What had I missed?

I reached for the Bible. Uncle Hermann and Mrs. Jenkins said Zelophehad's daughters were mentioned in Numbers and I was determined to read through all of it this time. I concentrated on every list of names—the longer the better. The longest started in chapter twenty-six—the tribes that came from Jacob's twelve sons. Finally I got to:

> 28 The sons of Joseph after their families were Manasseh and Ephraim.

Sons and more sons. Naturally. Then, listed under the tribe of Manasseh:

> 33 And Zelophehad the son of Hepher had no sons, but daughters: and the names of the daughters of Zelophehad were Mahlah, and Noah, Hoglah, Milcah, and Tirzah.

Not spelled the way I had heard their names, but it didn't matter. I read through the verses listing the tribes, until I came to Asher.

> 46 And the name of the daughter of Asher was Sarah.

Serakh at last. I imagined Tirtzah and her sisters and Serakh sitting with me on the floor near my bed. Together again, here, in my time and place. I wiped my tears on my sleeve and started to read again, line by line.

Chapter twenty-seven told the story I had seen the second time I traveled with the blue thread, the time I stood before Moses. Tirtzah and her sisters asked for their inheritance and Moses gave it to them. Then he made it a law for every man who died with daughters but no sons.

What about that other ruling? I followed my finger down the rest of the column. I read chapter after chapter. And there it was in chapter thirty-six. Those angry men claimed that the land had to stay within their tribe. They made an argument about inheritance and something called the jubilee, which I didn't understand. But the rest of the chapter was all too clear.

> 6 This is the thing which the LORD doth command concerning the daughters of Zelophehad, saying, Let them marry to whom they think best; only to the family of the tribe of their father shall they marry.

Moses made it a rule for all time.

> 8 And every daughter, that possesseth an inheritance in any tribe of the children of Israel, shall be wife unto one of the family of the tribe of her father, that the children of Israel may enjoy every man the inheritance of his fathers.

And to top it all off:

> 11 For Mahlah, Tirzah, and Hoglah, and Milcah, and Noah, the daughters of Zelophehad, were married unto their father's brothers' sons:

Oh, for crying out loud! I was sorely tempted to hurl the Bible across the room, but you don't do that to holy books. I slammed it shut and commenced to pace. If Tirtzah and her sisters wanted their land, they had to get married. Plus they had to marry their uncles or cousins. Tirtzah had fought so hard, and in the end she lost Gabi the Reubenite, who was not a member of her tribe. Who knows what oafs she and her sisters got stuck with?

At dinner, it was as if nothing had happened the day before, as if the flash of blue and Papa's raving were long dead and buried. I studied my knife and fork and listened to my parents' polite conversation. I thought about families and tribes, and how little things had changed between men and women since Tirtzah's time, when men enjoyed "the inheritance of their fathers." I stabbed at my buttered baby turnips. Two of them skittered off the plate.

Tirtzah wanted me to be with her for that second decision, and I had let her down. Would Serakh have let me interfere, to stand before Moses again? Probably not. Could I have made a difference then? Probably not. But Papa was not going to stop me from making a difference now.

Twenty-Nine

ON TUESDAY, PAPA DROVE US TO work in the Oldsmobile. "I will be away with Mr. Jacobowitz most of the day. I leave you in the care of Miss Svenson."

He swerved to avoid a horse and wagon plodding across the intersection. The horse wore blinders. Maybe Papa did, too. "How are you feeling?" I asked. I hoped that we might talk about what had happened the other night.

"Fine," he snapped. "I will be back by three. Do you have money for lunch?"

"Yes, Papa." We rode the rest of the way in silence.

After Papa left, Uncle Hermann made a quick round of the production floor and then retired to the office to read *The Morning Oregonian*. I followed him in, closed the office door, and sat on the edge of his desk. I decided to be direct.

"I just want to ask you one thing about that prayer shawl." I barreled on before he could object. "What happened after Raizl died?"

Uncle Hermann folded the newspaper. He fiddled with his fountain pen.

I waited.

Finally, he said, "I was too young to know the details, but I shared a bed with your father and often he woke up screaming. After Raizl's burial, the rabbi came to the house and there was an argument. The rabbi asked Savta for the shawl. She refused. Then the shawl seemed to have disappeared. Rumors spread. People turned their backs on Savta. Merchants refused to sell her their wares. She stayed at home and helped Mama, Frida, and me. By then Julius was apprenticed to a printer. That had been our father's trade."

"What happened to your father?"

"He was killed when I was a baby. He...well, it's a long story, Miriam. Let's save that for another time."

"No more blue flashes?"

Uncle Hermann frowned with confusion. I struggled to strip away any emotion except curiosity. "Papa mentioned something about a blue flash," I said. "Who was Frida?"

"Frida? She was—is—our sister. There was your father, then Raizl—they were close. Then Frida, who is five years older than I. She married well, and later Mama and Savta went to live with her. The family decided your father and I should go to America."

"And that's when you got the prayer shawl?"

Uncle Hermann nodded. "We had no idea Savta still had it. She gave it to us at the train station. Savta said she would die soon. She pleaded with us to name a daughter Miriam in her memory and to give that daughter the prayer shawl."

"And you kept the prayer shawl because Papa was afraid to give it to me."

"Yes." He put his hand on my knee. "Let matters rest, Mim."

I slid off his desk and gave him a quick hug. "Thanks, Uncle Hermann. Everything's starting to make sense. I'd like to work with Miss Svenson today."

His smile was wide and welcoming. "Just be sure you are off the production floor by the time your father gets back. I'm in enough trouble already." Cousin Albert was lucky to have him for a father. "It should be an easy day," he added. "We've delivered most of the Hallowe'en work and there's no rush yet for Thanksgiving."

Hallowe'en.

Perfect.

"I'd wager Albert would like his very own Hallowe'en cards. Miss Svenson and I can make them if there's slack time today."

Uncle Hermann was keen on my idea. So was Kirsten when I explained my plan to use the Osborne's extra cardstock and learn how to compose, set type, and run the press.

She smoothed her apron. "I can give you the basics and test which ink works best on this cardstock. Hmm…I just used a black cat image for Mrs. Pettygrove's dinner party menu."

"When can we start?"

"A little after one, I should think."

At four minutes after one, I was at Kirsten's side. We stood next to the large cabinet in the center of the room. "This is called a California job case," she said. "Don't ask me why. Every letter and punctuation mark has its own little box, see? All the majuscules—the capital letters—are in the upper part of the case and the little letters—the minuscules—are in the lower part. And here are the rest, Miriam—strips that go between the lines, em spaces that go between the words, and slugs for other kinds of spacing."

"I get it. So that's why capitals are called upper case letters and the smaller ones are called lower case." Sister Margaret couldn't have given me a more approving smile. I handed Kirsten a scrap of paper. "Here's what I'd like on the card."

THE GOBLINS AT DARK EERIE MEETINGS
ON HALLOWE'EN SEND YOU THEIR GREETINGS!

"And let's put that black cat at the bottom."

"Good. Now watch this." Kirsten held a ruler-like gadget with a tiny shelf on the bottom edge. She picked up majuscules, minuscules, punctuation marks, and spacing leads and placed each line—with the letters backward—onto a marble slab, then into a heavy metal frame she called a "chase." She added the cat image from Mrs. Pettygrove's print job, extra pieces she called "furniture," and two pressure adjusters, called "quoins," for the vertical and horizontal aspects of the frame. I turned a quoin key to lock everything into place.

This is like my life. Odd pieces in a frame. Serakh and the blue thread are my quoins, holding me together.

The bell over the front door jingled. Papa was back early. Kirsten collected the chase, and I rushed to Papa's office. I'd have to finish with Kirsten later.

§

HALLOWE'EN WAS THE BIG TOPIC AT Neighborhood House the next day. A sign on the wall read:

COME TO A JOLLY HALLOWE'EN PARTY
GAMES AND DANCING
ENTERTAINMENT FOR THE YOUNGER SET
THURSDAY, OCTOBER 31ST
7:30 P.M.

Hallowe'en decorations hung from the kindergarten windows. The teacher pointed me toward a girl who had refused to join the others in making party hats and masks. I grabbed a piece of paper and colored pencils, and walked over.

"I'm Miriam Josefsohn. What's your name?"

"Bella Jacobowitz."

"Oh! Do you have a relative who works at Precision Printers?"

Bella frowned.

Perhaps not. "Don't you want to make a party hat?"

"Mama says Hallowe'en is about dead people. I won't go to a party with dead people."

"There won't be dead people, Bella. Let's make a special crown to protect you."

Bella's eyes widened. "Do you know magic?"

"Somebody once called me a witch, but I'm a regular person, just like you."

"I'm not a regular person. I'm going to have a magic crown."

I wished I had a magic crown too. And my prayer shawl. After I finished with Bella, I checked in the office. No Mrs. Rosenfeld. She wasn't in the clothing donation room either. I'd brought a bundle of outgrown clothes in which I'd hidden the shoes Serakh brought back from…when…where…I hurled them at that horrid man. Someone could use them and Mama would notice if I kept both pairs of black shoes.

Leaving my bundle on the donation table, I wondered when Mrs. Steinbacher would tire of her atrocious hat, and which poor immigrant woman would dare to wear it next. A familiar gray dress hung near the men's trousers. I stepped closer until I was sure, until I smelled goats. I pulled the dress from its hanger and crushed it to my chest.

I felt a tightness at the corners of my eyes. Was Serakh gone forever now? Had she given up on me because I didn't have my prayer shawl? What would happen if Papa got his way and the blue thread went up in flames?

I don't know how long I stayed in that donation room, waiting for answers that hovered out of reach. A woman came in once, said something in a foreign language, and walked out. I finally composed myself, fed Mama a tiny lie about sorting dusty clothes, and climbed into the front seat of Mrs. Steinbacher's Packard. I sat next to a new chauffeur who smelled of mothballs and had hair growing out of his ears.

I didn't ask Mr. Jacobowitz about Bella the next day. Maybe it was a common enough name. Besides, curiosity could not overcome my recent discomfort in his presence. While Papa was holed up in his office, I watched Kirsten insert our Hallowe'en chase into the press and align a piece of cardstock against tiny pins on a flat part she called a "platen." She put a pile of blank cardstock on the right side of a platform at the front of the press and opened a can of ink that looked like blue molasses.

"It's got to be thick to stick to the rollers," she said. "And to spread an even surface on the inking disc." She spread two lines of ink on the disc, moved a large lever forward, started the flywheel with her left hand, and pumped the treadle with her right foot. The press seemed to fold up on itself—*ka-chunk*—while forcing the chase against the platen and inking Albert's card.

"I already adjusted the packing under the tympan, and pulled a proof," she said.

I had no notion what she meant, but I nodded nevertheless.

"Stand away from the press," she continued. "See? My left hand removes the printed card to the left side of the platform. I separate the good cards from the ones that weren't inked properly. My right hand takes a blank card from the pile on the right side of the platform and inserts it against the pins."

She made it look easy. *Ka-chunk.* The press inked and printed another card.

"Some presses close up on you fast; we call them 'alligators.' You have to be very careful, Miriam. Once you engage the motor and start the treadle, the press keeps moving. Even if you pull the braking lever and disengage the motor, the press will finish that cycle."

"Here, I'll take a turn."

Kirsten folded her arms across her chest. "Didn't you hear me? You're not ready. Your father doesn't even want you on the production floor, remember?"

"I'm not exactly waiting for his permission. Besides, Papa won't know."

Another compositor asked Kirsten a question, and I saw my chance when she stepped away to answer him. This was like sewing class—you learned by doing. How hard could it be to print a few cards?

Operating the lever and the flywheel I ever so carefully printed one good card, then another. But the third piece of cardstock went in crooked. I reached in to fix its alignment. The machine began to close, and I pulled back—not soon enough. My index finger went numb, then flashed with a burning pain when the machine opened again.

I stood there, staring at my finger. Kirsten rushed me to the storage room. She told me later that I kept yelping like a kicked dog, but I didn't remember any of it.

"Ice! she shouted." I sat on a little bench, biting my lip against the pain. I squeezed my eyelids shut. The pain surged deeper. When I opened my eyes, Mr. Jacobowitz was wrapping my hand in a wet cloth with slivers of ice from the icebox at the back of the room. "Let me look at your hand. Please, just for a second." His palms were sweaty.

"Don't tell my father!"

"I won't," he said, touching my hand as if it were made of the most delicate porcelain. "Ah, the nail is still attached. No bones crushed. You will heal and be whole, thanks be to God." Slowly he looked from my hand to my face. There was such kindness in his eyes. Without thinking, I put my free hand on top of the one holding my injured one.

"Thank you," I whispered.

He blushed, and I admit I felt my cheeks grow warm. *Silly me, how unprofessional is that?*

"I'll take care of her now," Kirsten said, coming over with fresh ice.

Mr. Jacobowitz didn't argue, but as he left Papa appeared suddenly in the doorway.

"*Gott in Himmel*, look what you've done!" He cradled my injured hand in his own.

"She'll be fine, sir," Kirsten said. "Nothing is broken, I assure you. I am so terribly sorry. I shouldn't have let her near the presses. It's entirely my fault."

The vein in Papa's temple throbbed. "Miss Svenson, you will tell Mr. Jacobowitz to call my brother to bring his automobile to the shop. You will accompany Miriam home. When you return, you will empty your personals box, collect this week's pay from Mr. Jacobowitz, and leave."

I clutched his sleeve with my good hand. "No! Don't fire Miss Svenson, Papa. It's not her fault." I waved my injured hand in his face. "Look," I lied, "my finger hardly hurts now. By tomorrow it will be perfect." *Poor Kirsten. How could I have been such a clumsy fool?!*

"By tomorrow it will be black and blue and swollen, and you will not keep that nail. Is that not so, Miss Svenson?"

"Yes, sir," she whispered. "May I have until the end of the day to finish Mrs. Bloom's birth announcement?"

Papa jerked his head yes. After Kirsten left, he grabbed my shoulders. "You sit here and keep ice on your hand. Not one more word. *Ach!* Such foolishness." He stomped out.

That's when the shakes began. I'd ruined everything.

Thirty

ON THE RIDE HOME, I PLEADED with Uncle Hermann to see that Kirsten kept her job. He said he'd do his best. Mrs. Jenkins puffed her way down the front walk. Uncle Hermann got out of his automobile to talk to her.

While we were alone, Kirsten whispered, "Look in your personals box in the storage room. I'm at Mrs. Hardwick's boarding house on Third and Harrison. Ice your hand tomorrow. I am so sorry."

"I'm the one who's sorry," I said. "I'll make it up to you, I promise."

Mrs. Jenkins smothered me as if I'd broken my arm and come down with typhoid fever in the same instant. Later I let Mama bathe my hand in tincture of iodine, which stung like blazes. I dined in my room, which was just as well. Otherwise, I might have thrown something at Papa.

The next morning the top third of my index finger had turned an ugly bluish-black. But Papa was wrong—the nail didn't fall off. Mama scrutinized my hand and finally pronounced it on the mend. She produced a pair of white leather gloves with lace trim. "They're for the masquerade dance," she said. "Your hand might still look bruised."

She held me at arm's length and studied me like a printer's proof. "A hint of rouge and you will look stunning. A pity you have your father's nose instead of mine, but your eyes are captivating, and your skin is improving. You'll be the toast of the Concordia Club."

"I'm going to the party at Neighborhood House," I announced. "They need me." Whether they needed me or not, I refused to parade on Papa's arm now that he'd fired Kirsten.

"After all the trouble Mrs. Lowenthal went through to lend you her costume?"

"Poor people can't appreciate Marie Antoinette?"

"Don't be impertinent, Miriam."

I was not about to back down. Papa had gone too far. She finally agreed to have Mrs. Steinbacher's chauffeur fetch me at Neighborhood House at half past ten.

Mama brushed a stray curl from her forehead. "I'll ask Mrs. Steinbacher when we have tea with her this afternoon. You'd better come along, Miriam. I'm not about to leave you alone today. There might still be an infection under that fingernail."

I let Mama have her way, and I'm glad I did. As I visited Mrs. Steinbacher's guest commode, I overheard Mama ask about "that embroidered item."

"It's in my armoire," Mrs. Steinbacher said. "I'll go get it for you."

"Heavens no, Hilda. Julius still has a notion to burn it, and I'm not about to do that with a family heirloom."

My shawl! Safe. After we left, Mama remarked on my jolly mood at tea. I told her how much I enjoyed visiting the Steinbachers. I don't think she believed me.

The next day, I convinced Mama I was well enough to visit the Osbornes. Charity bubbled over with news. Mrs. Duniway's birthday rally was apparently a huge success. "And you should have seen the crowds at the Lincoln High School debate last night," Charity added. "Colonel Miller represented the Oregon Equal Suffrage League and he was fabulous."

Prudence yanked a spool of yellow ribbon off the shelf. "So was Judge Corliss from the State Association Opposed to Equal Suffrage. A judge, mind you. Plus, the liquor interests in this state think women will shut down the saloons. We've got powerful enemies."

"Why would we shut down the saloons?"

"Ask the Woman's Christian Temperance Union. They're huge supporters of suffrage for women. I wish they would hold their tongues until this election is over."

I explained what had happened with poor Kirsten. "But, don't worry," I said. "She showed me how to print the VOTE FOR JUSTICE cards. I'll make sure you have some. May I use your telephone?" I rang Uncle Hermann and asked to borrow an extra key to Precision Printers. I told him that Kirsten had left something for me.

"I can pick it up for you on Monday, Miriam," he said.

"Uncle Hermann, don't you think women should have the right to vote?"

"Certainly. But what does that have to do with a key to the shop?"

"I don't want to lie to you, and I don't want to get you into any more trouble with Papa. But I have to get into the shop tomorrow."

Silence. I clutched the receiver and stared at the ceiling.

Then he said, "There's a loose brick near the ground directly below our nameplate. We always keep a spare key there. I'm bringing a food basket to Miss Svenson tomorrow. If you can arrange it with your parents, I'll take you along."

"Absolutely!" *Thank you, Uncle Hermann.*

§

When Uncle Hermann and I arrived on Sunday, Mrs. Hardwick's boarding house smelled of mildew and cooked cabbage. The furnishings seemed unchanged since the Civil War. Kirsten met us in the parlor, the only place she said guests were allowed. Mrs. Hardwick's place, she explained, was listed as wholly "moral" on the new map that the mayor's vice committee had just published.

"This is extremely kind of you," she told Uncle Hermann. "I do have a little put aside for next month's rent, so I'll manage."

She examined my finger, now a greenish yellow and tender only to the touch, and we three chatted about nothing in particular. Then I asked Uncle Hermann to take a slow walk around the block so Kirsten and I could be alone. Kirsten cautioned him to watch his wallet. He was barely out the door before I asked her what she'd put in my personals box.

"Before I left, I managed to set up the VOTE FOR JUSTICE chase for you and printed the first batch of cards. Are you sure you can print the rest? I don't want you getting hurt again."

"What choice do we have?" I gave her a wry smile. "My father can't fire me."

Kirsten smoothed her skirt. "All right then. Watch closely." She moved her hands and feet as if she were operating an imaginary press. "Now you try. Feel the treadle. Take your shoes off, if it's easier. And mind your fingers!"

Uncle Hermann returned in the middle of my forty-third imaginary card. "If I didn't know better, I'd say you were dancing that newfangled turkey trot."

We didn't explain, and he didn't ask questions. Neither did he question me when I asked him to stop by the shop so I could pick up a package. I wrapped the printed cards in the brown paper we used for customers. My shoulders ached and the back of my legs burned from my dance with the imaginary press. Still, I hadn't had such a satisfying Sunday afternoon in ages.

Monday morning, I delivered Kirsten's package of cards to Osborne Milliners. "I'll print more this week," I told Charity, although I wasn't sure how I'd manage it. She showed me a gray and navy hat she'd made. "It's simple but elegant, don't you think?"

"Definitely. I really like it." I tried on the hat and admired myself in the mirror.

"I have a favor to ask," I said, returning the hat. "I need to be at Precision Printers as much as possible this week. Could you come tomorrow and admire my samples album? If customers are interested in the album, then I'd have an excuse to be at the shop."

Prudence looked up from her ledger. She agreed to come and to ask several other suffragists to help. On the way home, I imagined a long queue of women winding around the block waiting to admire my album.

§

As promised, Charity presented herself at the shop on Tuesday at half past ten. I made a great show of presenting the samples album to her. As Papa walked to the front counter, Charity thrust her hand toward him. "It's such a pleasure, Mr. Josefsohn. I am so impressed with the way Precision Printers has organized its offerings. I could have chosen any number of printing establishments, but now I shall tell all my friends and acquaintances about your friendly service."

She extended her hand again, and Papa shook it. "Good day to you, sir, and to you, Miss Josefsohn. It has been a pleasure doing business with you."

After Papa and Charity left, Mr. Jacobowitz walked over to me. "What did Miss Osborne order?"

Why the sudden curiosity? "Nothing yet. But she will, I can assure you," I said.

An hour later he stood in the doorway to the office. "There are two ladies asking for Miss Josefsohn," he said.

"Thank you," I said. I smiled at Papa, who didn't seem to notice. "You needn't escort me to my clients, Mr. Jacobowitz."

He gave me an odd look and returned to his desk.

"Hello from Prudence," one of the women whispered when I reached the counter. Then she added in a loud voice, "You have an excellent selection. We'll be back after Election Day to purchase thank you notes."

The other woman muttered, "Or condolence cards."

Several more women came to the shop throughout the day and admired the samples album. Papa didn't say anything, but they must have caught his attention.

As we were closing the shop, I put my hand on Papa's arm and he looked at me expectantly. "Seeing as so many people are interested in the samples album, I'd be happy to come in tomorrow, Papa."

"No, you are Tuesdays and Thursdays. Leave the samples album on the front counter. Mr. Jacobowitz will handle the customers."

Mr. Jacobowitz rushed to help me with my coat. "I will be as helpful as I possibly can with your new customers, Miss Josefsohn," he said. "You can rely on me."

Rely on you to do what? Watch out for me for my father's sake? For yours? For mine? I remembered Papa's comment that Mr. Jacobowitz was not the caliber of husband he and Mama had in mind for me. *He's nice enough when he's not hovering, kind even. But I've yet to decide what caliber of person Mr. Jacobowitz is, let alone what caliber of husband.* I put on my gloves, reached for my purse, and let him escort me to the door.

Wednesday I was back again at Neighborhood House. I told Mrs. Rosenfeld that I planned to come to the Hallowe'en party the next evening.

She arched her eyebrows. "I assumed that you would join the more prosperous members of the Jewish community at the Concordia Club."

"Frankly, I'd rather be here."

"Well then, I'm glad to have you." She looked at me, as if she were deciding whether to tell me something. Then she gazed at her wedding ring and said, "We do have some very promising young men who come to Neighborhood House, but most of them aren't American citizens yet."

I stuck my hand under my chin. "Mrs. Rosenfeld, I'm up to here with my mother's talk about promising young men. I won't get married any time soon. Not if I have anything to say about it."

"Clever girl," she said. "But you should know there's a federal law stating that when an American woman marries a man with foreign citizenship, she gives up her citizenship for his. The law applies only to women, not to American men who take foreign wives."

"That's ridiculous. I had no notion my government was so unfair."

§

I ALSO HAD NO NOTION Mrs. Jenkins made candy, since it was the first Hallowe'en that she had worked for my parents. The kitchen smelled like a confectionery when we got home. I worked out some of my frustrations by whipping nougat, pulling taffy, and cracking walnut shells.

"My brother Danny used to love Hallowe'en," I told Mrs. Jenkins. "He died of tetanus when he was ten and I was seven," I blurted out.

"Oh, I am so sorry."

I gave her a reassuring smile, having glossed over the painful details. "Danny would have adored your taffy. If he were alive now, he'd be in heaven."

We both laughed at how that came out. "Miss Miriam," she said, "he *is* in heaven."

I wasn't sure I believed in such a place, but maybe Mrs. Jenkins was right. Maybe my steadfast tin soldier was waiting there for his paper ballerina.

Thirty-One

HALLOWE'EN DAWNED BRIGHT AND PROMISING. I paced the front hall, eager to get to Precision Printers. When the clock chimed nine, I knew something was wrong. Papa was never this late.

I strode back into the kitchen and headed for the sweet rolls. Several long minutes later, Papa made his appearance in slippers and a dressing gown.

"I'm so sorry you aren't feeling well, Papa." I swept crumbs from my skirt.

He shook his head. "There is nothing the matter with me, Miriam. I gave everyone a holiday. I won't be going to the shop today."

"You *what?*"

Mrs. Jenkins took one look at my face and bustled out of the kitchen.

"Lower your voice, Miriam. My men have worked hard and tomorrow we start our Thanksgiving orders. So today the men get a holiday. Unpaid naturally."

"How could you?"

"Do not question my business practices, Miriam. I'll make it up to them with a Christmas bonus if business is good."

"I mean how could you give everyone a Thursday off and not tell me? Tuesdays and Thursdays are my workdays. Now I'd wager you won't let me go to work tomorrow because it's Friday."

"Young ladies do not wager. How many times must I remind you?"

"Papa, why didn't you tell me?"

"I told them at the shop yesterday. Didn't I tell you last night at dinner? No matter. You are dressed for the day, so take a nice outing before we are forced into our costumes."

My jaw tightened. "That's not the point, Papa. I had plans for today. Things I…um…things I need to finish."

"They will wait until Tuesday. Election Day. You should be proud I am a good American. I give the men an hour off work to vote. With pay, even. Many employers give no time off."

I willed myself not to strangle him. "Don't you want to get any work done there before the Hallowe'en party?"

"Not today. Your mama wishes to dress me as Napoléon Bonaparte, but first I spend a quiet afternoon at the Club." Papa poured a cup of coffee and walked toward the library.

I steamed off toward my room. Halfway there I cooled down and reconsidered. No one would be at the shop today. I'd have the presses all to myself. "I think an outing is a great idea," I told Papa while he sipped his coffee and leafed through some papers. "Please tell Mama I'll be back by three."

"Where will you be?"

"I haven't decided yet, Papa. But it's such a sunny day. Perhaps I'll stroll downtown."

He nodded and returned to his papers. Maybe he thought I was more mature than Mama did. Maybe I was making progress.

The key to Precision Printers was right where Uncle Hermann said it would be.

I sat at Papa's desk. The photograph by his pen-and-ink stand showed Mama and Danny and me having a picnic. I was all in white, and I was squinting in the sun and trying to look straight at the camera. My hair hung in stiff ringlets and I wore a big white bow, like a gift ready to be delivered—Papa's little girl in pretty little petticoats. *I'm not a little girl anymore, Papa.*

I eyed the machines. Neither Papa nor the presses were going to intimidate me today. I put on Kirsten's apron, cuffed my sleeves to my elbows and smeared cerulean onto the inking disc. I locked the chase in place and set up the pins for the cardstock. I practiced pumping a pretend treadle while feeding cardstock with one hand and removing it with the other. Step—put—*ka-chunk*—take—put—*ka-chunk*—step. It had seemed so easy at Kirsten's boarding house.

In practice, I was terrible.

Hours later, my reject pile had grown as fast as my keep pile. Still, I had done nearly another thousand acceptable cards, even with one bum finger. I cleaned the rollers and chase with kerosene, hid the cards and chase in my personals box, put the key back under the brick, and caught the streetcar home.

Later, Mama paraded me in front of Papa in my costume.

"Lillian, don't you think it is too revealing?"

"Julius, she's a young lady now," Mama said, as if I weren't in the room. "Imagine how lovely she will look in her holiday gowns in New York." Papa blushed.

We piled into the Oldsmobile, and they drove me to Neighborhood House. After I took off my coat, Mrs. Rosenfeld escorted me to the punch bowl. Two men stood nearby, dressed as peddlers. Or perhaps they weren't wearing costumes. Their eyes bored into my bare shoulders.

"You look lovely," Mrs. Rosenfeld glanced at the peddlers. "Perhaps a little too lovely."

I fetched a shawl from the donation room. Serakh's gray dress was still there. I breathed in the faint goat smell and resolved to concentrate on the suffrage campaign. Serakh would have wanted me to.

As I walked back toward the festivities, a girl shouted, "There's the witch. She's dressed like a princess." I turned and saw that kindergarten girl who worried about dead people. She tugged at a masked man dressed as a cowboy, dragging him to where I stood. A tin foil crown topped her everyday clothes, and her lips were smeared with chocolate. I squatted down to hug her, then looked up at the man's mustard-colored mustache.

No, it can't be.

"Miss Josefsohn," he said.

"Good evening, Mr. Jacobowitz," I said, although I wasn't sure anything good was going to come of the evening.

Bella was wide-eyed. "You know Uncle Ephraim?"

"Run along to the apple-bobbing, Bella," Mr. Jacobowitz said. "I have something very important to discuss with Miss Josefsohn." He cleared his throat.

Oh, damnation. Have I been too forward?

Bella scampered down the hall. I hid my bare shoulders in the borrowed shawl.

"Whatever business you have to discuss with me can wait until I'm in the office next Tuesday, can't it?"

He smoothed his mustache. "Pardon my insistence, but next Tuesday is Election Day, as you know. That's too late."

My stomach twisted. "What's Election Day got to do with me, Mr. Jacobowitz?"

"Please, Miss Josefsohn, I am not stupid. I am not without eyes and ears, or brains. Miss Osborne provides cardstock, but doesn't tell us what to print on it. Women look at the samples album, but order nothing. Miss Svenson uses cerulean ink, when the only job scheduled for her that day was Mrs. Bloom's announcement for a baby girl. The ink for that is deep rose with gold flecks, not cerulean."

"I don't know what you're talking about." My heart pounded.

He gazed at the floor. "Then I am forced to mention the items in your personals box."

"What? So this is the caliber of person you are? This is what I can rely on you for? You sneak! You've been spying on me for my father!"

"No. I assure you, it's not like that. I happened to see you operating the presses today," he said. "I restrained myself from entering the shop as you were there alone and that would not be appropriate. But now opportunity brings us together this evening."

He's saved the worst until last.

"Please." Mr. Jacobowitz reached a hand toward me. I stepped back. "I was not spying," he said. "I went to check some invoices at the office. When I came to this country, your kind uncle helped me settle with my sister and her children. He and your father gave me a good job. They bought me English lessons. I appreciate everything they have done for me."

I glared at him. "Now you will prove your loyalty to my father by exposing Kirsten and me. You are a true cad, Mr. Jacobowitz. I have nothing more to say." I strode down the hall.

Thirty-Two

"WAIT!"

I heard Mr. Jacobowitz shuffle toward me in his ridiculous oversized boots. "With Miss Svenson gone, you must be under considerable pressure."

Still furious, I turned and faced him. "That's none of your business. Sneak!"

He removed his cowboy hat and fiddled with the brim. His hair stuck out every which way. "My intentions are honorable, I assure you. You can put your trust in me."

"Trust? You must be joking."

"I think you are printing cards for the suffrage campaign— and, yes, women should vote. I do not discuss this with your father; I need my job because of my sister." He stood taller. "This does not matter to you, I know, but Bella is one of her three children. Their father was killed in the 1906 pogrom in Bialystok. So many Jews die for no reason. You know of this?"

I lied with a nod of my head.

"Your father assures me that Germany would have been a fine place for Jews now, that we did not have to come to America, but I think he is wrong. Still, life here is not easy.

My sister's oldest is only eleven—a newsboy. Every week he has a black eye or a bloody nose, defending his corner to sell to businessmen who do not even bother to look at him."

Newsies. "What is it you want?" I asked in a softer voice, my anger turning to confusion.

He cleared his throat again, and I waited impatiently. *Tell me the worst already!*

Mr. Jacobowitz took off his mask and smiled, revealing a chipped tooth. "I'm offering you a chance to print more cards. I am not as fast as Miss Svenson, but—if you will forgive my saying so—I am far faster than you. I think what you are trying to do is brave. I want to help."

I shook my head in disbelief.

"Mrs. Rosenfeld will watch Bella," he added. "You do not have to leave Neighborhood House. I can do the printing job on my own."

"And how do I know you'll do what you say? How do I know you won't dump Kirsten's chase in the river?"

He winced. "Your doubt is understandable, Miss Josefsohn, but I beg you to give me a chance."

I crossed my arms over my chest. I studied his pale face and stooped shoulders. He waited. He let me think. He didn't tell me what to do. That was something in his favor, I had to admit. Maybe he was telling the truth.

"I am not about to have you go to the print shop without me, Mr. Jacobowitz. However, we haven't much time. My parents are sending an automobile here at half past ten to take me to the Concordia Club."

His brown eyes took on a sparkle I'd never seen before. "I'll have you back here by a quarter past. Better yet, I'll drive you to the Club by then. It's closer to the shop. We'll have more time."

He seemed so intense, I had to look away. "You told me once I could rely on you, Mr. Jacobowitz. Is this what you meant?"

He cleared his throat. "You won't be sorry, Miss Josefsohn. I'll tell Mrs. Rosenfeld and meet you by the front door." He galumphed down the hall.

As I was leaving, I handed Mrs. Rosenfeld the borrowed shawl. "He hardly has two nickels to rub together," she said. "But he's a gentleman, and he's applied for American citizenship."

I buttoned my coat and said nothing. I had no intention of doing anything with Mr. Jacobowitz besides watch him run my print job. *But he might be proving himself to be a gentleman...* I couldn't argue with that.

His Model T Ford was spotless. I wondered whether he polished the brass on the print shop's front door. Mr. Jacobowitz offered his arm. I took it as I stepped onto the running board, but sat up against the passenger door and folded my hands in my lap. We drove in silence.

When we arrived, he unlocked the shop and held the door for me. "May I take your coat?"

Clutching my coat collar, I shook my head.

"As you wish," he said. "Pardon me, but I must move freely at the press."

He stripped down to his shirt and trousers. He removed his boots, revealing threadbare socks and smaller feet than I would have thought for a man his height.

Our eyes met. He touched his mustache nervously. "Had I known you would see my socks, I would have worn my, um... what is that expression?"

"Your Sunday best." I couldn't help but smile.

He bobbed his head several times. "Yes, my Sunday best. For you, my Sunday best."

He cleared his throat yet again, as if all his words and thoughts kept getting jumbled together in his voice box. I shoved my hands into my coat pockets. "I'd better fetch the VOTE FOR JUSTICE chase and the cardstock," I said. "Will you ink the press, Mr. Jacobowitz?"

"I'd work faster if you'd call me Ephraim." His voice had a pleasant trace of a tease.

I felt my shoulders relax. "Then it's for a good cause... Ephraim. Just for tonight."

Mr. Jacobowitz—Ephraim—stacked the cardstock and took the chase from me, his rough hand brushing against mine. He released the brake lever, tugged on the flywheel, and handed me the first printer's proof for my approval. I nodded and smiled. He got to work in earnest. The press spat out card after card after card. He started whistling. His face glowed.

I unbuttoned my coat, as the room was getting warm. He glanced at me, then consigned the next card to the reject pile. Later, when he took a short break, I asked, "Why did you reject this? We can't afford to waste a single card."

"It's off-center. Every card should look professional, so men will take you seriously." He wiped his hands and grinned. "Other men besides me. I always take you seriously."

That was kind of him. Or was he teasing me? "We haven't much time...Ephraim," I reminded him.

He nodded and headed for the storage room. "I've run out of your cardstock, but I'll borrow something similar from your father's supply. I'll replace it tomorrow and buy extra for you, in case you have time to print more over the weekend. I'd offer to help you then, but I go to services on Saturdays and my sister needs me this Sunday."

"Tell me how much you spend, and I'll reimburse you."

"It's not necessary. Let the cardstock be my gift."

"I insist."

He wiped his forehead with his handkerchief. "As you wish. You know, Precision Printers is more than a job for me. It's my second chance, my second home."

"Precision Printers is my world too, you know. You get to work here as many days as you wish. Why can't I?"

"But you don't have to work. Your father is comfortable financially, and then, when you marry—"

I put my hands on my hips. "My marriage is none of your business! You wouldn't understand anyway. I'm going to be a typographer. It's not about money. I want to do something on my own that I'm proud of."

"What's wrong with having someone take care of you, Miss Josefsohn? Especially someone who shares an interest in the business that you love? Someone as sturdy and reliable as the new Steel Bridge."

I didn't answer and there was an awkward silence. His eyes took on that dull look again. I adopted the teasing tone he had used earlier. "You may call me Miriam, for tonight, if it will make you work faster."

But I could not bring a smile to his lips. Instead, he said, "Thank you, Miriam." He pumped the treadle and set to work.

Half an hour later, I added the cards Ephraim had printed to the ones I'd managed to print earlier in the day. He cleaned the press and locked up for the night. He wanted to put the box of cards in the back of his Model T, but I insisted they stay up front with me—on my lap. When we got to my house, he rushed to open my side of the automobile. He hoisted the box of cards and offered me his arm. I took it.

I let him carry the box up the steps to the porch, but stopped him at the front door.

"I have no intention of stepping inside your house while no one else is there, Miriam." He sounded offended. "What kind of a man do you think I am?"

Ephraim was so different from Richard. There was nothing enchanting about him, no excitement. Still, he wasn't the glob of porridge I first thought he was. When I came back to the porch, he was leaning against the pillar. He smiled when he saw me. I walked to him and let him guide me down the steps, his hand under my elbow, my skirt a jot higher than necessary. I let him help me into his Model T.

He cranked the automobile to life, slid into the driver's seat, and put on his cowboy hat.

"Do you like lima beans?" he asked as we motored to the Club. "We had a fine crop this year—the last of the season—and they are particularly sweet—for limas." *What an odd conversation topic*, I thought. Still, I answered amiably.

"Well, I prefer lima beans to a dose of cod liver oil. But fresh baby limas might be delicious, Ephraim."

His cheeks lifted against the laugh lines under his eyes. "I've finished printing now. You are no longer obliged to call me Ephraim."

"Well, then, let's see what I call you when I see you again."

"In front of your father, I will be Mr. Jacobowitz, and you will be Miss Josefsohn."

The laugh lines vanished. Ephraim seemed almost wistful, as if he would never again have the right to call me Miriam. *Aren't I worth fighting for?* I thought, but I said nothing more about it then. Maybe, when I saw him at the shop on Monday, we'd talk about it.

He pulled to the curb a block from the Club, lest my parents question why he had been my escort instead of Mrs. Steinbacher's chauffeur. A cowboy ushered Marie Antoinette onto the sidewalk. We must have looked like the mismatched pair we truly were.

"Thank you for the help," I repeated. I really was grateful.

"My pleasure." I felt his eyes on me as I walked the rest of the way alone.

Mrs. Steinbacher's chauffeur—the handsome one—did meet me just outside the door to the Club. "Now perhaps I'll steal a half an hour to myself," he said, with a grin.

The Concordia was loud and festive, filled with the sort of people I'd known all my life. Wrapping my fingers around a glass of mulled cider, I zigzagged my way across the ballroom to an Oriental woman standing with Napoléon Bonaparte.

"A kind person from Neighborhood House dropped me here," I told Mama.

"Oh, how nice." Mama was flushed and smiling. "Who was she?"

She. Naturally. "Mrs. Jacobo...farb." It sounded Jewish enough.

"Hmm...I don't recall a Mrs. Jacobofarb," Mama said, but she didn't pursue the matter.

Papa patted my arm. "You make a lovely Marie Antoinette."

Except no one's chopping off my head. I intend to keep it squarely on my shoulders.

§

FRIDAY MORNING I SPIRITED A PICNIC basket of nougat bars, and biscuits, and VOTE FOR JUSTICE cards to the Osbornes. Prudence brewed tea while I unpacked the goodies. She was surprised that I had printed so many cards. I nibbled on a biscuit and didn't mention Ephraim.

We made up VOTE FOR JUSTICE packets for out-of-town suffrage leagues and the shop's pro-suffrage customers who lived out of town. Prudence wrote notes for each packet. "You can't say we haven't tried," she said. On the way home, the sky threatened rain and the start of a long winter.

Papa came home early and deposited a plain paper bag on the kitchen table. "One of my employees brought me something from his garden," he told Mrs. Jenkins and me. "Do the best you can with it." He left us to shell two pints of baby lima beans. I covered my smile. Dressed in butter and a dash of nutmeg, they were surprisingly good.

Saturday was a frustrating waste—no chance to get out from under my parents. But Sunday they motored to Multnomah Falls for a last trip out to the Gorge before winter set in. I had hours and hours to myself. At the shop, I found a new package of cardstock labeled "Osborne"— Ephraim's doing no doubt. My batch of cards wasn't as large or as well printed as his. Still, I wasn't bad for a beginner.

The next morning I woke to the sound of the back doorbell. I peeked out my bedroom window at two men unloading firewood from an old wagon, as they'd done on the first Monday in November since I can remember.

By the time I got down to breakfast, a letter from Florrie lay on the table in the front hall. I savored her words along with my sweet rolls.

Fie on Richard! Come visit me, there are lots of fellows here you'd like. I can't wait to hear about the prayer shawl, and I promise to believe every word. The election is big news here, too. People argue about whether to vote for Taft, Roosevelt, Wilson, or Debs. Women seem to favor Roosevelt and Debs, although some think that Wilson is also sincere about suffrage. Oh, Mim, I do hope all your efforts in Oregon are not in vain.

I downed my hot chocolate and raced to Osborne Milliners. Charity looked glum.

"Prudence is truly downhearted," she said. "Despite what Mrs. Hirsch and Dr. Lovejoy say, she is convinced we don't have the numbers."

"What does Mrs. Duniway think?"

"She's of the notion that we pushed ourselves too hard on the public."

Prudence came in, her face pale, her lips a tight slash. I'd never seen her look so haggard.

"We'll never carry Portland," she told me. "And if we lose badly here, we'll never win statewide."

I knew then what I had to do. "Well, then we'll have to work harder in Portland," I said. "Let's distribute the rest of the VOTE FOR JUSTICE cards here."

"Don't go crazy, Miriam," Charity looked at me as if I already were. "Suppose your father finds out?"

"VOTE FOR JUSTICE cards are just what we need to boost our chances at the polls," I said, trying to sound confident. "How will we distribute them?"

Prudence straightened her bun. She didn't tell me I was crazy. "A group of campaign workers are meeting here tomorrow morning. If you can get us the rest of the cards, we'll figure it out then. Are you sure you want to do this?"

"I'm certain of it. We've come so far. We can't let my father stop us now."

§

"I WILL GO TO THE POLLS tomorrow after work," Papa told Mama that night at the table. "And I would like fish for dinner."

Fish and a slice of humble pie, I thought. Then I dared to ask, "Do you think the suffrage initiative will finally pass this time, Papa?"

He reached for the butter dish. "Why repair what is not broken? Women should care for what is inside the home, and men for what is outside the home. A good division of labor."

I tore my dinner roll in two. "Florrie writes that women in the Democratic Party are holding a political convention in California. Californians believe in progress. By the by, I'm not coming into the shop tomorrow after all. I have other business to attend to—outside the home."

Silence. Papa eyed Mama as if it were her fault. My left hand curled into a fist in my lap.

Thirty-Three

ELECTION DAY DAWNED OVERCAST, WITH STORM clouds gathering in the east. I met Mrs. Jenkins at the front door and shared a cup of coffee with her in the kitchen.

"I'll have to miss your sweet rolls this morning," I told her. "I've got suffrage work to do at Osborne Milliners."

"Do your parents know about this?"

I collected a piece of cheese from the icebox. "They might have guessed." I smiled at her and added, "I can't rightly say."

"Well, you do look lovely. Isn't that the navy outfit that you wore to your temple some weeks back? Only now you're wearing a new hat."

"It's not new exactly, Mrs. Jenkins. Charity Osborne just added a bit of ribbon." I thought of Serakh asking me about the "small ornaments" I had put on my "head covering," back when the daughters of Zelophehad were only a name on a suffrage banner to me. Would I ever see them again? Today was the day I would campaign in their honor. Especially Tirtzah's.

"Wish me luck," I said, grabbing another piece of cheese for the walk. "I'll see you tonight." I grabbed my coat and gloves, and nearly slipped on the early morning frost covering the front steps.

I thought I'd be the first to arrive at Osborne Milliners, but a dozen women had already crowded into the hat shop. Most of them looked about Charity's age, and they chatted as excitedly as my classmates and I used to before Sister Margaret called us to order.

Kirsten waved me over and introduced me to two of her friends. Then she took me aside. "Prudence just told us that we'll be handing out VOTE FOR JUSTICE cards at the polls. You know how foolish that is, but you won't listen anyway, right?"

"Right." I grinned, despite my nerves.

"You printed an amazing amount."

"Frankly, Kirsten, Mr. Jacobowitz helped me."

"Mr. Jacobowitz? Do you trust him not to say anything to your father?"

"He won't tell my father; he's not that kind of man. But I don't know if he helped because of me, or the campaign, or both." I blushed.

"That's how Nils and I used to be."

I touched her sleeve. "Is Nils an American citizen?"

"Yes, he is. Why do you ask?"

"Good, because an American woman loses her citizenship rights when she marries a foreigner. Isn't that the most unfair thing you ever heard of?"

Kirsten practically snorted. "I can list dozens of unfair things about how we treat women, children, immigrants, and the working class in this country. But, yes, that law would be one of them. Sorry, I can't stay and talk." She showed me a hand-drawn map of polling places.

"What about these two spots on the west side by my neighborhood? I don't see a checkmark by them for the afternoon. I'll distribute our cards there."

"Absolutely not. You've done enough—more than enough—what with these cards showing up all over

Portland. I just pray your father doesn't bother to look at one too closely."

"Kirsten, I met someone once. Her name was Tirtzah. It's a long story, but she stood up for what she thought was right—for what *I told her* was right. Now I'm going to do the same, for her sake, for us—for everyone. How many cards can you spare?"

She stared at me. I stared back.

"We'll give you about a hundred," she said finally.

"Fair enough," I agreed.

I spent the morning at the shop talking with other suffragists, brewing tea, answering the telephone, distributing votes for women sashes and my own vote for justice card, and mending torn placards.

Around noon, a woman rushed into the shop, waving a telegram. We crowded around her. "Dr. Shaw sent this to the suffrage campaign committee at the Portland Woman's Club," she announced. Then she read, "The women of the world are looking to Oregon for hope. May Oregon women win their deserved success, and Oregon men prove worthy of their heritage."

When the woman finished, we clapped and cheered. Even Prudence, worried as I knew she was, managed a smile. She made me eat a liverwurst sandwich for lunch and drink a cup of hot broth. "It's cold out there, and you'll need your strength."

"I'm only going to two polling places in the neighborhood," I said.

"That's two places too many as far as I'm concerned. But here are your cards. Stay back from the voting tent a few feet—that's the law. Don't give your cards away unless someone wants to keep one. Don't bother with drunks—they're in the pocket of the liquor bosses, so we've lost their vote already. Be polite. Don't raise your voice, or they'll mark you as another hysterical woman, and that hurts the cause. Promise me that if you see your father coming, you'll disappear into the crowd."

Not wanting to lie to Prudence, I simply shrugged. I hoped I wasn't going to see Papa, but I wasn't going to run away from him either. I had as much right to be at the polling tent as he did. She looked at me hard and then handed the cards to me anyway. I touched the suffrage bow on my coat, felt my left nostril for the gold nose ring that wasn't there, and walked out the door.

My feet were the first to feel the chill. I hailed every likely-looking man near the polls at Twelfth and Burnside. "A vote for women is a vote for justice!" I called out. "You know it's the right thing to do. Your mother had the good sense to raise you. She's got the good sense to vote. Make this a better world. Vote for justice!"

I said those lines over and over, until my voice grew hoarse. Most men ignored me. Some held up their hands to shield themselves from my cards and my words. One man took my card and threw it on the ground. Another asked to walk me home in a way that made my stomach crawl.

Two hours later, I trudged to Twenty-second and Hoyt. The wind had picked up and a late afternoon shower left me wishing for an umbrella. I said my lines over and over. There were fewer men here. One of them ripped the card in front of my face and hissed a word at me that I would not repeat.

None of you spit at me. Or hurl stones at me. I've seen worse. I thought about how hot I had been back then, with Tirtzah and her sisters. I stamped my icy feet and smiled. Compared with Tirtzah's argument before Moses, this was a cakewalk.

Then I saw Papa. Huddled under his umbrella, he might have gone right by me. I made my decision then and there.

"Mr. Josefsohn," I said, stepping in front of him with my packet of VOTE FOR JUSTICE cards.

"Miriam, what are you doing here?" He looked dumbfounded. Astonished. *Isn't it obvious?* I took a deep, shaky breath and repeated my lines the way I had to dozens of men before him. Then I handed him a card.

He stared at the card. He drew closer to me so that we were both under the umbrella. "This looks like it came from my presses. Where did you get it?"

I stood as tall as I could under that umbrella. Papa was not going to intimidate me. "The paper is not from our stock. The ink is one we used on another job. I might have printed this particular card myself, Papa. As God is my witness, I hope I did."

He clenched his jaw. "Come home with me now."

"No, Papa. I'm not finished here."

"You make a fool of me standing by the polls, wearing politics on your coat."

"And you didn't make a fool of me, Papa, when you printed the VOTE NO cards in 1906?" I heard myself getting louder and shriller. Prudence said not to argue, but Papa was too close. I felt stifled under that great black umbrella, with the smell of his pomade and cigars. I wanted to keep everything under control for the sake of the campaign. But my stomach twisted. I felt fury growing inside me.

He grabbed my arm. "You will do as I say. You should be grateful I put a roof over your head and give you everything you could want. Dance lessons. French tutors. A girl's academy. Instead you act like a spiteful child who knows nothing of this world."

"Nothing? Did the big breweries make it worth your while, Papa? Or was it just a business deal, like printing a dinner party menu?"

His grip tightened. "How dare you insult me! I printed that card at my own expense. I am my own man."

"And I am my own woman, Papa. A businesswoman one day, despite you." With my free hand I raised my skirt a few inches above my ankles. "Take a good look at that petticoat, Papa. Petticoat government, is that what you're so dead set against? Women who might challenge your opinions or question your judgment?" I hiked my skirt higher.

Papa let go of my arm. "Brazen hussy," he growled.

He slapped my face. "What decent man would wish to marry you?"

My cheek burned and my mouth turned sour. "It's always about men, isn't it? As if I couldn't survive without someone in trousers. As if I couldn't manage without his money—or yours."

"I would disown you if it wouldn't break your mother's heart." Papa's accent thickened and his face was livid.

"You can't disown what you don't own," I said, deliberately twisting his words. "You don't own me, Papa."

I willed myself not to cry. I was no longer his little girl. I was Serakh's Miriam, Tirtzah's Miriam. *Brave Miriam, sweet and strong.*

I wrenched myself away. "Leave me alone!"

The grocer from across the street came out of his shop and strode toward us. "She's my daughter," Papa called out to him.

"In that case, I wish you luck, sir. She's quite a handful."

I marched up to that grocer and slapped a VOTE FOR WOMEN card against his chest. "I wish you luck, too, sir," I hissed. "When you have to pay fair wages to everyone, keep rats and vermin out of your store, and send your children to school!"

My heart pounded in my throat. I wanted everything to change for the better—right now. I turned back to take my place at the polls, but Papa stood in my path.

"I'll help you get her home," the grocer told Papa. "Now, missy, let's be reasonable," he said to me, staking a step closer. Angry and frightened, I dodged both men and ran down the street. A newsie slouched against the doorway of a warehouse, a grimy woolen scarf half covering his equally grimy face.

"Want to make fifty cents?" I asked.

He was on his feet in half a second. You'd think I had offered him manna from heaven.

"Take these cards and hand them out to every man you see. Say 'Vote for justice, sir.' Don't forget the 'sir' part. Here are your quarters. I trust you won't throw these cards in the gutter."

He grabbed my money and my cards and dashed away. I heard footsteps behind me. It was Papa. The grocer was gone. I stood my ground.

"Foolish girl," he said, catching his breath. "You've wasted my hard-earned money again. You eat sweet rolls, thanks to me. I have worked since I was thirteen for my family. I kept my mother in bread, and my brother and sister. They thanked me for every crumb. Not once did they throw my money away."

I rounded on him, eyes blazing. "And your grandmother, Papa? What did you do for her? Call her crazy? Accuse her of killing Raizl? Turn your town against her? Oh yes, Uncle Hermann told me all about that."

"Hermann knows nothing."

I paced in front of him as he stood under his umbrella. I felt like a lioness in her cage. "You're the one who knows nothing, Papa. You ruined Savta's life, I won't let you ruin mine. Your sister Raizl wanted to wear that shawl. She begged to wear that shawl. She yearned to see Jerusalem and she got her dying wish."

Papa's eyes narrowed. *Jerusalem.* I sucked in my breath. Prudence had warned me against acting hysterical. Now, without thinking, I'd gone too far.

Thirty-Four

I LOOKED AT THE COBBLESTONES AND softened my voice. "I'm sorry about Raizl," I said, hoping he wouldn't ask about Jerusalem. "I understand how you must feel. I lost Danny, too—remember? He wasn't just your son—he was my brother. But I'm not sorry about printing those cards, Papa. And I'm not sorry about wanting to learn the printing business and wanting to join you in your shop. Don't wrap me up in petticoats and then a wedding veil and pass me along to another man. I'm not a job you can finish and present to a satisfied customer. I'm me!"

He shook his head. "You are not a job, you are my daughter. I love and protect you. I want only the best for you, to give you away to another man who will do the same when I am gone."

"Miriam Josefsohn, marriageable maiden…I am sick of it! I'm more than that, Papa."

He took a step closer. I stepped back. He was not Moses. He was my father. I refused to wait any longer for the blessing I wanted, the blessing that would never come. I gathered up my skirts and rushed away.

The rain seeped through to my shoulders and down my back. I hugged myself and kept walking, down alleys, across streetcar lines, past warehouses. I stayed away from the main streets, lest Papa try to track me down in his Oldsmobile.

I walked past houses, churches, and corner shops. I stopped in front of Osborne Milliners—dark now—and wondered where Charity and Prudence might be waiting for the election returns. I fetched a handkerchief from my soggy handbag and wiped my nose.

Sweet rolls got the better of me. Cold, wet, and hungry, I finally headed for home.

By the time I reached Nineteenth and Johnson, the light was on in our dining room. Mrs. Jenkins met me in the front hall.

"Look at you! Mr. Josefsohn said you'd be right along, and that was over an hour ago. Get out of those clothes before you catch your death. I'll put the kettle on for tea."

"If you wouldn't mind, I'll have dinner in my room tonight." Papa was not about to ruin one more meal.

By the time I got into dry clothes, Mrs. Jenkins had left a dinner tray on my desk. Beef stew. Sourdough bread. Poached peaches. Chamomile tea. A regular meal for me, a feast for that newsie.

I had a walk-think in my bedroom. Seven strides to the north wall. *Old World ways—ha! I've been back to a biblical world far older than Papa's Bavaria.* Turn. Ten strides to the south wall. *I wasn't born to be passed along from father to husband.* Turn. Ten strides to the north. *I'm me, Miriam Josefsohn, the daughter of Julius, but also a person in her own right, a person who aims to be a typographer.* Ten strides to the south. *And if Papa won't let me work in his print shop, I shall have to find another printer who will.*

Four strides to my bedroom door. I stomped downstairs.

My parents had closeted themselves in the library. I fetched a valise from the basement and returned to my room to pack.

"You barely touched my stew," Mrs. Jenkins said when she collected the dinner tray. She glanced at the valise. "Now don't you do anything foolish, Miss Miriam. I expect you to be here come morning."

"I'll be here," I assured her. But I had already made up my mind. I strode into Papa's upstairs office, reached for the telephone, and wondered how much money telephone operators earned.

"Western Electric. What number, please?"

"Long distance, please. Berkeley, California." Was Florrie staying with the aunt on her mother's side or her father's? "Steinbacher residence," I guessed.

"One moment please, and I'll connect you." I had guessed right.

"Good evening, Mr. Steinbacher," I said, trying to keep my voice steady. "This is Miriam Josefsohn, a friend of your niece Florence. May I speak with her please?"

"Certainly. I'll fetch her from the back garden."

She took forever.

"Miriam!"

Florrie's cheerful voice was too much to bear. "I've got to come see you," I said, my voice cracking. "I can't stay here a moment longer." I told her everything. Well, almost everything. Serakh and the blue thread would have to wait until I could speak to her in person. I couldn't bear to hear any doubt or hesitation in Florrie's voice now.

A quarter of an hour later, I hung up, dried my tears, and counted my rainy day fund. Fourteen dollars. It would have to do. The valise was packed full to bursting, but I could still manage it. I shoved it under my bed.

The grandfather clock chimed eleven. Mama knocked on my door and let herself in before I answered. "The election returns for president should be in by now," she said, her voice ragged. I followed her to Danny's old room.

Papa was there, his back to me. I doubted that we three had been together in that room since Danny died so many years ago, but Danny's window gave the best view of the Journal Building.

Red lights on the corners of the building's massive tower flashed the signal that Mr. Wilson had won the presidency. The red and white lights on *The Morning Oregonian* tower and the horizontal sweep of searchlights across Council Crest confirmed the news. Papa muttered "*Gott in Himmel*" and left the room. I grabbed Mama's hand as she turned to follow him.

"Wait. I have to talk to you."

"If it's about that disagreement with your father, I have heard enough. I'm tired. Whatever it is, it can wait until morning."

I blocked the door. I could see the weariness in her face, and I knew she'd rather be any place else in the house than in Danny's room. Still, if Danny hadn't died, maybe things would have been better. Danny had made us a four-square family. Now I was the odd one out.

"Mama, this is very important. *Très important.*"

The corners of her mouth curved up slightly at my French. She leaned against the windowsill. Now that I had her attention, I wasn't sure where to begin. So I started in the middle.

"I'm buying a train ticket tomorrow for Berkeley. Well, for Oakland, actually. To see Florrie. She knows I'm coming, and I have a place to stay."

Mama pursed her lips. I waited until she composed an answer. "You've never traveled anywhere alone," she said.

"You've never even set foot in California. You haven't the slightest notion of what you're getting yourself into."

I crossed my arms over my chest. "You said yourself I'm nearly seventeen, Mama. I'll manage. I'll write when I'm settled."

"Settled?" She looked away. When she turned back, her face was pinched and pale. "Surely this is just a visit to Florrie—and a well-timed one, I should say. You and your father have got to calm down. I expect you'll be traveling back to Portland with Florrie when she returns for Thanksgiving."

"Florrie's not sure whether she's coming home then."

"Well, you'll just have to travel home regardless. There's our trip to New York City. It's all arranged. And I'll see to it that you can re-enroll at St. Mary's when we return."

Her offer surprised me. I bit my lip and thought a minute. I loved St. Mary's Academy. Still… "And after that, Mama? What happens after I leave St. Mary's for good? I'll never get to work in the print shop. You and Papa will still want to marry me off and make me another man's responsibility."

"It's not like that, Miriam. Please stop pacing."

I willed my feet to stay in one spot—my tiny spot on the *olam*, my here and now, my life. "I need to be on my own," I said.

Mama's voice was flat. Distant. "Where will you stay?"

"With Florrie's aunt and uncle in Berkeley," I repeated. "They have a spare room."

Suddenly Mama seemed to wilt completely. Stuck in Danny's room, maybe she was remembering Danny's last days, the smell of the doctor's carbolic acid. Maybe she was remembering Danny's face in a tight grimace, his jaws locked, his back arched, his legs shaking. I can't imagine she was worried about me.

Nobody had worried about me on the day after Danny died. The windows were shut tight. Grandma Goldstein took Mama for a long walk. Papa was on the telephone. Mrs. Steinbacher was in the kitchen. I snuck into Danny's room and found his favorite tin soldier. I wrapped the soldier in my best paper ballerina doll and cradled them all the way to the fireplace in the library. Then I kissed them and threw them into the flames.

Mama's soft sniffling brought me back to the present. I shuddered, and then stared at her bowed head. Maybe Mama was worrying about me now. About losing me, as she had lost Danny.

"Wait here," I told her. "I'll be right back."

I returned with Baloo. Mama buried her face in his tattered fur.

"It wasn't my fault," I whispered. "I was so little. I didn't know Danny could get hurt jumping out of the window."

She looked up at me. "Who ever said Danny's death was your fault?" She wrapped her arms around me, crushing Baloo between us. "Oh, my dear Miss Marmalade, it was never your fault. Not ever. How could you believe that?"

I stood there, feeling hollow inside. I searched for a way to make her understand what these last nine years had been like for me with Danny gone.

At last she released me. "You'll have your prayer shawl in the morning." She kissed my cheek.

"Thank you," was all I managed to say.

§

MRS. STEINBACHER'S PACKARD ARRIVED SHORTLY AFTER Papa left for Precision Printers. By the time I finished bathing, there were six five-dollar bills on my coverlet and two new petticoats with money sewn into a seam. The embroidered bag with my prayer shawl inside slouched against my headboard. I kissed the bag and packed it in my valise. And I made room for Mr. Gress's typography book. Now that I had the blue thread, I might stay in California for quite some time.

Mama was practicing the piano when I came down to breakfast. Mrs. Steinbacher was gone. "Telephone us when you get to Florrie's," Mama called from the parlor, as if I were going on a long-planned vacation.

Mama made mistake after mistake with her music, but she kept at it. I remembered how she banged on the piano for hours each day after Danny died, leaving me to muddle through those first weeks with Grandma Goldstein.

I called Osborne Milliners. Prudence answered the telephone.

"Any news about the suffrage amendment?"

"Frankly, I'm not optimistic, Miriam. Would you like to join us for tea? Charity could use a bit of cheering up. And I would enjoy your company too."

"I…I'm going away for awhile. I'm taking the train to visit my friend, Florence Steinbacher, in California."

"A well-deserved break. When will you be back?"

"I'm not sure. It's a long story, Prudence."

"Your father?"

"Yes, and I don't want to go into it now."

"I see," she said softly. I gave her the details about the train, and she wished me a safe journey. I returned to my room.

And just like last time, there she was.

She sat next to my valise. Beside her were the robes and sandals I had worn twice before in the back-there-and-then.

"You look pale, Miriam. Are you ill?"

I shook my head and tried to get my thoughts in order.

Serakh embraced me—Serakh, with her precious smell of goats. I clung to her for a full minute.

"Can you come with me now to see Tirtzah?"

I simply nodded. I didn't ask how she knew this was the perfect moment to come back. I unpacked my prayer shawl and shed my 1912 self, piling my clothes on the valise.

"I have a train to catch," I said, reaching for the headscarf. Then I felt a grin pull at my cheeks. "No matter," I said. "I know this will take no time at all."

Thirty-Five

SERAKH SHADED MY FACE. I BLINKED my eyes and caught my breath, taking in the high desert country she called Canaan.

"I promised Tirtzah you would return," she said. "But our meeting must be brief. She is great with child, and I do not wish to tire her."

I rubbed my forehead. "How long have I been away?"

"Through many harvests. Tirtzah and her sisters have wed among their cousins—even little Makhlah, although the custom of women is not yet upon her."

"That's terrible! I'm so, so sorry. If only I'd had my shawl, I could have persuaded Moses to let them choose anybody they wanted to marry. Tirtzah could have had Gabi."

She patted my shoulder. "No, Miriam. Had you come for the second ruling, you would only have been an observer. The daughters of Zelophehad won a great victory. One step in the pursuit of justice, and then another. Tirtzah and her sisters married well, as will you one day."

I sighed in frustration.

"Oh, but you must marry. How else will the blue thread pass through the generations? Come, are you able to walk now?"

I nodded and covered my head. I leaned against her on the uneven ground. "Tell me about Miriam Seligman, my great-grandmother," I said, hoping for more answers. "My father hates her."

"Your father's hate comes from fear. Do not condemn him. It is easier for him to believe that his *savta* caused Raizl's death than it is to believe that he could have saved her and did not."

"Could he have saved Raizl?"

"No, surely not. Her illness was too grave. His *savta* forgave him for all that he did after Raizl's death. He was a boy struggling to do a man's job."

I wiped the moisture from my forehead. "But he could have saved Danny. He could have trusted Mama's instincts and fetched the doctor sooner."

She nodded. "He knows that. He lives with that pain. He does not have your great-grandmother to share in the blame."

We had reached the crest of a small hill. She pointed to a tent not far from where we stood. I touched the blue thread hanging at my side. "You once told me that Rashi's daughter embroidered this shawl, but my uncle said that Rashi lived hundreds of years ago. Tell me how did the shawl get from Rashi's daughter to my great-grandmother?"

"By ox cart."

"Serakh!"

She grinned. "I am teasing you. It was a long and wondrous journey. The new shawl went from Miriam to Miriam, from generation to generation. Each traveled as you have done, each with a purpose. Each like you—strong."

"And where did you travel with my great-grandmother besides Solomon's temple?"

Serakh shook her head. "Enough of your curiosity! Tirtzah can wait no longer. Drink the water she gives you and let her bathe your feet. She will offer you food."

"Two bites. Yes, I remember." *Will I ever get the whole story?*

The tent smelled of spices and lamb stew. Tirtzah lay in the corner, her belly huge, her hands and feet swollen. The gold ring was gone from her nostril. Still, she looked beautiful. Hurrying to her before she could rise, I fell to my knees and crushed her against me.

"Oh, my sister of the heart," she said. "You brought me the courage to stand before Moses and the elders. I cannot thank you enough."

"I'm sorry about Gabi," I said.

"No matter," she said. "I am content. I am provided for and so shall my children be. Help me to rise; soon Miryam will be back from the well."

"Who?"

Tirtzah beamed. "The daughter I have named for you and for the prophet Miryam. Listen, do you not hear her singing?"

A child's voice sounded outside the tent. I looked at the opening and there she was, hugging an earthen pitcher. Four years old, maybe five—a tiny version of the Tirtzah I remembered from Serakh's cave. She wore a loose shift, ochre-colored, with a thick blue stripe on one side. As she stepped closer, the blue stripe faded away.

I stared in disbelief. Tirtzah's daughter smiled at me and spoke gibberish.

"Touch her cheek and greet her," Serakh said. "She bears the blue threads that came to Miryam the prophetess through the tribe of Levi. As Miryam the prophetess had no children, she wished to pass the blue threads to a daughter of Tirtzah. When this Miryam reaches womanhood, at the time of her first blood, we will weave the threads as fringes into the four corners of her garment."

"What blue threads? I thought I saw them a second ago, but now…"

Serakh pointed to my prayer shawl. "Now you are the bearer of the one blue thread that remains of the threads of Miryam the prophetess."

"Wait. You mean…this girl is my great-great-great-great…so many I can't count…"

Serakh nodded. "Your ancestor, the Miryam of all those Miriams until you. Touch her."

I bent down and put my fingers on the little girl's bronze cheek.

"Peace unto you," she said. "I have brought water for you to drink. Mama will bathe your feet."

Tears streamed down my face.

The little girl frowned in confusion.

I stroked her hair. "Peace unto you," I said. "Peace and blessings."

Then Serakh put her hands on my shoulders. "Miryam the prophetess would have been proud of you. And the many others. And your great-grandmother. Proud of you, as am I, Miriam sweet and strong."

I drank the water. Tirtzah bathed my feet—it would have been futile to refuse. While she touched my toes, she chatted about good harvests and a kind husband, about a goat lost to a mountain lion, and about the woman who would help her as the new baby struggled into life.

"Another daughter, perhaps," Tirtzah said. "I would be content. She will own land if she marries within the tribe. For this, I am grateful."

"It will be a boy this time," Serakh said. I didn't doubt her.

Tirtzah smiled at me, her fingers on my ankle. "What shall we name the boy, my sister of the heart?"

"Daniel," I whispered. "Name him Daniel."

It happened so fast after that. Tirtzah's face creased with pain. She put her hands on the small of her back. Serakh told little Miryam to fetch the midwife. She insisted that my time with Tirtzah was at an end—at least for now.

I kissed Tirtzah. "Peace unto you. Maybe one day…"

§

A BLUE FLASH. THAT TAFFY-PULL FEELING, and I was back in my bedroom. I heard Mama pounding the piano.

"Be quick," Serakh said, yanking the headscarf from my shoulders.

"No, wait. There's so much I still don't know. I have to ask you—"

"Not now. Another time."

I grabbed a sandal as hostage. "When? I'm going away today. For a long time."

She paused. "What of your passion for your father's printing presses?"

I hugged the sandal. "I did what I thought was right. I pursued justice and now I don't really know what's going to happen."

"Miriam, I cannot stay."

"Will I ever see you again?"

"I pray it shall be so." Her eyes seemed older. Sadness creased her face.

I returned the sandal. Serakh stood on tiptoe and kissed my forehead. "May The One shine upon you and give you peace."

I closed my eyes against the flash.

Mama struck another wrong chord.

Thirty-Six

I PUT MY PRAYER SHAWL IN my valise, washed my face, and went to the kitchen to say good-bye to Mrs. Jenkins. She was stuffing freshly baked sweet rolls into our picnic basket. "Now don't you buy anything from those food sellers at the stations. You can't trust them. How long is your trip?"

"About twenty-seven hours," I said, trying to control my nervous pacing. Mrs. Jenkins, of all people, might have believed me if I told her of the longer trip I'd just taken, to the Promised Land. I wondered what would have happened if I had confided in her all along.

"Lordy! Give me back that basket. I haven't packed enough."

Charity surprised me at the front door a little after three. "Prudence is sorry she can't come, but someone has to mind the store." She handed me a hatbox. Inside was a VOTE FOR JUSTICE card and the gray and navy hat I had admired at their shop.

Tears again. The past weeks seemed to keep pouring over my eyelids. I felt ridiculous.

"We did our best, Charity, didn't we?"

She nodded. "The morning papers say the suffrage vote is too close to call. Mrs. Duniway says she wouldn't be surprised if we failed in Portland."

"Damnation!"

She reached into her handbag. "You take care in California. And come back soon, no matter which way the vote goes." She handed me an envelope. "Here's enough for a comfortable berth in the Pullman car. The least we could do is see that you get a good rest tonight."

"I can't take your money."

"Consider it a payment for your first printing job. The Everybody's Equal Suffrage League can afford four dollars and fifty cents."

Mama came to the front hall. She insisted that Mrs. Steinbacher's chauffeur drive Charity and me to the railroad depot. Sure enough, a few minutes later the Packard was once again in front of our house. I feared for a moment that Mama would come with us, but she didn't. Instead, she gave me the pearl necklace I'd worn as Marie Antoinette.

"It looks better on you, anyway," she said. "Don't sit next to strange men. Order chicken in the dining car. Send a telegram as soon as you get to Oakland."

The front doorbell chimed. Mrs. Jenkins answered it, and the chauffeur—the handsome one again—took my valise, hatbox, and basket. Mrs. Jenkins squeezed me to her bosom. Mama and I hugged briefly. Musical scales started before I crossed the front porch.

I bought a ticket for the Shasta Limited, due to leave Portland at 5:50 that evening and arrive at Oakland Pier at 8:20 the next night. I begged Charity to leave because I couldn't stand to see her waiting with me until the last minute. She finally did. I bought a lower tourist berth for two dollars and fifty cents, saving the extra two dollars for food and necessaries. I dabbed my nose with my handkerchief, slouched against the wooden bench in the waiting room and stared at the floor.

Some moments later, I realized that the man who had come to sit next to me was Papa.

"You want to go away," Papa said, in the same tone he would have used to tell Kirsten to set letterhead in twenty-four-point Caslon Bold.

"Yes, Papa," I whispered. I straightened my posture, ready to confront him, yet wary of making a scene. "I've already purchased my ticket."

"Tickets can be returned."

I clenched my jaw.

"You are young and stubborn as a goose," he said. "No, I am wrong. It is silly as a goose, stubborn as a mule, yes?"

I nodded. *Why did he come?*

"I was also stubborn when I came to America—a nothing, a nobody with a younger brother to feed and clothe." He patted my knee. "Stubborn is sometimes a good thing. But do not be too stubborn to ask for help. You will make mistakes, as I have. We care about you."

"Yes, Papa." I looked at the station clock. Nearly an hour and a half before the train was due—too much time. I wondered if my parents had told Uncle Hermann I was leaving and if Uncle Hermann would try to stop me. *Oh, please no.* My resolve might crumble if I saw Uncle Hermann.

"Shouldn't you be back at the shop, Papa?" I ventured.

He took off his bowler hat and ran his fingers through his hair. "Mr. Jacobowitz will handle everything."

Mr. Jacobowitz—Ephraim. My stomach lurched. He was expecting me on Thursday. What would he do when I didn't come to the shop? What would Papa tell him? What would he think of my leaving without a word?

"Uncle Hermann does not know," Papa added.

I closed my eyes and felt my shoulders relax.

"Miriam," Papa started again.

Then silence.

I said nothing.

"Miriam." He cleared his throat, so like Ephraim. "You must remember that you will always have a place in my home." His voice cracked. "And in my heart." He patted my knee again, but he did not look at me. Then, without so much as a good-bye, he stood and walked toward the depot doors.

I thought of Tirtzah, my sister of the heart, and what it meant to be brave. I thought of Danny, and Papa's Raizl. My shawl was safely hidden in my valise. I was going away, I was sure of that. Now was my chance. What did it matter if Papa thought me mad? If only he'd listen.

"Papa," I said, working up my courage. "Papa, wait! Please! It's about Raizl. Believe me, there was nothing you could do. It wasn't your fault!"

He kept walking. He didn't look back.

§

THE HUGE SOUTHERN PACIFIC STEAM ENGINE pulled in right on time. A porter hefted my valise and showed me to my seat. I put the hatbox on the overhead rack and opened the basket Mrs. Jenkins had prepared. Inside were a napkin and paring knife, a copy of the *Ladies' Home Journal*, Mrs. Jenkins's address, and a bushel of food: hard boiled eggs, cheese, a tin of lemon drops, a salami sandwich, two apples, six sweet rolls, and a paper cone of licorice nibs.

The little girl across the aisle watched me pop a nib into my mouth. "Molly, you shouldn't stare." I heard her mother—or older sister—say.

"May I offer you both some licorice?" I said. "They are quite safe."

The woman looked up from her Bible. Her hands were rough, a farmwoman's hands.

"Dark manna," I said. She crinkled her brow. "Begging your pardon," I said. "I didn't mean any blasphemy."

She nodded and took a nib. I offered some to Molly. Her stockings were mended at the knees. "Take five. It's going to be a long ride." Her freckles squished together in a smile.

We rolled south. Crawling into the lower tourist berth that night, I settled into the rocking motion of the rails, not unlike the *ka-chunk ka-chunk* of a printing press. I retrieved my typography book, comforting as cocoa. I took off my shoes and socks and massaged my feet. Not one grain of sand under my toenails, yet Tirtzah seemed nearby. I wished that instructions for designing a fair and just world could be as clear and straightforward as those for printing a well-proportioned handbill. I eased into sleep.

The next morning I stepped off the train at Davis with my food basket, while they switched engines. The day was warm and sunny, as I imagined California would be. Just a few more hours to Oakland and to Florrie. Newsies hawked the *Sacramento Bee* and *San Francisco Chronicle*. "England welcomes Wilson victory! Democrats gain big in Congress! Suffragists win in Arizona, Kansas, Michigan, and Oregon; Wisconsin votes no!"

What? I waved a nickel. The nearest newsie was almost my height, with a hint of brown fuzz over his upper lip and a scar under his right eye. I wondered what he'd had to suffer through to secure such a profitable spot at the depot. And I thought of Ephraim's nephew. The newsie handed me a *Chronicle* and I soon found the sentence that set my heart racing.

> Suffrage is running behind in the City of Portland, but very
> incomplete returns from the outside counties indicate that
> the women are in favor there, and that the amendment will
> receive good majorities.

Oh, yes, and *hallelujah*! I sat on a bench and dug into my basket. Sweet rolls always taste better when served with a slice of good news. After my second roll, I closed my eyes and tilted my face toward sun. That's when I smelled goats.

"Serakh?" I jerked my eyes open and scrambled to my feet. Dozens of people crowded the platform. I grabbed my basket and wove in and out among them searching for her.

"Did you see a bronze-skinned girl?" I asked the conductor. "About my age, long white hair, short and thin, hazel eyes like mine?"

"No, miss." A few minutes later he called "All aboard."

I searched the platform until the conductor practically hoisted me onto the train. No Serakh. Yet I felt sure that I had just missed her somehow.

I gave Molly another licorice nib and decided to save the last few to celebrate with Florrie. But first I'd send a telegram to Mama, as promised. And I'd splurge on a "we-did-it" telegram to Charity and Prudence and ask them to hug Kirsten for me. I wished I had Ephraim's address. I still owed him for the extra cardstock he had bought for the campaign. Perhaps if I wrote to him in care of Mrs. Rosenfeld at Neighborhood House—but what would I say? "Dear Ephraim" would be enough for him. *Do I mean that? Maybe.*

I looked at my valise and thought of Papa. As much as he infuriated me, he had come to the station to see me off. I did have a place in his heart. I folded the newspaper and stared out the window. Mostly, I saw me staring back in my new hat.

Papa never would have let me run Precision Printers or in-herit his shop, I reminded myself. I remembered the "cursed rag" that Papa was afraid to give me. Still, I had asked for my inheritance, and there it was, in my valise, tucked safely inside its embroidered bag.

I straightened my suit jacket and opened the newspaper to the employment section.

> Shaker Press. Wanted: Printer's apprentice.
> Apply in person. 1473 Channing Way, Berkeley.

Shaker Press. I thought of Serakh. Maybe I'd find her at the Oakland depot eating a cucumber sandwich. Maybe she would stroll alongside me as if she had all the time in the world. Maybe she does.

Author's Note

THIS BOOK TOOK ROOT WHEN I saw the real picture of the 1908 suffrage banner Miriam sees, the one that reads: LIKE THE DAUGHTERS OF ZELOPHEHAD WE ASK FOR OUR INHERITANCE. It's the last banner in the parade on the opposite page. I had no idea that American women a hundred years ago still talked about five Israelite sisters whose story was set thousands of years earlier. These sisters are not among the well-known women in the Bible, but are five relatively minor characters. They might have been the kind of sisters who could have lived across the street—the kind you might want to meet across the *olam*.

Olam. That's an ancient Hebrew word used in many Jewish prayers. It is sometimes translated as "the universe," sometimes as "eternity" or "forever." Time and space collide in that one tiny word. A traveler across the *olam* could go anywhere in history—or in the future for that matter. You have a spot in the *olam*, along with your grandmother and your grandchildren.

Hebrew has two main regional accents: Askenazi ("German"), with roots in northern and eastern Europe, and Sephardi ("Spanish"), with roots in southern Europe and the Mediterranean region. Sephardic Hebrew is spoken in present-day Israel, and many American Hebrew schools and Jewish worship services now use that accent. In 1912, Miriam Josefsohn's congregation—primarily of German immigrants—would have said *Adonoi* ("Lord"). For contrast, Serakh speaks to Miriam in English and in Sephardi-accented Hebrew, saying, for example, *Adonai*. As a magical character, Serakh could have spoken any language.

Blue Thread follows the story of Zelophehad's daughters fairly closely—although I made up Zelophehad's widow, Tirtzah's daughter, and Gabi, as well as the reactions of the crowd. Miryam the prophetess is in the Bible. Rashi and his three daughters did live in eleventh-century France, and it's possible, though not at all probable, that Rashi's daughter, Miriam, embroidered a woman's prayer shawl. Savta— Miriam Seligmann—is purely fictional.

The Bible barely mentions Serakh, although it does list her in two places about four hundred years part. For thousands of years, people have spun tales about her. According to one story, the Jews of Isfahan (now in Iran) believed Serakh lived among them until she died in a synagogue fire about nine hundred years ago. Some say that Serakh was exceptionally beautiful, that she played the harp, and that she told Jacob that his son Joseph was still alive and later told Moses where Joseph's bones were buried in Egypt. So I, too, have spun a tale about Serakh as the "wise old woman" of Jewish legend.

Abigail Scott Duniway might have been called the wise old woman of Portland in 1912. Shortly after moving there in 1871, Duniway started a newspaper for women, the *New Northwest*. She worked with Susan B. Anthony and others in the women's movement, and managed to get women's suffrage on the ballot in the 1884 election. The measure failed then—and four times more—before it came up for a vote, and passed, in 1912.

One of Duniway's staunchest opponents was her brother, Harvey Scott, who fought against suffrage in the newspaper he edited, *The Morning Oregonian*. In 1912, Scott had been dead for two years and Duniway, nearly eighty, was often bedridden. Younger women from many different backgrounds worked together on the campaign. They organized rallies, parades, and media events such as Blotter Day. They had handbills, posters, banners, and newspaper ads—but, as far as I know, no VOTE FOR JUSTICE cards. The petticoat card is real. Two cards are pasted into Abigail Scott Duniway's scrapbook archived at the University of Oregon.

National leaders, including Anna Howard Shaw, campaigned for the vote in Oregon, and many "equal suffrage leagues" sprang up in the state. Among them were the Portland Equal Suffrage League, founded by Josephine

Mayer Hirsch, and the Everybody's Equal Suffrage League, founded by Esther Pohl Lovejoy. The amendment finally passed statewide (61,265 to 57,104), although it failed in Miriam Josefsohn's "Nob Hill" section of Portland. On November 30, 1912, Duniway co-signed Oregon's suffrage proclamation with Governor Oswald West and became the first Oregon woman to register to vote.

Following the lead of the national organization, the Portland chapter of the National Council of Jewish Women decided not to endorse suffrage for women—officially, that is—and instead devoted itself to charitable causes. Among them was Neighborhood House, which offered classes, well-baby clinics, and other services to poor families in an area known as South Portland. Neighborhood House had the city's first public kindergarten. Many Council members did support suffrage, among them Josephine Mayer Hirsch, the chapter's founding president and a member of Temple Beth Israel, which was founded a year before Oregon became a state. Other Jewish congregations followed, including Ahavai Sholom and Neveh Zedek, now combined as Neveh Shalom. Beth Israel's building at SW Twelfth and Main burned down under suspicious circumstances in 1923, when the Ku Klux Klan was powerful in Oregon.

Many other parts of *Blue Thread* are true. Edmund Gress's typography book still lives in the closed stacks of Multnomah County Central Library. In 1912 there were still a few horse-drawn fire engines competing with cars on the streets of Portland. Portlanders learned who won the 1912 presidential election by watching for different colored lights. Children like fictional Danny Josefsohn might have died of a tetanus infection—commonly called "lockjaw." The antitoxin for tetanus was isolated in the late 1800s, but the tetanus vaccine we have now was not developed until 1924.

I made up Miriam Josefsohn and the particular prayer shawl she found. Although there is a biblical mandate to tie a blue thread at the corners of a garment, most prayer shawls now have only white fringes at the corner. There's a lively and ongoing debate about the origin and current availability of that particular blue dye. The most recent research favors dye from a snail—*Murex trunculus*. In 1912, Jewish women would not have worn a prayer shawl—for centuries that custom was reserved for men. Some Jewish women wear these shawls in synagogues now, often after they become a *bat mitzvah*—a daughter of the commandment.

Make no mistake, though. The magic in Miriam's prayer shawl is real. It is that quality of something inside us that pushes us to do the right thing when we least expect it.

Acknowledgements

MANY PEOPLE LENT A HAND WITH weaving the fabric of *Blue Thread*. Miriam Josefsohn's passion for typography and her experiences at Precision Printers could not have found their places in this story without the help of printmaker and artist, Emily Riley.

The background for Miriam's religious experiences in 1912 and in the "back-then-and-there" came in part from: Judith Baskin, Knight Professor of Humanities at the University of Oregon; Sylvia Frankel; Anne LeVant Prahl, curator of collections at the Oregon Jewish Museum; and Rabbi Joseph Wolf. Miriam's involvement in the 1912 suffrage campaign for Oregon women grew with the help of: Janice Dilg, professor of Women's Studies at Portland State University; and Kimberly Jensen, professor of History and Gender Studies at Western Oregon University.

The story took shape thanks to the many resources of the Multnomah County Library, and the pleasures of working in the library's Sterling Writer's Room. I wrote and revised with the support, inspiration, and expertise of Viva Scriva— the best writer's critique group in the galaxy: Addie Boswell, Melissa Dalton, Amber Keyser, Michelle McCann, Sabina

Rascol, Mary Rehmann, Elizabeth Rusch, and Nicole Schreiber. And I am particularly grateful to my husband and beta-reader Michael Feldman, who has shared his home with my imaginary friends for so many years that they feel like part of the family.

Editor and instructor Linda Meyer and her Winter 2010 Book Editing class at Portland State University unraveled a draft of *Blue Thread* paragraph by paragraph and suggested valuable ways to weave it back together. And re-weave I did, guided and encouraged by the many editors, designers, and marketers at Ooligan Press, whose rare blend of education, enthusiasm, and persistence are any author's dream. Dozens of people have helped along the way at Ooligan, starting with Janie Webster. A special shout out goes to Sylvia Spratt on the editorial side, to designers Brandon Freels and Kelsey Klockenteger, and the marketing team leaders Laura Gleim, Sara Simmonds, Brittany Torgerson, and Tracy Turpen.

OOLIGAN PRESS is a non-profit, general trade press located in the Pacific Northwest and dedicated to advancing the craft of publishing. Ooligan's staff consists of educators, publishing professionals, and students within the graduate publishing program at Portland State University. We are a press committed to providing education, publishing sustainably, and producing quality books that represent the unique landscapes, communities, and people of the Pacific Northwest.

Project Managers:
Michelle Blair
Kelsey Klockenteger
Anne Paulsen
Stefani Varney
Marc Lindsay
LeAnna Nash

Editing Managers:
Erin Clarkson
Julie Flanagan
Ashley Rogers
Tanna Waters

Developmental Director:
Sylvia Spratt

Developmental Editors:
Katelyn Benz
Leah Brown
Julie Flanagan
Sarah Heilman
Stephanie Kroll
Susan Wigget
Travis Willmore
Amanda Winterroth

Editors:
Kathryn Banks
Kyle Brittain
Erin Clarkson
Heather Frazier
Cheryl Frey
Leah Gibson-Blackfeather
Ben Hamlin
Kenneth Hanour
Taylor Hudson

Diane Shadwick
Kristen Svenson
Christopher Thomas
Robin Wilkinson
Cheri Woods-Edwin

Proofreaders:
Kathryn Banks
Kelsey Klockenteger
Isaac Mayo
Anne Paulsen
Ashley Rogers
Diane Shadwick
Kristen Svenson
Safa Sofia Ghnaim

Design:
Brandon Freels (interior)
Kelsey Klockenteger (cover)
Mandi Russell
Elisabeth Wilson

Digital:
James Avery Wilhelm

Marketing & Sales:
Laura Gleim, Marketing Manager
Chelsea Pfund, Sales Manager
Sara Simmonds, Marketing Manager
Kristen Svenson, Sales Manager
Amanda Winterroth
Brittany Torgerson, Marketing Manager
Tracy Turpen, Marketing Manager
Jeremy Coatney
Lacey Friedly
Indu Shanmugam
Lucy Softich
Stephanie Kroll

RUTH TENZER FELDMAN is an award-winning author of numerous nonfiction books for children and young adults, including *The Fall of Constantinople, Thurgood Marshall,* and *Don't Whistle in School: The History of America's Public Schools.* Ruth has also published articles on a variety of subjects, ranging from leeches to Einstein's refrigerator. Originally from Long Island, New York, she studied at the American University Washington College of Law and has worked as a legislative attorney for the U.S. Department of Education. She now lives in Portland, Oregon, where she is a member of the League of Women Voters, the Oregon Historical Society, and the Institute for Judaic Studies. *Blue Thread* is her first novel.

For more information, visit her website at
www.ruthtenzerfeldman.com
and her blog at
www. bluethreadbook.com